ANGELS ADRIFT

ALSO BY ALICE DUNCAN

The Mercy Allcutt Mystery Series

Lost Among the Angels

Angels Flight

Fallen Angels

Angels of Mercy

Thanksgiving Angels

Angels Adrift

Christmas Angels

The Daisy Gumm Majesty Mystery Series

Strong Spirits

Fine Spirits

High Spirits

Hungry Spirits

Genteel Spirits

Ancient Spirits

Spirits Revived

Dark Spirits

Spirits Onstage

Unsettled Spirits

Bruised Spirits

Spirits United

Spirits Unearthed

Shaken Spirits

Scarlet Spirits

ANGELS ADRIFT

A MERCY ALLCUTT MYSTERY, BOOK 6

ALICE DUNCAN

ACKNOWLEDGMENTS

As ever, thanks to the most wonderful beta readers in the world: Lynne Welch, Sue Krekeler, Gina Gilmore, Margaret Cronk and David Bedini. Don't know what I'd do without you guys.

Thanks to my great great-niece, Sara Krafft. Sara helps me *all the time* with research, English usage, etc. I don't know how she's come to know so much so young, but she has, and I really appreciate her!

Thank you, also, Nina Paules of eBook Prep, and Brian Paules of its sister company, ePublishingWorks for wanting to publish more Mercy books. Nina makes gorgeous covers, and I do so appreciate everything Nina and Brian do.

ONE

December, 1926, had rolled in, bringing with it dreary, gray and icky weather. Mind you, since I'm originally from Boston, dreary weather was nothing new to me. But I'd been living in Los Angeles since June and had become accustomed to the warm, idyllic skies in Southern California. I guess even paradise has its off days.

This particular day was more than usually off. I'd pretty much recovered from Thanksgiving, which had almost been spent in my parents' new "winter" home in Pasadena, about twenty miles from Los Angeles.

Disaster had been narrowly averted, however, and I'd managed to slither out of Thanksgiving dinner itself by taking my battered self away from my parents' home, only gratified by their threats never to allow me to cross their threshold again. Unfortunately, they probably didn't mean them. So I was home again in Los Angeles, which was a good thing, but not as good as it might be, as noted above.

Not only had the weather turned on me—and my parents turned up—but my job, in which I generally took great delight, had become downright dull. You see, I am secretary to Mr. Ernest Templeton, P.I. P.I. means private investigator, in case you didn't know it. I didn't until Ernie told me. Anyhow, when he hired me I'd envisioned an exciting employment opportunity, filled with fascinating cases and interesting individuals.

Silly me.

It was now Thursday, and I hadn't had a thing to do all week except chat with Ernie and Lulu LaBelle, the receptionist in the Figueroa Building where Ernie had his office; Mr. Emerald Buck, the janitor at the Figueroa Building; and the rest of my tenants. Oh. Perhaps I'd better explain the last sentence.

You see, my sister Chloe and her husband Harvey had sold me their lovely house on Bunker Hill (the one in Los Angeles, not the one in Boston), and I'd turned it into a sort of boarding house. Lulu was one of the tenants in my home, and Caroline Terry was another. Caroline worked at the hosiery counter at the Broadway Department Store on Fourth and Broadway.

Recently I'd also rented a suite of rooms to a young lady named Sue Krekeler pronounced KREKler), who worked as a receptionist in a nearby dentist's office. I hadn't visited her employer, Dr. Philby, and hoped I wouldn't have to any time soon, not being that keen on dentists. But Sue was a nice girl, only twenty years old, and a great improvement over my last tenant who had turned out to be a remarkably poor choice.

But my housing arrangements have nothing to do with the cheerless December day. To put it simply, I was bored almost to tears. Therefore, after tidying and dusting the office, sharpening my already-sharp pencils and straightening the floor rugs and the various pictures on the wall, I got up from my desk, wandered into Ernie's room, and gazed out the window of same.

Lately Ernie had mainly been tailing—my new employment had enhanced my vocabulary quite a bit—wives cheating on husbands and husbands cheating on wives. I considered such cases sordid. So did Ernie, but he needed the money they garnered so he took them. Jobs like those didn't need me, though, more's the pity. Therefore, I stood, arms crossed over my chest, staring out the window and wishing Ernie had clients with more absorbing cases to solve. I had the sudden thought that Ernie might allow me to bring my sweet little apricot toy poodle, Buttercup, to work with me. If I didn't have any work, at least I'd have company.

He probably wouldn't approve of the notion. Ernie seemed determined to put a damper on most of my bright ideas.

As I contemplated Buttercup and how detectives' offices would appear friendlier if dogs were allowed in them, two men came into view walking down the unpaved alleyway behind the Figueroa Building. Ernie's office is on the third floor of the building—which sits on Seventh and Hill in the fair city of Los Angeles, in case you care—so I couldn't see their faces. Both men wore cloth hats. There was nothing distinctive about either one of the men whom I could see from my vantage point.

One of them wore a garish checked jacket over what looked like corduroy trousers, and the other wore what looked like an ill-fitting tweed suit. When another man, similarly attired in working-class duds—to wit, a cheap sack suit—came up behind the first two, I thought nothing of it, although I did wonder vaguely why three men had chosen to take a walk down a bumpy dirt alleyway when there were perfectly good sidewalks in the area upon which to walk.

And then the third man took something out of his coat pocket. I didn't think anything about *that*, either, until he slipped the some-thing—it looked like a thin cord—over the head of the man who wasn't wearing the garish jacket, crossed his hands, and tightened his grip on the cord. At first I was puzzled by this action on his part. Then my eyes must have nearly bugged from their sockets when I understood what I was watching. The attackee struggled and reached up to try to pry the cord from his neck.

As the full horror of what I was witnessing dawned, I know I pressed my own hands flat on the window pane, leaned closer until my nose almost squashed against the glass and gaped down at the scene below. The choking man kicked and squirmed and, I presume, gurgled, as I watched, aghast, scarcely able to believe my eyes.

But my eyes weren't lying. The man eventually stopped struggling and sagged to the ground. As he did so, his hat fell off, and his face tilted upward. It looked blue from where I stood, and his tongue stuck out from between his lips. Only then did I gather my scattered wits together and run for the telephone in my office. Don't ask me why I didn't use the telephone on Ernie's desk, because I'm not sure. I was upset and rattled, and I was accustomed to using my own telephone; so I presume those factors account for my behavior.

When the operator answered my frenzied clicks, I fairly shrieked, "I need the police!" Almost instantly, I was connected with someone at the Los Angeles Police Department.

For only a second, I thought to demand I be connected with the office of Phil Bigelow, Ernie's best friend and an L.A.P.D. detective. My state of nerves, though, was such that I only screeched, "I just saw somebody being murdered!"

As luck would have it, Ernie walked in through the outer door of the office in time to hear my announcement. I glanced up to see him, long and lean and eternally insouciant, stop dead in his tracks and stare at me as if I'd lost my mind. It wasn't the first time he'd looked at me thus, but I was too upset to take him to task for it then.

The policeman on the other end of the wire, a fellow whose name I never did learn, asked me to calm down.

"I *am* calm!" I bellowed back. Then I took in a deep, soothing breath and continued. "I beg your pardon. I'm not calm. I just saw someone being murdered in the alleyway behind the Figueroa Building on Seventh and Hill."

The policeman asked for a few more significant details and then told me someone would be at the office shortly to look into the matter and take a statement from me.

As the telephone receiver clunked into the cradle, I sagged into my swivel chair and pinned my gaze on Ernie. I'm pretty sure I looked like a madwoman.

Ernie said, "What the hell's going on? What murder? Have you gone nuts?"

I glared at him, my hand pressed to my still-thundering heart, and tried to keep in the scream clamoring to get out. In measured tones, I said, "No, Ernest Templeton, I have not gone *nuts*, whatever *nuts* means. A modern slang expression meaning crazy, I suppose."

"You suppose right." He removed his hat and plunked himself down on one of the chairs in front of my desk. "Now how about you tell me what's going on?"

The full horror of what I'd witnessed smacked me in the same heart still thundering in my chest, making it lurch painfully. I buried my face in my hands, ruining the image of a composed young secretary I so valiantly attempted to convey. "Oh, Ernie!" I cried. "It was *awful!*"

"Yeah," he said in his dry, professional P.I.'s voice. "I get that part. But what was awful? Care to share before the coppers come calling?"

"Share?" I cried, irked by his attitude. "I'll *show* you!" I lifted my head from my cupped hands, hopped up from my swivel chair and charged past my desk and into Ernie's room. There I headed for the window, Ernie hot on my heels.

"Look!" I said dramatically, glaring at Ernie and gesturing at the window. "Just look down there, and then tell me if I'm nuts or not."

Ernie obliged me by looking out the window. Although I'm loath to admit it, I hadn't glanced out said window myself, because I didn't want to see the poor dead man sprawled in the dirty alleyway again.

"Okay," said Ernie. "I'm looking. What am I supposed to be seeing?"

What was he supposed to be *seeing*? Indignant, I hollered, "The *body*, you numbskull! You're supposed to be seeing the *body*!" You can tell how upset I was by my phraseology. Never, in all my days, which included enough of them to cover almost twenty-two years, had I ever called anyone, much less my boss, a numbskull.

"Um...maybe you'd better point it out to me, Mercy." Now Ernie sounded kind, as if he were attempting to humor an invalid.

This seemed odd behavior on Ernie's part. Ernie wasn't a bad man; far from it. But he was definitely not one to throw cosseting tones of voice around, especially at me.

I eyed him suspiciously. Ernie wasn't above a practical joke every now and then, although if he was joking now, he was showing extremely poor taste. "You can't see the body?" I demanded.

"Show me," said Ernie, still in his kind-sounding voice.

With some trepidation, wondering what was going on—for the good Lord's sake, a man was *dead* down there—I joined him at the window and peered down…upon an empty alleyway. I leaned closer and stared harder, again pressing my palms to the window glass.

Nothing.

"But…but I saw it," I said, confused as well as filled with leftover revulsion. "Two men were walking, and another man came up behind them and put a cord or a wire or something of the sort around one of the men's necks and strangled him. I saw it, Ernie. I didn't imagine it! It was awful." I shuddered, remembering.

Curses. Wherever had the dratted body got itself off to? This didn't make any sense, unless…

"I know! Obviously, the other two men were in cahoots. They must have dragged the body off somewhere."

Ernie only gazed at me, his almost turquoise eyes sorrowful.

"Darn it, Ernie. Don't look at me like that!"

"Like what?"

"Like you're placating a lunatic!"

"Wouldn't dream of it."

It was probably fortunate for both of us that the police showed up just then, or I might have compounded my use of the word *numbskull* with battery upon Ernie's person, which would never do.

To my great relief, Phil Bigelow, the aforementioned L.A.P.D. detective friend of Ernie's, entered the office accompanied by two uniformed officers of the law. Phil was a middle-sized fellow with brown hair and a nondescript face. Ernie claimed he was the only copper in the entire Los Angeles Police Department who wasn't as dirty as mud. I had no reason to doubt him, although his claim seemed unlikely. I didn't think Phil was a wrongdoer, of course, but surely an entire city department couldn't be stocked only with crooks and liars, could it? As my father claims the United States Congress is? Revolting thought.

Suddenly I felt like crying. I'd never do such a thing in front of these men. Therefore I squared my shoulders, lifted my chin, and said, "Good morning, Phil. I just witnessed a murder."

The words were true, but they shocked me with their baldness, so I more or less staggered into my own room, groped for my desk and collapsed into my chair once more.

Phil was a nice man. He said, "So I hear. I'm sorry, Mercy." We'd been on first-name terms for several months by then. He wasn't taking liberties. "Can you tell me where and how the crime was committed?"

I glanced at Ernie, who offered nothing by way of supporting words or gestures. Figured. So I just told Phil the truth. "I was looking out the window in Ernie's office and saw two men walking down the alley. Then another man came up behind the first two, slipped a cord or a thin string or a wire around one of the men's necks and strangled him."

"Show me, all right?"

Ah. There was the rub. I allowed myself a grimace of distaste. "I can show you where I saw the crime committed, but the body's gone. Ernie and I just looked."

Ernie and Phil exchanged a speaking glance which I resented like fire. Nevertheless, I rose from my chair and again walked into Ernie's office. There I gestured down at the scene of a crime which seemed not to have been committed, for all anyone could tell from Ernie's window.

"Um..." said Phil.

"I know," I said crisply. "You can't see the body. It doesn't seem to be there any longer. But *I* saw it." The memory made me give another involuntary shudder. "It was awful. He fell down when he quit struggling against the cord around his neck, and his cap fell off. His face was all blue, and his tongue stuck out of his mouth, and it looked swollen." I shook my head violently, wishing the vision in my mind's eye would go away.

"Maybe we'd better go down there and you can show us exactly where all this took place," said Phil. Now he was sounding like a kindly uncle, just as Ernie had.

"I'll be happy to. It appears as though the body's been removed, however."

"Ah…yes. I noticed that," said Phil.

"But it happened!" I said, indignant as all get-out. "Whether or not the body is still there, surely there must be signs of a struggle or something left behind."

"Let's go look."

Because of the chilly weather, I got my cloche hat and gloves from my desk drawer and put them on. No sense getting a cold on top of witnessing a murder. I also grabbed my black woolen coat from the rack beside the door and shoved my arms into it as we left the office.

So the five of us—Phil, Ernie, the two uniformed coppers and me—trekked downstairs and through the Figueroa Building's lobby. I said, " 'Lo, Lulu," on my way out.

Lulu stopped filing her blood-red fingernails to stare at us, and said, " 'Lo, Mercy," as we walked out the front door and headed for the side of the building, where we turned right and walked to the alley.

Gazing upward, I found Ernie's office window and stopped underneath it. "It was right here," I told the four men with me. Violating every stern lecture my mother ever gave me about proper etiquette, I even pointed, this time at the ground. Squinting hard, I tried to discern any hint of the struggle I'd witnessed or any other sign that a man had lost his life there. All I saw were ruts and potholes in the dirt. Fiddlesticks.

"Um…" said Phil.

"I don't see nothing," said one of the uniforms.

"I know," I said crisply, understanding his meaning in spite of his grammar. "Someone must have taken the body and carted it off somewhere."

This time several speaking glances were exchanged among the assembled men. Gritting my teeth in exasperation, I leaned down and scoured the unpaved alleyway with my gaze. As hard-packed as cement, the dirt didn't take kindly to footprints. For instance, none of our little group's had made any impression at all. Darn it, there had to be *something* to show a man had lost his life on that spot.

"Are those drag marks?" I asked after a moment or two, again pointing, this time at two faint parallel scuff marks that might have been made by the heels of a shod body being hauled away from a crime scene.

Ernie bent down to examine the marks. "Maybe," he said. I heard doubt in his voice.

This was getting downright frustrating. "Darn it, I know what I saw!" I glanced around at the buildings on either side of the alley-way. I gestured at the one directly opposite the Figueroa Building. "What's that place? Is it an office building?"

Phil said, "I don't know, but we'll find out. In fact, we'll question everyone on both sides of the alley. Still…well, Mercy, do you think you can give us descriptions of the people involved? The murderer and the murderee, for instance? Descriptions would help us a lot."

Bother. Here was yet another rub. "I was on the third floor, Phil. I'll do my best, but I only saw the dead man after he was…well, dead. I'm sure he didn't look like that in life. At least I hope he didn't. If you know what I mean."

"I know what you mean."

Phil gave instructions to his underlings to conduct a door-to-door inquiry of tenants in the buildings on the block. Then he, Ernie and I traipsed back into the Figueroa Building.

As soon as we walked into the lobby, Lulu said, "What's up, Mercy?"

I decided I might as well be blunt. "I saw somebody being murdered in the alleyway behind the building, Lulu. I can tell you all about it at lunch." It had taken me at least a month to stop refer-ring to the mid-day meal as *luncheon*. I was getting better at this being-of-the-people thing every day.

Lulu's mascaraed eyes grew huge. "A *murder!* You bet you'll tell me all about it at lunch! I can't wait."

"We'll all three go to lunch and talk about it," said Ernie. Perhaps he was beginning to take me seriously. We'd see.

When we got back to the office, Phil drew out a notebook and pencil. This looked like a good idea to me, so I, too, got one of my own stenographic pads and a pencil. I always kept a supply of sharpened pencils in a Chinese cup on my desk, just in case. One never knew. Ernie might get a slew of important cases any old time. Or even one, if I was lucky. Anyhow, Phil sat in the chair beside my desk, and Ernie plopped himself back in the one he'd occupied when he'd first arrived, shoved it back a yard or so, and allowed his long legs to stretch out in front of him.

I told Phil everything I could remember about the three people involved in the crime I'd beheld being committed. I included the cloth caps on all three men's heads, and one of the men's garish checked jacket.

"Come to think of it," I said at one point, having remembered a detail, "the first man's—I mean the one who walked into the alley with the murdered man—plaid cap clashed horribly with his check-ered jacket."

"What colors were the hat and jacket? Could you tell from where you stood?" asked Phil.

I thought. And thought. Finally, I admitted, "I...well, I can't really remember. All I remember is being dismayed by the combina-tion of colors. I have a vague memory of red and purple. Or some-thing of the sort. Two colors that didn't belong together, at any rate."

Phil and Ernie exchanged another glance. I suppressed my mounting wrath. After all, it wasn't their fault I hadn't been close enough to see the crime more clearly, any more than it was mine.

"Did you notice the color of anyone's hair?" Phil asked me.

I thought about it. "Um...well, not really. Oh, wait. I do remember that when the dead man fell down and his hat fell off, he had reddish hair...well, I mean he had reddish hair before he fell down, but..." I sensed I was losing my audience, so I refrained from continuing along those lines and only said, "I remember his hair being red, because it contrasted hideously with his blue face." Another shudder shook me. "It wasn't a carroty red, but rather a darker red. Perhaps strong tea only a little redder. As if someone had added some cherry juice. Or something."

"That's a big help," muttered Ernie. "Now the guy's hair looks like tea and cherries."

"Darn you, Ernie Templeton! How dare—"

"It's all right, Mercy," said Phil, in a hurry to interrupt a contretemps. "I'm sure it was an awful thing to witness."

His kindness and evident belief in my story bucked me up some. "Yes. It was." I cast a disparaging glance at my employer, who didn't acknowledge it. It was probably just as well.

"What about the other two guys?" asked Ernie. "Did you notice their hair color or anything?"

I wracked my brain and dug down deep in my memory for any details I could possibly find. There weren't many of them. Heck, I'd been watching from a third-story window, and the weather had been gloomy. My eyes are good, but they can't see through cloth caps and so forth. It wasn't long before my store of information ran out. As I glanced down at my stenographer's pad, the sum total of my memories appeared mighty slim.

Discouraged, I said, "This isn't much to go on, is it?"

"Not much," said Ernie.

"But we'll see what we can do," promised Phil.

I wasn't altogether sure I believed him. After all, crimes were committed every day in the City of Angels. I expected the Los Angeles Police Department would spend its time on crimes more easily solved than the murder of an unidentifiable man observed being strangled by another unidentifiable man in an alleyway from a window in the third floor of the Figueroa Building on Seventh and Hill.

Phil left shortly thereafter. I assumed he would question his men about what, if anything, they'd discovered in their building-to-building survey of the neighborhood. Nevertheless, I felt discouraged, as well as all atremble from leftover distaste and revulsion, when Lulu, Ernie and I got into Ernie's battered Studebaker. He drove us down Hill Street to Chinatown, where we ate at a little noodle shop run by a Chinese man named Charley. We all ordered Ernie's favorite: pork and noodles, with a lot of vegetables to round out the meal and make it wholesome.

The noodles, etc., were delicious. My story, such as it was, was grim enough to fit the dismal weather.

At least Lulu was eager to hear all the grisly details. I could tell, however, that she was as sorry as Phil and Ernie had been when I couldn't provide more of them. Actually, so was I.

TWO

Of course, the hot topic around my own personal dinner table in the evening was the murder of the disappearing man. Our cook-housekeeper, by the way, was Lottie Buck, wife of Mr. Emerald Buck, the maintenance man at the Figueroa Building. Mr. Buck did an excellent job of keeping the Figueroa Building—and my house repaired and in spiffy order. Mrs. Buck made sure the house was clean as a whistle, and she also served the most delectable meals available anywhere.

It was Caroline Terry, a nice girl and usually quiet and who worked the hosiery counter at the Broadway Department Store on Fourth and Broadway, who surprised me by asking, "Golly, Mercy, do you suppose some company might have been filming a picture there? Maybe it was only a scene from a motion picture."

I would have opened my mouth and stared at her, agog at her insightful question, if my mouth hadn't been full of delicious roasted chicken.

Before I had a chance to swallow, Lulu piped up. "We didn't even think about the pictures, did we, Mercy? I wonder if that's it. A picture being filmed would make more sense than a real murder. I guess." Her eyes lit up, and I could tell she cherished the idea of a movie being filmed at the Figueroa Building. Lulu wanted to be a star in the flickers.

Thinking hard as I gulped down my bite of chicken and then took a swig of water to hurry it on its way, I said, "Um…I don't know. I hadn't considered the pictures. You're right, Lulu. It would make more sense than a murder." Recalling the morning and how long it had taken the coppers to come to the office and then how much time had passed before we all trekked down to the alleyway to look, I frowned, disappointed at the conclusion I'd come to. "But I don't think so. I've been to sets where pictures were being shot before, and it takes a long time to set everything up and take it all down again. Besides, there are always crewmen and cameras everywhere, and they almost always have the actors repeat the scene forty or fifty times before the director's satisfied."

Lulu said, "Huh."

"Oh, my, Mercy, have you really seen pictures being filmed?" This, from Sue, whose big green eyes went round with fascination.

"You didn't know?" asked Lulu with seeming incredulity. "Mercy's sister is married to Harvey *Nash*, for Pete's sake!"

Sue's eyes grew even rounder. She whispered, "Really? I had no idea."

Oh, dear. I guess I'd forgotten to tell Sue about how I'd come by the house. To this day, it passes my understanding why people are so in awe of picture folks. I mean, I loved Harvey like a brother. He was a great guy. But face it, the pictures were…well, the pictures. They didn't have anything to do with real life. They were little pieces of fantasy, where every crime was solved and true love conquered everything from poverty to tuberculosis.

Nevertheless, I didn't want to disillusion poor Sue, so I told her my story. "Yes, indeed. Harvey Nash and my sister Chloe have been married for several years. They're going to have a baby in May. We think. Maybe April or June. Harvey's very excited about it. Well, so is Chloe." For the record, Chloe is a lot prettier than I am, with beautiful blond hair and heavenly blue eyes. I'm not bad looking, but my hair is brown, and my blue eyes are just…well, blue. "This used to be their house. I bought it from them when they moved to Beverly Hills."

For a moment I feared poor Sue might faint from the shock brought about by the sudden knowledge she now lived in a home formerly occupied by one of the most famous producers and directors in the picture biz. She didn't, for which I was grateful. She did whisper, "Oh, my," in an awed-sounding voice.

Since she was impressed, I decided to add to her listening pleasure. "Yes, indeedy. In fact, you and Caroline share the suite of rooms formerly occupied by Chloe and Harvey."

Sue slapped a hand to her bosom in a gesture so dramatic, I wouldn't have believed it if I'd seen it on screen. She seemed in danger of being overwhelmed.

I guess Caroline, a prosaic, God-fearing girl whose parents lived in Alhambra—not that Alhambra has anything to do with anything, I only mention it—said, "It's not as if they're royalty, Sue. They're only wealthy moving-picture people." Caroline went to church every Sunday of her life, and she had her priorities in the proper order. Well, I think she did anyway.

"*Only?*" Sue goggled at Caroline.

Lulu, who was in her own way as star-struck as anyone living, had resided in Los Angeles for several years. She wasn't precisely jaded, but she knew what was what. She said, "I'd like to be a wealthy picture person. But it's a tough business. You have to look really good on the screen in order to make it in the pictures. Half the time, if you see the people who are big stars in person, they don't look like they do on-screen."

She knew this from experience, having been out to dinner with none other than John Gilbert a month or so earlier. John Gilbert looked just as good off-screen as on. But I'd told her about others whom I'd met and whom you'd never recognize as being stars if they hadn't been introduced by name. Before they moved to Beverly Hills, Harvey and Chloe used to entertain a lot, so I got to meet a ton of movie folks. They still entertained in their home in Beverly Hills, but I didn't live with them there, so I didn't see as many flicker people as I used to.

"Oh, my," said Sue again. "Who all have you met, Mercy?" From her voice, you'd have thought Jesus and the twelve disciples had been on Chloe's guest list.

Thus it was that dinner-table conversation veered away from murder and on to the picture people I'd met during my short time in Los Angeles. I was more than a little glad the conversation had tilted away from murder, mainly because the morning's murder was such an inconclusive one, yet still absolutely horrible.

Anyhow, the next morning, Friday, the weather still lowered and loomed. I wished it would do something positive, like rain. But no. It just sulked and pouted and maintained its dismal and gloomy mood, which transferred itself to those of us below. At least it did to me. I'm not sure about the rest of the residents of Los Angeles.

Mrs. Buck had prepared a delicious breakfast fit for a gloomy day. I knew I was an extremely lucky person because I could afford this house and Mr. and Mrs. Buck to keep it tidy and us fed.

I didn't feel lucky that morning. I felt as depressed and cloudy as the weather.

After breakfast Lulu, Sue, Caroline and I all walked the two blocks from my lovely home on Bunker Hill to Angels Flight, the darling, almost vertical funicular railroad that ran from Olive to Hill and back again all day long. Although I now owned and even knew how to drive a motorcar, I loved Angels Flight and took it every morning and evening when I traveled to and from my place of employment.

When Harvey had given Chloe a brand-new Rolls Royce Silver Ghost, complete with chauffeur so she wouldn't be distracted from caring for the baby whilst driving, they'd gifted me with Chloe's 1924 Moon Roadster. I enjoyed driving, but I clung to Angels Flight as my vehicle of choice when getting to and from work.

"Cheer up, Mercy. I'm sure they'll find the body one of these days," said Lulu. This morning she wore a vivid purple dress with a lowered waist and a big bow that tied on the side. With it she wore a black hat on her bottle-blond hair. Her nails were still bright red. I loved Lulu, but I didn't think I'd ever quite reconcile myself to her taste in fashion. She wanted to be an actress and was only awaiting her opportunity to be "discovered" and thereby become a bright light in the motion pictures.

Although Lulu was a pretty young woman and might look fine on the silver screen, I had my doubts about the way she seemed to be pursuing her goal—filing her nails all day, every day, in the lobby of the Figueroa Building seemed a rather passive way to go about being discovered—I'd never say so to Lulu. Let the girl have her dreams, was what I believed.

I had dreams of my own, which featured me as a best-selling novelist of detective fiction. What's more, I worked on my dream a little bit every day, on my sturdy Underwood typewriting machine at home. As far as I could tell, the only thing Lulu did in pursuit of her goal was read movie magazines. Ah, well. Such is life.

"I hope so, Lulu," said I, resigned to the fact that the crime I'd seen with my very own eyeballs would probably never be solved. Heck, nobody could even find the body of the man I'd watched being murdered.

Sue, as ever, was clad in her tidy white uniform that looked like one a nurse might wear, although she wasn't one. A nurse, I mean. But Dr. Philby chose to have everyone who worked in his office dress in white uniforms, and I thought he was correct to do so. The white uniform made Sue appear respectable and proficient.

As for me, I wore a suit appropriate for the consummate professional secretary. Which I would be if Ernie ever had any work for me to do.

I'd taken typing and shorthand classes (Pitman Method) at the Boston Young Women's Christian Association, much to the consternation of my parents and assorted kinfolk—well, I didn't even tell them about the shorthand classes, since they'd made such a fuss about the typing. Anyhow, I was prepared if I ever needed my secretarial skills in the office, something I had begun to fear would never happen.

Caroline, who came to Angels Flight with us, had her mind on loftier matters I guess, because she didn't add to the conversation.

We walked the few blocks from where the Angels Flight car let us off—this morning we rode on the car called Olivet. The other car was Sinai—first to Fourth, where we said good-bye to Caroline, who walked along Fourth to the Broadway Department Store. Then we continued on to the Figueroa Building, where Sue left us to hike another block to her place of employment. Before she parted from Lulu and me, she said, "I'm sure Lulu's right, Mercy. Eventually they'll find the body. And then Mr. Templeton can find the guy who did it."

"I hope you're both right," I said upon a deep and soulful sigh. The prospect of finding the body and then the murderer seemed slim to me that morning. Perhaps I was only reacting to the lousy weather, but I think the disappearing body had more to do with my mood than the overcast sky.

Mr. Buck stood outside when we got to our place of employment, polishing the brass plaque declaring our workplace to be the Figueroa Building. I'd seen him at my house earlier in the morning, but he left for work at least an hour before the rest of us did. He smiled at us, and we smiled back.

"Good morning to you again, ladies."

"Good morning again, Mr. Buck," said I.

"Hey there, Mr. Buck," said Lulu.

Deciding a compliment was in order, I gave him one. "You know, Mr. Buck, when I first began working in this building, it was a mess. You've tidied it up so much. That plaque, for instance, was sort of a muddy gray when I first saw it. Now it shines like anything."

"Thank you, Miss Mercy," said Mr. Buck. "I try to do a good job."

"You succeed admirably," I said firmly as Lulu and I pushed open the front door and entered the lobby. Lulu headed straight for her desk, and I headed for the stairs. The building had a self-operating elevator, but I didn't use it very often, having had a rather grim experience involving it shortly after my employment began.

"Want to go to lunch again today, Mercy?" Lulu called after me. "We could go across the street and get a corned beef."

Lulu knew I'd become partial to corned beef on rye since my move to Los Angeles. My mother had been appalled when she'd learned of this new dietary choice on my part, but she was pretty much appalled by everything I did, so her attitude didn't bother me. Well…perhaps I should say her attitude didn't affect my choices. Her attitude always bothered me.

I knew Lulu shouldn't be spending her meager pay on taking lunches out, but I also knew she wanted to chat some more about the murder and so forth. As for me, I'd inherited a nice legacy from my late great-aunt, Agatha, much to the displeasure of many members of my family, so I didn't have to worry about money. Told you I was lucky. Nevertheless, because I anticipated another boring day with nothing to do but peer out office windows or read the novel I'd tucked into my handbag, I said, "Sure. That will be fun, Lulu. See you around noonish."

She beamed as she stuffed her hat and handbag under her desk and turned to hang her coat on the coat tree behind her desk. "Good. We'll solve this thing. You just see if we don't."

Oh, boy. I wasn't sure if I wanted to include Lulu in a murder investigation. Providing there was one in the offing. Without a body, such an investigation seemed unlikely.

This unpleasant thought kept me busy as I trudged up the three flights to Ernie's office.

Most days Ernie strolled into the office around nine or nine-thirty, although I always made it a point to arrive at my job punctually at eight. I might not have much work to do, but I did what little I had to the best of my ability. My immediate goal, as opposed to my long-term goal of being a novelist, was to become so important to Ernie's business, he'd promote me to be his assistant. On this gloomy morning, such a thing seemed almost as impossible a prospect as Lulu being discovered in the lobby of our workplace and turned into a Hollywood star.

Much to my surprise, Ernie showed up shortly after I'd settled myself behind my desk and picked up my dust rag. I always put my hat, handbag and gloves in the lower right side drawer of my desk. I'd barely begun dusting everything when he pushed the outer door to the office open and stomped inside.

When I glanced at him, he looked peeved. He also seemed to be absent his perpetual copy of the *Los Angeles Times*. His habit was to enter the room, say hello to me, go to his own office, throw his hat at the coat rack, hang his jacket on the back of his chair, lift his feet to his desk, and read the *Times*. He appeared incompletely clad without his newspaper.

So I asked. "Where's the *Times*?"

Scowling hideously, he said, "Huey Davis wasn't at his news stand this morning. The damned thing's shut up like a furled umbrella."

I vaguely recalled Huey Davis. He was a middle-aged man who ran the news stand about a block down the street from us on Hill. He always wore a cloth cap like those yesterday's men had been wear—

"Ernie," I said abruptly. "Do you suppose it was *Huey Davis* who was murdered yesterday?"

He frowned at me. No surprise there. "Why would you think such a thing?"

"No particular reason, although if it was he who was strangled, he couldn't very well open his news stand this morning, could he? Besides, doesn't he always wear a cloth cap?"

"Cripes," said Ernie. He tramped to his office, where I heard him moving around for a minute or two before he came out again, *sans* coat and hat. "Dammit, I can't start the day without my newspaper."

"Perhaps Mr. Buck can get you one," I suggested. I doubted fetching newspapers for Ernie was in the custodian's job description, providing he had one, but Mr. Buck was a most obliging fellow. Heck, he always made sure Ernie got the parking space directly in front of the Figueroa Building, which was no mean feat in the bustling, crowded city of Los Angeles.

Still frowning, Ernie paused for a few moments before he said, "I'll go ask him." And he left the office as abruptly as he'd entered it. Well, blast. I wanted to talk to him about the murder some more. All right, I know there wasn't a whole lot to talk about, but still... perhaps the poor dead man *was* Huey David. Ernie would like to know it, if only to understand why his favorite news stand would remain unmanned for the foreseeable future.

Did Huey Davis have reddish hair? I couldn't remember, not having paid much attention to him as I walked past his news stand every morning. I frowned, realizing my lack of observational skills bespoke a hole in both my investigational prowess and my novelistic prospects. Then and there I vowed to become more observant.

When Ernie returned to the office a few minutes later, I asked, "Is Mr. Buck getting you a paper?"

"Yeah," he said. He walked past me and on into his office.

Drat the man! I followed him in and, before he could argue, plopped myself on a chair in front of his desk. "Ernie, we need to talk about the murder I witnessed yesterday."

He sat, too, and glowered at me. "Yeah? What's to talk about? You saw a murder, the body disappeared, you can't identify anyone involved in the crime, and the police are stuck. So what's there to talk about?"

"What do you mean, the police are stuck? Did you talk to Phil after his men surveyed the neighborhood?"

"Yeah, I talked to him."

"Well?" I demanded, becoming increasingly annoyed with my tight-lipped employer. "What did Phil have to say? What did his men find out? Who occupies the buildings on the other side of the alleyway from us?"

Ernie heaved a huge sigh and allowed his gaze to visit the ceiling, a gesture I resented.

"Darn you, Ernie Templeton! Stop rolling your eyes at me. I don't see murders being committed every day in the week! This is *important*! It was *upsetting*! The least you can do is tell me what Phil and his men discovered."

"They didn't discover anything," Ernie grumbled.

I guess Ernie saw me beginning to puff up like a blowfish because he held out a hand, palm forward. "All right, all right. I'll tell you what they *discovered*." The way he said the last word made me want to hit him.

"Thank you," I pushed out through clenched teeth.

"They didn't discover much." Again he rushed on before I could explode. "And the person who lives opposite the Figueroa Building is a lady named Mrs. Baker, who runs a boarding house. She appears to be extremely respectable."

Rats. I was hoping that building would be the one in which the culprit or culprits had their lair. "There are other buildings on the block," I reminded him.

"Yeah. I know. Next door to Mrs. Baker on the west is an office building full of doctors and lawyers and other professional people. On the east is another boarding house."

"Golly, I didn't know there were so many boarding houses so close to the office. I wonder if Lulu knew about them before she moved in with me."

"It wouldn't matter. Mrs. Baker and the other lady, whose name I can't remember, only take male tenants."

"That's not fair!" I said before I could ponder the matter thoroughly.

"Nuts, Mercy. Would you take male tenants in your house?"

Darn it. He would have to remind me my own personal rules forbade men as tenants. I frowned at him to let him know I didn't approve of his question. "No, I wouldn't, as you well know. And you're right. I suppose Mrs. Baker and the other lady—"

"Actually, the other boarding house is run by a married couple," said Ernie. He scrunched up his face as he tried to recall their name. "I think they have a German last name. Schmidt, Schultz or Schnitzel or something like that."

"I doubt it's Schnitzel," I grumbled.

"I doubt it too." He grinned at me. He would.

"So are you going to look into the matter yourself?" I asked.

He lifted his eyebrows in an *are you kidding me* manner. "Why should I look into it? Nobody's hired me. Besides, let the police do their jobs."

"I can't believe you said that, Ernest Templeton. You, who quit the police force because of the rampant corruption extant therein. Do you honestly think the police are going to look into a murder when nobody can find the corpse?"

"No. I doubt it very much."

"Well, then?" I demanded.

"Well then what?" he asked, all innocence.

"Well, then, *you* need to look into it!"

"Why?"

"Why? *Why?* Because a man was murdered right outside your office window, Ernie Templeton, in front of my very own eyes. *That's* why!"

"Three floors down," he reminded me.

"Yes, yes. I saw the crime from the third floor. So what? What kind of a feeble excuse is that?"

"How about the fact that you couldn't describe anybody involved in the commission of the crime?"

Hmm. This was a poser. Nevertheless, I had an answer. "Surely someone will report the murdered man missing one of these days. Then we'll know who he is, and you can work from there."

"Maybe. Maybe not. Not everyone has a loving family to report if one of its members goes missing."

What a melancholy thought. I frowned. "Still, I think you should look into the matter, Ernie. After all, it happened right below your office window."

He heaved a gigantic sigh. "If the police can't find a body, what makes you think I can?"

"You're a private investigator! You're good! You've solved cases that have stumped the police before now."

"Only because you made me and wouldn't leave me alone until I saved your hide. This time, there's not even a body to work with."

"Darn you, Ernie Templeton. If you aren't the most pigheaded, stubborn—"

"Here's your paper, Mr. Ernie," came Mr. Buck's voice after a brisk knock at the office door.

I guess Ernie and I had been so intent upon our conversation— perhaps it was more like an argument—we hadn't heard him enter. I turned in my chair and forced a smile to my face, which didn't want to wear it. It wanted to keep scowling at Ernie. Nevertheless,

Mr. Buck was a nice man. *He* hadn't refused to help me as Ernie had, the fiend. Ernie, not Mr. Buck.

"Thanks, Buck," said Ernie, getting up and taking the newspaper. I knew he was glad we'd been interrupted.

"Happy to help, Mr. Ernie. I'll do you favors any old time. You know I will."

Ernie did know it, because he'd help (helped) clear Mr. Buck's son, Calvin, from an accusation of murder a month or so back. Come to think of it, I'd been of more use in that particular case than Ernie. Yet Ernie had garnered the credit. Life can be *so* unfair!

"Where'd you find the newspaper, Mr. Buck?" I asked, curious to know if Huey Davis had perhaps come to work late and opened his stand.

"Walked over to Broadway, Miss Mercy. There's a boy there hawks papers every day."

"Ah. I see." So still no Huey Davis.

"Here. I appreciate your effort on my behalf. Thanks a lot." Ernie handed Mr. Buck a dollar bill, which he at first wouldn't take, but Ernie insisted.

I understood Mr. Buck's hesitation, but he had gone out of his way for Ernie, and it made me feel better about my sometimes annoying employer to know he appreciated people who expended extra effort on his behalf.

Nevertheless, no matter how much I cajoled, he refused to budge on the idea of looking into the murder of the missing man. Darn. I was beginning to think of the poor dead fellow as *my* murdered man. I'd never tell Ernie so, because he'd lecture me about how I shouldn't get involved in investigating a crime, especially a murder, because I was a helpless, hapless female recently come to the mean streets of Los Angeles from my ivory tower in Boston.

He was right about my relative innocence, curse it. Still and all, that didn't mean I couldn't do a little snooping on my own. I didn't like the idea of someone being murdered under my nose and someone else getting away with the dastardly crime.

Therefore, although I had originally opted not to include Lulu in my investigatory efforts, I decided she might just come in handy after all. Heck, if we did happen to stumble across the vile murderer of the anonymous man, it would be harder to get rid of two of us than one of us, right?

You needn't answer that question.

THREE

At a little after twelve o'clock that day, I walked down the staircase in the Figueroa Building and fetched Lulu so we could cross the street and have corned-beef sandwiches at the little diner situated there. It was a busy place, but we always seemed to find a seat at the counter, probably because people were always in a hurry in Los Angeles and diners didn't dawdle.

Ernie, by the way, was nowhere in sight and hadn't been for hours. After he'd perused the *Times* Mr. Buck had so kindly retrieved for him, Ernie'd gone out to tail another erring spouse. There were a lot of them around, erring spouses. The knowledge made me sad.

Oh, very well, so Ernie had a point about my relative innocence. Inexperience had never deterred me before in my pursuit of right and justice, and it wouldn't deter me this time either. If the L.A.P.D. didn't give a hang about the poor strangled man, I, Mercedes Louise Allcutt, did, darn it.

By the way, my sister Chloe's real name is Clovilla Adelaide, which is even worse than Mercedes Louise. Small wonder we called ourselves Chloe and Mercy. Of course, our overbearing mother refused to call us anything but Clovilla and Mercedes Louise. Our mother was *such* a Bostonian prig. And she and my father had gone and bought a house in Southern California. I swear. Occasionally I contemplated moving somewhere like Bermuda. Or maybe Timbuktu. I doubted they'd follow me there. Still and all, I liked Los Angeles. Phooey.

Lulu, who'd been seated at her reception desk and staring out the crystal-clear window at the murky day beyond, turned around as I hit the bottom step and smiled brightly. I guess her morning had been as boring as mine.

"Oh, good," said she. "Is it lunchtime? I'm about to fall asleep here with nothing to do."

"You too? I've been so bored lately."

"I thought you saw somebody being murdered yesterday. How much more excitement do you want?"

"Well, yes. That was awful. But then the body disappeared, and nobody can find it. I doubt the police are even looking."

"That doesn't surprise me any," said Lulu, who wasn't fond of the L.A.P.D. "But you like your job, don't you?"

"Well, yes, but Ernie never has anything for me to do. I've been wondering why he keeps me on"

Lulu rose from behind her desk, revealing herself in her startling purple glory. If anything could liven up a dull day, Lulu was it. She turned to get her coat and hat off the rack behind her desk. "Oh, Ernie will never let you go, Mercy. He's much too fond of you."

"Fond of me?" There was a new concept. "I don't know about that, but I have to tell you I haven't had a single thing to do all week long."

"Really? And it's Friday. I thought you said you loved your job."

"I do when there's anything (something for me to do."

"Well, cheer up, Mercy. This is the first dull patch in a long time, isn't it?"

Was it? Maybe she was right. "I guess so. He never really has much work for me to do."

"I thought you were busy all the time for a few weeks not long ago."

"Was I?" I thought about it. "I guess I was, but that's because I was investigating—Ernie'd call it snooping—on my own. Lulu, he doesn't even have letters for me to type! What good am I as a secretary if I can't use my skills?"

"Golly, Mercy, I'm sorry. Maybe you need to look for another job." She didn't sound happy about the possibility.

I wasn't either. I loved my job. For the most part. "I'm beginning to think Ernie doesn't even know how to use a secretary," I said with a dark note to my voice. "Shouldn't he at least send invoices to his clients or something? I could type those, couldn't I?"

"Um...I guess so."

Clearly, Lulu didn't know any more about the effective use of a secretary's skills than Ernie did. This being the case, I decided to ask Lulu about my idea of investigating yesterday's murder.

"Say, Lulu, since neither one of us has anything to do, would you like to do a little snooping with me after lunch?" I bit my tongue so the *eon* wouldn't leak out after the word *lunch*.

"You betcha! I love helping out with your cases."

My cases, were they? Well, I guess she was right. Ernie sure didn't have any for me.

Can you tell I felt as dreary as the weather?

But feeling gloomy didn't negate the fact that I aimed to do some prying during my lunch hour. And Lulu wanted to help me. It wasn't as though I was dragging her along against her will or anything.

Ernie would be furious. But, blast it, Ernie wouldn't have to know, would he?

Therefore, after we downed our corned-beef sandwiches and chased them down with hot tea (me) and lemonade (Lulu), I said, "Would you be willing to visit a couple of the buildings behind the Figueroa Building just to ask the owners a few questions? Two of the buildings are boarding houses for young men—well, maybe old men, too. I don't know the age group of the tenants. The other one is full of doctors' and lawyers' offices."

"Sure. What are we going to ask them?"

Good question. "I'm not sure. Maybe I'll tell them what I saw and ask if they noticed anything out of the way yesterday."

"But what if one of them is the murderer? You don't want to let on you saw them do the deed, do you?"

Yet another good question. "Gosh, you're right."

I looked at Lulu. Lulu looked back at me. Then Lulu who, while she might not look it, is truly as bright as the clothes she wears, said, "I think we should start at the boarding houses. We could tell the landlords my brother Rupert is looking for a place to rent."

"Brilliant!"

"He already has a place, but we can lie as well as anybody else, can't we?" said Lulu.

When she put it that way, I felt kind of funny about it.

But how stupid of me. "You're absolutely right!"

So we crossed the street, detoured around the Figueroa Building, and ended up in the alley where I'd witnessed the dastardly deed take place the preceding day. We both gazed up at the towering buildings in front of us.

"Um, I think we'll have to walk around the block," said Lulu. "I don't think people usually knock at the back doors of places when they're trying to pretend to be innocent."

"I think you're right."

So we walked around the block and made our way to the first of the boarding-house buildings. A tall, beige brick place, it looked as if it had been in its current location forever, although such a thing was impossible. As Mother was always telling Chloe and me, Los Angeles was an upstart of a place and had no business existing, much less prospering. There was a small porch with two steps, so Lulu and I gamely trotted up the two steps and looked for a knocker or a doorbell. We found one of those old-fashioned twist-type bells, and I twisted it. We both leaned forward to listen, and sure enough, a raspy noise sounded within the building.

"One of the landladies is named Mrs. Baker, but Ernie couldn't remember the name of the couple who runs the other boarding house," I whispered to Lulu as we stood. The wind had whipped up, and both of us hugged our coats tightly against our bodies. I don't know about Lulu, but I inwardly cursed the wind. The day was plenty cold enough without it.

As we waited, Lulu suddenly said, "Say, Mercy, maybe we should bring Buttercup down here tomorrow. She's got a good sniffer. Maybe she can sniff around in the alley and figure out which way the body went."

I gazed at Lulu, bug-eyed. I already knew the girl was bright, but she was bordering on genius today. "Lulu, I swear, *you're* the one who ought to be a private investigator. I'd never have thought of bringing Buttercup here."

A slight blush stained Lulu's cheeks, even through pounds of makeup. "Well, it would be better if you had a bloodhound, I guess, but most dogs have good noses."

"And poodles were originally hunting dogs who retrieved birds from lakes and so forth," I said. Then I wondered if I'd just lied. I remembered reading somewhere the big poodles were originally bred to be water dogs, but I wasn't sure about the toy members of the breed, of which Buttercup was a superb example.

"Yeah? I never knew that. They look so…I dunno. Like prissy ladies who wouldn't pick up a dead duck, much less wade into a lake to get one."

I laughed a little. "True."

The door in front of us opened so abruptly, Lulu and I both jumped an inch or two. Before us stood a gray-haired woman who was large in all directions. Not only was she tall, but she was about as broad as the refrigerator in my lovely kitchen, wore a flour-stained apron and carried a dish towel upon which she seemed to be drying her hands. I don't know about Lulu, but I'd have been intimidated if she hadn't produced a beaming smile and blessed us with it.

"Well, goodness gracious sakes alive, what do we have here? What can two fine ladies like you be doing, ringing my doorbell?"

Lulu started the conversation. "We heard you run a boarding house, ma'am, and my brother—his name is Rupert—will be needing a place to stay when he gets here. He's moving to Los Angeles from Oklahoma."

"Well, my goodness gracious sakes alive!" cried the woman, which seemed a trifle excessive under the circumstances. "Why don't you two come right on in and have a cup of tea, and we can talk about your brother Rupert."

"Um, we don't have much time, ma'am," I said with more haste than propriety. "We're on our lunch hour."

"Working ladies, are you? Well, now, isn't that fine?"

My word, I don't think I'd ever met a person with a more positive outlook on life. Most people felt sorry for young ladies who had to labor for their livings. Or disdained them, as did my mother. "Um," I continued, "we work across the alley from your building."

"Is that so?"

"Yes. At the Figueroa Building."

"My goodness."

Lulu jumped into the muddle I was making. "Anyhow, after a... disturbance the other day, one of the fellows in our building told us your building was a boarding house, and we thought we'd ask about a room for Rupert."

"Aren't you the nicest thing, to think about your brother like that? My name is Mrs. Baker, but you sweet things can call me Dolly. And you are?"

"Lulu LaBelle, ma'am," said Lulu, her voice sinking in the presence of so much overt jollity.

"I see. And your brother is Rupert LaBelle? What a lovely name."

"Actually—" Lulu began, but I broke in. I know, how impolite, huh?

"Yes. And I'm Mary Alden, Mrs. Baker. I mean Dolly."

Don't ask me why I'd just adopted a couple of aliases for Rupert (whose last name was Mullins, as was Lulu's, although she'd chosen the last name LaBelle for herself because she thought it would look better on a theater marquee), but prudence had at last nudged me on the shoulder and told me I should. This lady didn't look like a murderer, and I knew darned well she wasn't one of the threesome I'd seen from Ernie's window the day before, but...well, you just never know. The two killers had been big men, and this woman was huge.

That's not much to go on, is it? Hmm.

"Anyhow, we thought we'd pop by on our lunch hour," I continued, "to see if you have any rooms available, and what services you offer."

"And how much you charge," added Lulu, ever the practical woman of the working classes. Sometimes I longed to be more like her—as long as I didn't have to adopt her mode of dress. Or, to be brutally honest, have to live on what she made as a receptionist at the Figueroa Building.

"Exactly," I said. Then I did a little beaming of my own at the woman, although I had to direct my beam at her from approximately a foot below her face. Mrs. Baker was *big*.

"Well, Lulu and Mary, you've come to the right place. I have an open room right now. My two boys are painting it this very minute. We had a tenant leave us suddenly only a few days ago, and I never rent out a room unless it's spick and span, you know."

And exactly how, why and when did her tenant leave? I wondered. I decided to try some subtlety on the matter. "Oh. Did your tenant move to another city or something?"

"Can't really say, dear. He just up and left." Mrs. Baker snapped her fingers. "Like that. Here one day, gone the next."

Lulu and I glanced at each other. I said, "Um…"

"I wonder if he was the man Mary saw being attacked in the alley," said Lulu before I could think of a delicate way of finding out the same thing. Restraint wasn't one of Lulu's more prominent qualities.

Slapping a hand to an enormous bosom, Mrs. Baker cried, "You saw someone attacked in the alley? How awful for you, Mary."

"It was pretty awful," I said, wanting to elbow Lulu, although we'd come here to find facts, and I guess blurting out our mission was one way to do it. Anyhow, Mrs. Baker didn't know why we were there. She'd bought the Rupert story. I hoped.

"I don't suppose the man Mary saw being attacked was your former lodger?" said Lulu in a questioning tone.

"As to that," said Mrs. Baker, back to being practical again—but beaming still—"I couldn't say. I certainly hope not. Anyhow, all of his belongings are gone, so I suspect he just left in a hurry."

"Without paying the rent, I imagine," said Lulu, implying she knew all about such things.

"Alas, yes." Mrs. Baker laughed as she said it, as if she and Lulu shared a certain camaraderie. "But that sort of thing doesn't happen very often, I'm glad to say. At all odds, the room and board for a single gentleman—an *employed* single gentleman. I don't cater to folks who can't pay their way, you know—is seventy-five dollars per month."

"And how many meals does the seventy-five bucks include?" asked Lulu. I'd never have thought to ask such a pertinent question. It would have been pertinent if we were telling Mrs. Baker the truth, anyhow.

"Breakfast and dinner, dear, and even though I say it as shouldn't, they're mighty fine meals. Why, you can ask any of my other tenants about the meals I serve if you care to."

And how, I wondered, would we go about talking to her tenants, not having been told the names of any of them? I didn't ask.

"That sounds fair," said Lulu.

It didn't sound awfully darned fair to me. I charged my tenants less than that, and I'd bet anything that Mrs. Buck was as good a cook as, if not better than, Mrs. Baker.

On the other hand, Mrs. Baker rented to men, and men, as we all know, make more money than do women, another inequity in this big bad world of ours. Also, they eat more.

"May we see the room?" I asked, aiming for a wide-eyed innocence I didn't particularly feel.

"I'm sorry, dear. As I told you, my sons are painting it this very minute, and I'm afraid I can't allow you into the house right now. I don't allow females abovestairs, don't you know. It wouldn't set the right tone. However, I'd be very glad if Miss LaBelle's brother would come by to take a peek. And, as I said before, I'll be more than happy if the two of you would like to take tea in the parlor."

"I see." Blast. Then again, I don't know what we'd learn by looking at a room, so it probably didn't make any difference. Besides which, we didn't even care about the stupid room.

"What time do you serve the meals?" asked Lulu, all business again. I guess she was trying to drive home the point we were really there for Rupert's sake.

"Breakfast is at six-thirty in the morning, and dinner is at seven in the evening."

Hmm. Same hours as those in my own home. Maybe all boarding houses kept similar rules for mealtimes. Made sense, I reckon. After all, boarding houses catered to single working folks.

Lulu and I stood on the stoop, mute, for another second or two longer as Mrs. Baker smiled down upon us like a benevolent Buddha.

Finally Lulu said, "Well, thanks, Mrs. Baker. I'll tell Rupert about your place. It sounds like it might be right up his alley."

"You do that, dear. Thank you for calling."

I could feel Mrs. Baker smile burning into our backs kind of like a ray of sunshine—or maybe a blowtorch—as we turned and walked down the porch stairs. When we were once more on the sidewalk, Lulu said, "Do we have time to ask at the other boarding house?"

"Don't think so. I think we're a little late already."

"Golly, I don't want to get canned. Let's get back to work."

So we did. And I was right about us being a little late coming back from lunch. I left Lulu at the reception desk and ran up the stairs to the third floor. I'd no sooner stuck my key in the lock of Ernie's outer office door than I heard his booming voice.

"Where the devil have you been?"

Blast. Since Ernie'd already unlocked the door, I removed my own key, shoved the door open and marched in. He stood there, hands on lean hips, glaring at me.

I glared back. "What do you care? It's not as if you have anything for me to do."

"For your information, I pay you to work eight hours a day. I don't pay you to take long *luncheon* hours, whether we have any work or not."

I gave up. He was right. I told him so. After hanging up my coat, I walked to my desk, removed my hat and shoved it and my handbag and gloves into the desk drawer. "You're right. I'm sorry,

Ernie. Lulu and I lost track of time." I glanced at my pagoda-shaped clock and sniffed. "Although we didn't lose track of awfully much of it. Why are you in such a foul mood, anyway?"

Sitting with a *whump* on one of the chairs in front of my desk, Ernie continued frowning, although I sensed I was no longer the object of his ill humor.

He squinted at me. "Any time you're not where you're supposed to be, I suspect you've started snooping into things you shouldn't be."

"Piffle. That's not true, and you know it." I was intensely concerned about a murder I'd witnessed with my very own baby-blues.

His frown abated. "Ah, hell, Mercy. I'm sick of not having decent work to do. I'm a P.I. I'm not a tracker of straying spouses. I hate that kind of work."

"I know you do. Which is one of the reasons I don't know why you don't want to investigate the murder I saw being committed."

"How the devil can I investigate a murder when nobody can find the body?" he demanded, his scowl back and in full glower. "There's nothing to go on. You know it as well as I do." Then his eyes narrowed. "That's what you were doing, wasn't it?"

"Wasn't what?" I asked, although I feared I knew what he was about to say next.

"You were snooping into the murder, weren't you?"

"Why do you think that? According to you, there's nothing to investigate."

"I suppose you dragged Lulu along with you, too, didn't you?"

"Darn you, Ernie Templeton! There was no dragging involved. Lulu wanted to go with me to visit one of those stupid boarding houses! And on Monday, we're going to visit the other one, too. So there! If you and the L.A.P.D. don't care about the poor dead man, Lulu and I do!"

Ernie held up his hands in an "I give up" gesture. "Mercy, I know you don't want to believe me, but I'd rather be investigating the murder you saw than spying on wandering spouses. But there's no *evidence*. And there's no body. Not to mention the fact that there's no client to pay my bills if I did investigate. Can't you get it through your head? You can talk to all the boarding-house owners in the entire city of Los Angeles, and what'll it get you?

I sniffed again. "I don't know, but at least I'm doing something." Heck, I'd pay him to investigate the crime. Mind you, he wouldn't take my money, but I could probably think of a way around his scruples.

"Not to mention the fact," Ernie went on as if I hadn't spoken. Nothing new there. "That if you did happen to knock at the right door, what would happen to you? Do you suppose the people who've murdered another person and covered up the dire act as successfully as these people evidently have would hesitate to do the same thing to you and Lulu? Those two men you saw with the victim were big, weren't they?"

A violent protest bubbled to my lips, but then my logical mind got in the way and made me swallow it. I thought about Ernie's question. "Were they big? I...um...yes. I guess they were. Kind of big. The man with the murdered man was taller than the murdered man, and the man who sneaked up behind them was as tall as the other man—not the murderee, I mean." Befuddled probably best describes my state just then.

Nodding as if to say he'd thought as much, Ernie muttered, "So you and Lulu, both of whom are approximately as big as a couple of minutes, went haring off to face two huge men—"

"I didn't say they were huge!" Even I knew I was fudging the issue.

Naturally, Ernie rolled his eyes. "Hell's bells, Mercy Allcutt, a couple of well-toned midgets could do you and Lulu in without half trying."

"You're not being fair. We didn't ask any probing questions or anything. We only asked about a room."

"Oh, there's a fine investigative technique. Walk up to a house where a murderer might be lurking and don't ask anything to the point."

"Curse it, Ernie! We mentioned a disturbance!"

"I'm sure that'll make any murderer quiver in his boots."

"Her boots," I muttered, stung.

"Her boots. I beg your pardon."

"Well, you and the police don't seem to be doing anything!" I once more pointed out, feeling stupid and resenting Ernie like fire for it.

He heaved a huge sigh, which only made me feel stupider. "If the police ever find a body, they'll investigate, believe me."

"Humph."

"In the meantime, how about you take a letter. Taking letters is what secretaries are supposed to do, isn't it?"

I'm sure my eyes grew huge. "You want me to take a letter? Oh, Ernie! Do you have a real job?"

He grimaced. "I've been working at *real* jobs, Mercy. Only those jobs haven't required letters to be written. However, while you were extending your lunch hour by jabbering with landlords—"

"Landladies," I corrected. "One landlady. And I was only five minutes late getting back to work."

"Cripes. Anyhow, I've got a new client. Her name is Lillian Swale—rather, Mrs. Richard Swale—and I need to write a letter on her behalf."

"Oh, Ernie! I'm so glad you finally got a real—I mean another kind of job!" I rushed to my desk, where I snatched up my stenographer's pad and two sharpened pencils. With any luck, Ernie's letter would be a long one.

FOUR

I t wasn't a long letter. Rather, it was a particularly esoteric one, at least to me.

Propping his feet on his desk and leaning back in his swivel chair—which, thanks to me and my trusty oil can, no longer squealed like a stuck pig. Not that I know anything about pigs, stuck or otherwise—Ernie cupped the back of his head in his hands and studied the ceiling.

"Very well," he said after thinking for a moment or two. Take this down. 'Dear Mr. Gallagher'—that's G-A-L-L-A-G-H-E-R— 'Thank you for your recent communication. Due to the nature of your request, I have secured a gentleman of my acquaintance to meet with your agent and make the transfer.' "

Looking up, I asked, "What transfer?"

Ernie scowled at me. "Don't interrupt my train of thought, dammit."

Scowling in my own right, but knowing he was the boss and, therefore, had the right to scold me for interrupting him, I turned my attention back to my pad and murmured, "Sorry."

"I'll bet," said Ernie, and recommenced thinking. " 'My agent will meet with your agent in the lobby of the Melrose Hotel on

Thursday next at nine o'clock p.m., as you requested. The exchange will be made there and at that time.' "

Ernie paused for so long, I darned near interrupted him again but held in my words. I could see he was thinking. I'd say something sarcastic about how difficult the process was for him, but I'd be lying. Ernie was smart as the proverbial whip. I had to bite my tongue to keep from speaking, however.

" 'Once the exchange is made, I expect you to keep your word about this matter and never refer to it again. It would not be in your best interest to continue to blackmail'—No. Strike that."

Blackmail! How exciting! But I remained mute.

"All right, write this: 'Once this exchange is made'—blah, blah, blah. The next part's okay. Then say, 'It would not be in your best interest to contact me again.' "

"Is 'to contact' a verb?" I asked, unable to stop myself.

Ernie's hands fell to his sides and his head lowered as he stared at me. "Hell, how should I know? People say it all the time."

"Well, perhaps it would be better to say 'It would not be in your best interest to get in touch with me again.' "

Ernie thought for a moment. "I don't like it. Too wordy. I want it to be simple and emphatic. What we want is for the bastard to stop blackmailing her once I give him the money."

Oh, my! It took all my willpower not to shower Ernie with questions. We'd handled two blackmail cases so far in my career as Ernie's secretary, and they were much more interesting than spouse-snooping.

After musing for another few seconds, Ernie said, "Let's try this: 'It would not be in your best interest to call me again. If you persist in annoying me with more demands, I shall involve the police, regardless of any consequences to myself.' "

"I think it should be 'to me,' " I said, and then wished I'd kept my mouth shut.

"Cripes. All right, all right, 'to me,' then. Does that satisfy your majesty?"

"I can't help it if my parents sent me to good schools," I said, miffed.

"Right. How could I forget?"

"Can you tell me about the case yet, or is there more to the letter? Oh, and to whom should I address it?"

"Gimme a minute, will you?"

I clammed up and decided to give him as many minutes as he required. He'd brought a real *job* to the office, and it sounded like a job meant to thwart a blackmailer! Now that's the kind of thing I'd signed on for.

After pondering his letter for another few seconds, Ernie said, "Ah, hell, that's enough. Sign it, 'Your's truly—' No. To hell with politeness. Just sign it 'Lillian Swale.'"

"Will Mrs. Swale come to the office to sign the letter, or will we take it to her?" I asked as I rose to return to my typewriter.

"What's this 'we' of whom you speak?" asked Ernie. His voice sounded as if he'd dipped the words in alum before delivering them.

I frowned, irked. "Very well. Will she come here or will *you* take her the letter to sign?"

"She's scheduled to come to the office at two-thirty, so you better get the letter typed pronto."

"For heaven's sake, Ernie Templeton, I'll have it ready in five minutes. Do you have Mr. Gallagher's address? For the envelope?"

"Oh. Yeah." He reached into his coat pocket and pulled out a crumpled sheet of lined paper. Squinting at it, he read off a post-office box address in Los Angeles, Silverlake District.

"Are you going to go to the post office where that will be delivered to see who opens the post-office box?" I asked eagerly.

"Why should I go to the trouble? I'm going to meet the guy at the Melrose on Thursday."

I gaped at him. "You mean you're not even going to *try* to see what the man looks like? If you went to the post office, you could at least tell what man it is you're going to be seeing. He might be a dangerous criminal, for Pete's sake!"

"Mercy," Ernie said in a syrupy voice, "I don't know when the guy will pick up his mail. You don't know when he'll pick up his mail. Do you suggest I hang out at the Silverlake post office for the next two or three days?"

"It might be more fun than sneaking around taking pictures of straying husbands and wives," I muttered, slightly miffed because he didn't consider my idea a good one. *I* thought it made sense. On the other hand, if Ernie was going to meet him at the Melrose, I don't suppose it would matter much where the fellow picked up his instructions. Now, if the police were involved, it would be a different matter. Bet they'd be happy to get their hands on a blackmailer. However, whoever Lillian Swale was, she evidently didn't share my opinion that blackmailers should be locked up as a menace to society. All things considered, I guess her attitude was valid or she'd have bypassed Ernie and gone to the police in the first place.

"Well then, may I go with you to the Melrose on Thursday? Just to see how you handle the matter of finding the blackmailer and giving him the mazuma?" Even as I asked the question, I knew it was futile. Ernie never wanted to share the excitement, what little there was of it, in his job.

"You already know the answer to your question, Mercy," he said, his voice having lost its syrup and now sounding like a couple of granite slabs rubbing together.

After heaving a big sigh, I said, "Right. I'll go type the letter." As I headed to my desk, however, it did occur to me that, as long as I knew when and where the meet was to take place, there wasn't any reason I couldn't hie myself down to the Melrose Hotel myself—maybe taking Lulu with me for company—and watch the exchange from behind a potted palm or something. I was much more interested in the action side of the business than I was in the letter-typing part.

It took the five minutes I'd told Ernie it would take for me to type the letter, neatly centered on Ernie's small stock of letterhead paper—he'd told me previously that his business required so little correspondence, it wasn't profitable to buy the stuff in bulk—and then type the envelope taken from a similarly small stack of letterhead envelopes. Naturally, I made a carbon copy of the letter, pulled out a pristine manila folder, typed up a label reading SWALE, LILLIAN, pasted the label to the file, and stuck the file in my desk drawer, where it shared space with the precious few other files in the same drawer.

When I took the missive to Ernie for inspection, he asked me to go back and type the letter again on plain white paper. "Why should I advertise my role in the case? We don't want the blackmailer to have any more information than he needs."

I looked bleakly at my handiwork. "You're right. I should have known to type it on plain paper, shouldn't I?"

He patted me on the shoulder. "It's okay, kiddo. We haven't had enough of this kind of work for you to learn the ins and outs of a P.I.'s correspondence."

His words perked me up slightly, although I did wish Ernie wouldn't call me "kiddo." When he did, I felt as though he considered me nothing more than a kid sister or a cousin, and I wanted to be a *partner*, curse it! Then again, I'd only worked for Ernie for a few months. There was plenty of time for me to achieve my goal.

Still and all, at the moment I was his secretary, so I did my duty, returned to my typewriter, and retyped the letter on anonymous white paper and used a plain white envelope for the address.

Ernie was pleased with my efforts, and his gratitude pleased me, so I went back to sitting at my desk, wishing I had more work to do, and looking forward to the advent of Lillian Swale. So far, all of our blackmailed clients had been women, one of them a slinky blonde, and the second of whom—but she'd been a sham in truth and not a blackmail victim at all. I'd have held her fibs against her if she hadn't ended up being murdered. At any rate, I wanted to see if Mrs. Swale fitted the picture I'd formed of all female blackmail victims being svelte, glamorous types.

Boy, I couldn't have been wronger, if that's a word. My little pagoda desk clock had just clicked its minute hand to the six when the outer office door opened and a block of a woman walked inside. I'd been typing away at my novel, having nothing better to do, and when I glanced up, I trust I hid my surprise.

"Mrs. Swale?" I smiled a charming smile at her.

She did not return the favor, but frowned at me as if she hadn't expected anyone but Ernie to be in residence upon her arrival and resented me like fire. "Who are you?" she demanded, her voice matching her appearance, being deep and fat—if that makes any sense.

"My name is Miss Allcutt," I said primly, arranging the brass plaque on my desk proclaiming my name, if she'd bothered to look at it. "I am Mr. Templeton's confidential secretary."

"Humph. I didn't expect to have to go through underlings."

Well, of all the nerve!

It's probably a good thing Ernie opened his own office door just then, or I might have reacted. Shoot, this woman could have rivaled my own mother in the rudeness department. An underling, my left hind foot!

"Come right on in, Mrs. Swale," said Ernie in as suave a voice as I'd ever heard issue from his mouth—never, naturally, directed at me. He might bark at me, or roar or even occasionally be nice, but he had yet to show me an ounce of suavity. "Miss Allcutt has prepared the letter for you to sign, and then we'll get it posted right away."

"I hadn't anticipated having to deal with a secretary," Mrs. Swale groused, frowning at me as she walked to Ernie's office.

He politely stood aside to let her pass before him. "Miss Allcutt is discretion itself, Mrs. Swale. You have nothing to fear from this office. Our business is as private as it gets." Then he tipped me a wink and entered his office after the offensive woman.

"Pooh," I muttered to myself after the door closed. Then I wondered what the woman had done to get herself blackmailed. After meeting her—sort of—I couldn't imagine her being wooed by some bounder who then threatened to tell her husband she'd succumbed to his advances. Who'd want her? On the other hand, why was she being blackmailed? Our first blackmail victim had been denuded of her toy poodle during an illicit tryst. I, by the way, had been instrumental in recovering the lost poodle.

Fortunately for me, Mrs. Swale only stayed in Ernie's office long enough to sign the letter I'd typed, and then she left. As soon as Ernie'd seen her out the front office door, he said, "Will you take this downstairs, please, Mercy? I think the afternoon mail pickup is at three or four, so this should make it into today's mail with no problem."

"Will do," said I in my eager secretarial mode, figuring that if I was agreeable, Ernie'd be more likely to tell me Mrs. Swale's tale than if I badgered him right off the bat.

So I took the letter, stamped it, left the office, tripped down the stairs, and handed it to Lulu at the front desk. "Afternoon, Lulu. The mailman hasn't been here yet, has he?"

"Only for the noon pickup and delivery. He'll be back again at three-thirty or four." She took the letter I handed her. "Was that buffalo of a woman here to see Ernie?" she asked as she put my letter onto the pile already accumulated in a wicker basket. Naturally, Lulu held a fingernail file in her hand. No matter the hour, Lulu either held a fingernail file with which she filed her brilliantly colored nails, or she had an open bottle of nail varnish on her desk with which she touched up any nail the polish of which had become chipped.

"Buffalo's a good word for her. She was rude, too."

"In Oklahoma they say buffaloes are mean as rabid dogs," said Lulu.

I laughed. "This one sure was. And yes, she was here to see Ernie."

"How come?" Lulu leaned over eagerly to hear why Mrs. Swale had come to call on Ernie.

"I'm really sorry, Lulu, but I don't know. Ernie didn't tell me her story." That wasn't even much of a lie. Yet. Besides, Ernie was a private investigator, and I took the "private" part of his job description seriously.

"Nuts," said Lulu, straightening in her chair again.

I shrugged. "Sorry. I just hope she doesn't come back again, because she's not nice at all. She called me an 'underling.' "

"Shoot. You're right. That wasn't nice."

"I guess it takes all kinds."

"You betcha." She paused for a second, then said, "Did she look familiar to you?" in a puzzled-sounding voice.

I thought about it. "No."

Lulu sighed. "I just thought for a minute…But you're probably right. She didn't look familiar to me, either."

I stared at Lulu for a moment, but she said no more, so I left her opening her desk drawer, undoubtedly to remove a bottle of nail varnish.

As soon as I got back to the office, I tackled Ernie. Not in the literal sense. He sat in his office chair, staring out the window, so I didn't interrupt him doing anything important. He heard me coming. I could tell, because his shoulders kind of hunched, and I suspected he knew why I was there.

"I can't talk about my clients' private cases," he said before I could begin grilling him.

"Nuts. I'm your confidential secretary. I won't tell anyone. But I can't believe that woman has had an illicit adventure with some man who's blackmailing her so he won't tell her husband."

His head swiveled so fast, I feared for his neck muscles. "An illicit adventure?" And he began laughing at me.

I took his amusement at my expense for as long as I could, then snapped, "Darn you, Ernie Templeton, quit jeering at me and tell me why that horrid woman is being blackmailed!"

He'd managed to turn his chair around so his body and his head were once more in alignment. After he wiped his eyes on his handkerchief, he said, "Aw, hell, I don't really care. She bribed a judge at a dog show, this Gallagher bimbo saw her do it, and now he's blackmailing her. Says he'll report her to the Beverly Hills Kennel Club if she doesn't pay him a bunch of bucks."

I more or less collapsed into one of the chairs sitting before Ernie's desk. "She's being blackmailed because she bribed a judge at a *dog* show?" I could scarcely believe my ears.

Ernie held up his hands in an "it's not my fault" gesture. "Hey, some people are really in to the dog-show world."

"Well…I guess I already knew that. Heck, some of my parents' friends actually *hire* people to show their dogs in various dog shows. But…she bribed a judge?" I contemplated the boxy, stern Mrs. Swale. "Somehow, she doesn't look the type."

"Looks can be deceiving. She said the dog world is nothing but politics, and she wants one of her mastiffs to go to Westminster. Said if the one she entered didn't win that particular show, he wouldn't make it."

"Good Lord."

"My sentiments exactly."

After thinking about the matter for another moment or two, I said, "I'm not surprised she has mastiffs. She's built kind of like one."

My unkind comment, however true, set Ernie off again. So I left him laughing in his room and went back to work on my novel. It was kind of nice to be able to write on the job, but I'd just as soon have more investigatorial work to do. After all, my novels of mystery and suspense would be much more believable if I knew what I was writing about.

Ah, well. Such is life.

A little after five in the afternoon, I said good-bye to Ernie, left the office, joined Lulu in the lobby of the Figueroa Building where Caroline met us, and the three of us walked to the dentist's office where we met up with Sue. Then we all trudged to Angels Flight, where we took the one-block ride up the hill, then walked another two blocks to my lovely home on Bunker Hill.

After dinner, I asked Lulu if she'd like to ride with me to the Melrose Hotel on Thursday next to watch Ernie meet with a black-mailer. Naturally, she said yes.

You'll notice I didn't mention a thing about Mrs. Swale, mastiffs, or anything else likely to give the game away. Discretion itself was I.

FIVE

The day after the Mrs. Swale incident was Saturday, and neither Lulu nor I had to work. Caroline and Sue weren't as lucky as we. However, their having to work a half-day suited our plans admirably, since we aimed to do more snooping into the murder of the vanished man and didn't require their company. Or maybe we just didn't want anyone else to tell us we were being silly.

Although Ernie had taught me how to drive my lovely almost-new Moon Roadster, I wasn't precisely an expert at the driving arts by then. However, Lulu had braved my driving before, and she claimed to be undaunted by the prospect of sitting next to me, Buttercup on her lap, whilst I navigated the heavy Los Angeles traffic.

Truth to tell, traffic wasn't bad in my neighborhood. It was only after I got to Hill Street that things got thick. Literally. Hordes of people used their Saturdays to visit the Grand Central Market on Broadway to do their weekly marketing. Lulu and I enjoyed investigating the Grand Central Market from time to time. You could find anything from a side of beef to dozens of tortillas (which I'd never seen before moving to Los Angeles) to pounds of fruit and vegetables to clothing, and even have a sandwich or a bowl of chop suey there. The place was always abustle with vendors and shoppers.

On Saturday, however, my little Moon Roadster chugged its way through the swarming automobiles and people as I did my best to get us to the Figueroa Building without mowing anyone down or hitting anything. Naturally, since Ernie didn't work on Saturdays, either, the convenient parking space smack in front of the building wasn't available, and I had to search high and low to find another place to park. Well, there were spaces available, but I'd have had to back in to them, and I wasn't ready for quite that much adventure yet.

Finally, about a block away from the Figueroa Building and around the corner, on Spring, we found a space conveniently vacated by a Packard just as we showed up. I was able to nose the Roadster into the space. By the time I got the car parked, I was a nervous wreck and perspiring freely in spite of the chilly weather.

Lulu patted me on the back. "You did good, Mercy. I know parking's hard. At least Rupert tells me it is. And you dodged all those people swell, too."

"Thanks," I whispered, wishing I possessed a braver soul. Perhaps all it took was practice when it came to driving a machine in the City of the Angels. No. Practice would help, but one also needed nerves of steel. Mine definitely weren't steely enough yet.

Anyhow, after wiping my glowing brow and clipping Buttercup's blue leash to her adorable blue collar (decorated with rhinestones), I got out of the car on the driver's side, Lulu exited on the passenger side, and we began our stroll to the alleyway behind the Figueroa Building.

I'd had the forethought to wear sensible shoes and insist Lulu do likewise, although she didn't generally go in for sensible clothing. For instance, while I wore a plain blue skirt, white blouse and a blue sweater along with shoes suitable for walking, and hoped the sweater would keep me warm enough, Lulu had chosen a less sober costume. As soon as I stepped foot out of the machine, I felt chilled. Of course, that might have been due to my bedewed brow encountering the open air. With any luck, after I dried out, I wouldn't be cold any longer.

One might say Lulu, too, had on clothing suitable for exercise. But for heaven's sake, she wore trousers! Mind you, some of the most dashing ladies of the day were revealing themselves in trousers, but nobody I knew wore them, except for the lounging pajamas Chloe and some other fashionable ladies wore indoors. Not Lulu. She claimed they were amazingly comfortable.

She was probably right, but I admit to being shocked when she first descended the staircase in the morning. I'd never tell her so. Anyhow, she also had a heavy gray sweater on top of her violently pink blouse so, except for exposing the shape of her legs to the world, she didn't reveal any of the rest of her anatomy. And really, Lulu's trousers were wide enough not to show too much of her shape unless the wind decided to blow. At least her shoes were suitable for walking. I only hoped we wouldn't attract too much attention. It probably wouldn't matter, though, since we were ostensibly doing nothing more intriguing than walking the dog.

Buttercup, always suitably clad, loved taking walks, so she was a happy toy poodle as we meandered over to the Figueroa Building, attempting to appear casual. It wouldn't do for the murderer, if he was there, to catch sight of us and realize we were attempting detection. Provided we could find anything to detect.

Such an event—detecting anything, I mean—appeared less than probable as we started down the alleyway behind the row of structures comprising the Figueroa Building. In fact, there wasn't a soul to be seen. Not even a rat. Or a cat, for that matter.

"Well, this doesn't look very promising," said Lulu when we were almost directly behind our building.

"No." I heaved a sigh. "I guess I knew we wouldn't find anything, but I can't help being a little disappointed. I mean, if we could have—*eek!*"

My squeal had been prompted by my very own, extremely proper and well-behaved toy poodle, who'd suddenly yipped in delight and started tugging on her leash. Mind you, she was a small dog, but she was strong and, once determined upon a course of action, wasn't easily distracted.

"Crumb," said Lulu. "What's up with Buttercup?"

"I don't know. Maybe she saw a stray cat or something."

As we approached the corner of the building next to ours—rather quickly, thanks to Buttercup—my nose wrinkled.

I guess Lulu's did, too, because she said, "Ew. What's that awful smell? Smells like when a 'possum died under the outhouse once."

And what a pleasant visual image *this* piece of information evoked. Still, Lulu was right about the stink. "I don't know about dead rats, but something sure smells," I said.

Buttercup, on the other hand, leaped and yipped as if she were inhaling the aroma emanating from a bed of violets. Dogs, even adorable, superior ones like Buttercup, occasionally enjoyed the vilest things.

Then we got to the space between the buildings, and Lulu and I emitted a duet of piercing shrieks. Maybe Buttercup did, too. I wasn't keeping track.

"It's the man!" I cried, horrified and dumbfounded and all the other things one is when one discovers a two-day-old corpse one had assumed had been hauled away and dumped in the Pacific Ocean.

"Good Lord!" cried Lulu in her turn. "We'd better go get the coppers!"

I considered this a brilliant suggestion.

Buttercup didn't, but I was bigger than she, so I scooped her up, and Lulu and I raced back to the Roadster. Thanks to a curious incident in which the two of us had participated (against our will) a few weeks prior to this incident, I knew exactly where the nearest police station lay, and I drove straight there. Fortunately for all of us, I avoided all pedestrians and automobiles along the way, and even found a convenient parking space when we got to the police station. We all but stumbled over ourselves getting out of the car, and then ran to the front door.

We'd barely made it inside when Lulu screeched, "We found the body! We found the body!"

The police officer manning the front desk looked at us as if we were insane. I sucked in about a gallon of police-station-scented air—which is rather unpleasant, by the way—and, with a hand covering my thundering heart, said, "I beg your pardon, Officer, but we just discovered a dead body in the space between the Figueroa Building on Seventh and Hill and the building next to it to the north. It's the body of the man I saw being killed on Thursday. But it had disappeared when the police came to investigate."

"Maybe you better go a little slower," said the policeman, eyeing us doubtfully. "Who'd you say you were?"

I took in another deep breath and told myself to cease panicking and get a hold upon my nerves. It wouldn't do to alienate this police officer, even if he did seem to be a dim example of the species.

"I saw a man being murdered on Thursday in the alleyway behind the Figueroa Building. My name is Miss Mercy Allcutt, and this is Miss Lulu LaBelle. When I called the police and they came to investigate, the body had vanished. But we just saw it again!" My voice had begun to rise on the last sentence, and I once more lectured myself to calm down. Slowly and deliberately, I said, "You might want to telephone Detective Phil Bigelow. He was called out on Thursday, and he can give you all the details." So could I, but I sensed this man would be more likely to accept the truth from Phil than from me.

"Bigelow, eh?" he said, as if the name were familiar to him.

"Yes. I am secretary to Mr. Ernest Templeton, and—"

A loud guffaw broke my chain of thought. I frowned at the policeman. "Do you find the idea of murder amusing, Officer?"

He shook his head. "Naw. It's not that. It's Ernie. He's a good guy. I just can't see you as his secretary, is all."

"And why is that?" Ice had crept into my voice.

"You're too...I don't know. Too classy for old Ern, is all, I guess."

Darn it! Why was it, even when I tried with all my considerable talent to appear as one of the working-class masses, people always pegged me as a moneyed young woman? Piddle on them all.

Steaming by then, I said, "Be that as it may, I witnessed a

murder committed, and I expect you to do your duty. Telephone Detective Bigelow right this minute, and get some of Los Angeles's finest out there to collect the body! Now!"

When Boston creeps into my voice, I guess I take on a powerful air, because people generally do what I want them to do. A legacy from my ghastly mother, no doubt.

"Yes, ma'am," the officer said. He picked up the receiver and spoke into it. "Millie, get me Bigelow at First."

Lulu whispered in my ear, "Shoot, Mercy, I didn't know you could sound so ferocious. Good going."

"I learned from my mother," I said glumly. I had *so* hoped to avoid any of mother's Boston manners. On the other hand, some of them came in handy every now and then. Take the current situation, for instance.

After another minute or two, the policeman started speaking quite politely into the receiver of his 'phone, and I presumed he was talking to Phil.

Tugging on my sweater sleeve, Lulu said, "C'mon, Mercy. We might as well sit down." She jerked her head at a row of hard metal chairs.

I remembered those chairs. They were extremely uncomfortable. However, Lulu was right. We might as well get off our feet, as we'd used them quite a bit already. So we sat, and Buttercup politely sat still at my feet.

After what seemed like three hours, but was probably only about three minutes, the officer hung the receiver on the hook and glanced our way. "Bigelow says you're telling the truth."

Bridling instantly, I asked frigidly, "And why, pray, would we lie about something so horrible?"

He shrugged. "You'd be surprised what people do sometimes."

"I assure you, Officer, I'm not likely to joke about something as dire as murder."

"Yeah. That's what Bigelow said."

"Stop grinding your teeth, Mercy," Lulu whispered. "It's bad for them."

Buttercup decided just then to jump onto my lap, and I decided

Lulu was right. Why let this oafish man upset me. According to Ernie, most of the officers in the L.A.P.D. were stupid and at least an equal number of them were crooks.

After another moment or three had passed, two more uniformed officers shoved through the door behind the reception desk—if that's what you call it in a police station—and came up to us.

"You ladies say you seen a body?"

Deplorable grammar! Nevertheless, I said, "Yes, we did. We found the man whom I saw murdered on Thursday morning. He was lying in the space between the Figueroa Building and the building to its north when we were walking my dog this morning. In the alleyway there."

"You walk your dog in alleys all the time?" the same man asked.

"No. I do not. However, I was curious to see if we could find any remnant of the crime the police might have missed."

"You don't trust us, eh?" said the second man.

I glared at him. "No. I do not. I've heard and seen too many things about the Los Angeles Police Department to put much credence in anything they do."

"That's not very nice," said the first man.

"She's Ernie Templeton's secretary," offered the fellow behind the desk.

The two officers nodded, as if those simple words explained my attitude. Which they did. I still resented them.

"And I work in the lobby as the Figueroa's receptionist," Lulu piped up. I guess she didn't like being ignored. Can't say as I blamed her, although I'd just as soon be ignored by these three brutish men.

"Well, you'd better come along with us and show us this body," said the first uniform. I noticed his shield proclaimed him as Gerald Potter. The other guy was John Smith. I'm not kidding.

"Thank you." My voice brittle, I gently set Buttercup on the floor and rose from my uncomfortable seat. Lulu stood, too.

"Do we have to ride with you? Mercy's got her Roadster out there."

The two men exchanged a glance then refocused on the three of us. "You better come with us so we don't get separated."

"Very well," I said, aiming for regal and achieving it, to judge by the looks of disgust on the two men's faces. Very well, so my mother's attitude was annoying. I already knew that from years of bitter experience.

We all left the station together. Officer Smith opened the back door to a nearby prowl car. "You two ladies and the pup can get in the back seat," said he. Then he added, "Cute dog," and I didn't hate him quite so much anymore.

"Thank you," Lulu and I said together. We made a pretty nifty duet sometimes.

It didn't take long for the policeman to drive us to the alleyway behind the Figueroa Building. As he turned into it, he said, "Point out the building, please. I'll stop the machine before we get there, and we'll walk the rest of the way. Don't want to mess up any evidence if there is any."

Sound reasoning, even if it did come from Officer Potter, who hadn't impressed me as a fellow of any great perspicacity.

"Here. Stop here. It's the next building," Lulu said as I was busy contemplating the state of education in the United States, thereby reminding me to pay attention to the business at hand and not get sidetracked.

Officer Potter pulled the police car to the side of the alley, and Officer Smith politely opened the back door for Lulu, Buttercup and me. We got out.

"Show us where you saw the body, please," said Officer Potter. "You lead the way, and we'll follow."

"Very well."

We were only a few yards from where we'd discovered the corpse, but I sensed something amiss even before we got to the space between the two buildings. For one thing, Buttercup wasn't yanking me along on the lead. For another thing, the smell was gone—or maybe the wind had changed direction.

"I don't like this, Mercy," Lulu muttered. "It doesn't stink anymore."

"I'm afraid you're right, Lulu," I replied in a similarly subdued tone.

Buttercup, while not as exuberant as she'd been the first time we'd traversed this alley, still seemed interested, so perhaps our forebodings were for naught.

I should have known better. Although Buttercup, leading with her nose glued to the filthy alleyway the whole time, led us directly to where we'd discovered the corpse, the corpse itself had vanished as neatly as it had done on Thursday.

"Blast and heck," said Lulu.

"Nuts," said I.

Buttercup started rolling where the corpse had been. I guess she, with her superior scent-sniffing ability, could tell where the body'd been.

"Stop it, Buttercup." I pulled on her leash. She gave up reluctantly, but she obeyed. "Good dog."

The policemen had come up behind us. "I don't see no body," said Officer Potter.

"Neither do I," said Officer Smith.

"Neither do we," I said in my turn, and I sighed deeply. "Somebody's taken it away again."

"You're sure it was there?" Potter.

"Yes." Me.

"Yeah?" Smith.

"Yeah." Lulu.

Silence ensued. It was broken by Officer Potter a few moments later. "Well, I sure don't see nothing resembling a body."

The validity of his observation couldn't be denied. I not only didn't see nothing resembling a body, I didn't even see anything resembling a body.

"Yes," I said. "I know. But it was there."

"It sure was. Scared me to death," said Lulu.

"Hmm."

Frustrated and annoyed, I said, "It was there, I tell you! If you don't believe me, look at this." And I loosened my grip on Buttercup's leash and let her have at the empty space once more. Again, she rolled in what must have been the delicious odor left by the decomposing corpse. Ew. The notion made me shudder. Not so Buttercup, who rolled and rolled in an ecstasy of doggie delight.

"The dog sure smells something," said Potter.

I regret to say I rolled my eyes, although I didn't speak. I figure one bad deed and one good deed probably canceled each other out.

"Yeah," said Smith.

Then both officers walked over to Buttercup and knelt on the ground. I pulled Buttercup to my side once more.

"You, young lady, are taking a bath as soon as we get home," I told her severely.

"Don't be too hard on her," Lulu advised. "It'll be harder for the coppers to disbelieve the nose of a dog than the statements of a couple of girls."

She was right, curse the male sex to perdition.

Smith, his nose almost bumping against the ground, grunted and gestured at Potter, who bent over and did likewise. I saw his nose wrinkle.

Aha! So there lingered a scent even a policeman couldn't miss! I loved my dog a whole lot just then. I still aimed to bathe her before I picked her up and hugged her.

We heard the engine of another motorcar, and when Lulu and I turned, it was to see one more police car, this one driven by a man I didn't recognize. Phil Bigelow sat in the seat beside him, and darned if Ernie wasn't slumped in the back seat. The sight jarred me a bit, since the last time Ernie'd ridden in a police car, it was because he was suspected of murdering a woman. Another jumbled job by the police department I need not say, I'm sure. In fact, it has been I, Mercedes Louise Allcutt, who'd solved that particular case.

But prior cases were neither here nor there. I lifted an arm and waved at Phil and Ernie.

"What the blazes are you two doing here on a Saturday?" asked Ernie, sounding vexed, if not downright surly.

I straightened my spine. "Lulu and I were taking Buttercup for a walk, and we found"—I paused to swallow—"the body of the man I saw being murdered."

"Where is it?" asked Phil. He didn't sound at all peevish, bless him.

"I don't know," I admitted.

Lulu shrugged.

"Cripes," said Ernie. "You just can't keep your nose out of police business, can you, Mercy?"

"It's not my nose, but Buttercup's in this instance," I said with dignity.

"Huh."

Officers Potter and Smith arose, turned, and saluted Phil. At least I'm pretty sure it was Phil whom they saluted, since he was their superior officer, and Ernie didn't count for anything as far as the L.A.P.D. was concerned.

Potter spoke first. "The dog's nose is right, Detective Bigelow. A rotting corpse of something dead was laying there not long ago."

"Lying," I murmured, unable to help myself.

Ernie frowned at me.

Phil didn't. "Yeah? Well, hell."

We stood in the alleyway, a quintet of puzzled humans—the driver of Phil's machine had stayed therein—and a brilliant toy poodle, staring at the spot where a body had lain. Unfortunately, it wasn't there any longer, and there didn't seem to be a soul anywhere nearby who could tell us what had happened to it.

After several seconds of silence, Phil said doubtfully, "Well, I guess we can question the neighbors again."

"Probably won't do any good," said Ernie, the perennial pessimist.

"Won't do any harm," I countered instantly.

"She's right, Ernie," said Phil.

"Mercy's always right," said my staunch friend Lulu. "Well, usually, anyhow," she added. The qualifier didn't make her less staunch.

Ernie, as might have been expected, said, "Huh."

So Phil directed Officers Potter and Smith to query neighbors on all sides of and behind the Figueroa Building. Ernie continued frowning. Lulu, Buttercup and I hiked all the way back to the police station to fetch my lovely Moon Roadster, and I drove us home.

The first thing I did once we got there was give Buttercup a bath. She wasn't pleased with me, but I was absolutely delighted with her. If it hadn't been for her superior sniffer, no one would have believed Lulu and me when we reported finding the body.

Not that a perpetually disappearing corpse did anyone any good. Drat.

SIX

The rest of the weekend passed peacefully enough. I read and wrote. Lulu read, too (her preferred reading material consisted of movie magazines), Caroline and Sue came home at noon on Saturday and rested in their rooms.

Caroline went to church on Sunday and then took a red car to visit her parents in Alhambra. Sue left the house early. I don't know where she went, but I'm sure she was doing something equally respectable.

As for Lulu and me, although we'd visited the Angelica Gospel Hall a few times a few months earlier, we lazed around on Sunday morning and didn't attend any church service at all. I know. Sinful. Still and all, it was pleasant for a working girl to have a whole day to herself.

Along about four on Sunday afternoon, Lulu and I took a sweet-smelling Buttercup for a walk around the neighborhood.

"What I can't figure out," said Lulu as we moseyed along, Buttercup sniffing joyfully at the plant life and telephone poles on our way, "is what happened to that darned body. *Again*, for cripes' sake."

"I know. This whole case is terribly frustrating. We don't even know who the murdered man is—was—for heaven's sake. And his body keeps vanishing."

"Yeah," grumbled Lulu. She brightened minimally. "But at least we can watch Ernie deal with a blackmailer on Thursday."

"Yes. Something to look forward to," said I, not particularly cheered by the notion. True, I was interested in witnessing an exchange between Ernie and a blackmailer, but because if the coming week was anything like the last one, I'd have nothing to do between Monday and Thursday.

"Somebody's bound to find the body someday," said Lulu with more hope than I felt.

"I suppose so, although we're really close to the Pacific Ocean. Somebody could put it in cement overshoes and dump him in the ocean."

After a short spate of silence, I glanced at Lulu, who gaped at me, big-eyed.

"What?" I asked.

"I think you've been reading too many detective books," she said. "Cement overshoes?"

"I got the expression out of the newspaper. Gangsters in Chicago are always sticking people's feet in buckets of cement. Then they throw the bodies into Lake Michigan after the cement sets. With the feet cased in cement, the bodies don't rise to the surface."

Lulu's nose wrinkled and her lip curled. "I'm glad we live in Los Angeles."

"But there's still the Pacific Ocean," I reminded her. "There's as much cement in L.A. as there is in Chicago. And there are probably sharks and other predatory creatures in the Pacific Ocean."

"I guess so."

The rest of the day passed approximately as productively as the first part had. In other words, nothing happened.

On Monday Lulu, Caroline, Sue and I all began our weekly routine: eating a delicious breakfast prepared for us by Mrs. Buck, walking to Angels Flight, taking same to Hill Street, and thence on to our respective places of employment.

Mr. Buck, who had waved farewell to us as we ate our breakfast earlier in the morning, greeted Lulu and me when we arrived at the Figueroa Building a little before eight o'clock. There we bade good-bye to Sue and entered the building.

"Good morning again, Mr. Buck," I said, happy to have such a tidy gentleman maintaining both my home and my workplace.

"Morning again, Miss Mercy. Miss Lulu."

"Hey, Mr. Buck," said Lulu, aiming herself at the reception desk as I headed for the staircase.

Oddly enough, a letter awaited me on my desk when I unlocked the office door and entered. I picked it up saw the note clipped thereto. It said: *Mercy, please type this up. I'll be in at nine or so. Ernie.*

Work! Ernie had given me *work* to do! Mind you, it wouldn't take me an hour to type the puny little letter he'd left for me, but its presence signified business might be picking up. This being the case, and because I was so glad to have something to do, I sat myself down and typed the letter before even I dusted the office and straightened the pictures on the walls.

It wasn't much of a letter. Still, I was encouraged as I typed it, because it spelled out the terms by which Ernie was willing to accept another job for a person named Mrs. Benjamin Hallowell, who'd evidently misplaced a child.

Dear Mrs. Hallowell:

Per your request, I am willing to attempt to locate your daughter, Gladys. Naturally, I can guarantee no specific results. My fee is twenty-five dollars per day plus expenses, and I require a fifty-dollar retainer before I begin my search.

In order to conduct a proper investigation, I will need the names of your daughter's friends, their addresses and, if possible, any of her friends' telephone numbers. It would behoove you to contemplate any unusual behaviors you have noticed with regard to Gladys in the past month or so. Then please tell me anything, even if you consider it trivial, that might assist me in locating her.

If these terms are agreeable to you, please telephone my office at

the number printed above. My secretary will set up a convenient time for you to come in with the information I have requested.
Sincerely,
Ernest Templeton, Private Investigator

A missing child! How fascinating! And how awful for Gladys's parents. On the other hand, perhaps the girl had run away from home because they beat her. My bet, however, was that silly Gladys had run off with an unsuitable lover. Perhaps I was maligning the child. Darn it, I wished Ernie would come in so I could get his thoughts on the Gladys matter.

Anyhow, it took about five minutes for me to type the letter (on letterhead this time) and the envelope to enclose it, and to put it on Ernie's desk along with the carbon copy. Although Ernie didn't think so, *I* believed it was important to have his signature, even his carbonized one, on all correspondence. After all, in some respects, we were an arm of the law, and one had to cross one's T's and dot one's I's in order to maintain credibility in the eyes of the police.

Oh, very well, our being an arm of the law was a stretch. Still and all, Ernie and the police—primarily in the person of Phil Bigelow—worked closely together from time to time.

I'd already dusted Ernie's desk and had begun dusting my own when he strolled in a little after nine that morning, a newspaper snugged under his arm. I glanced at the newspaper and said, "Mr. Davis is back on the job, I presume?"

He eyed my dust cloth with misgiving, as if he feared I'd get carried away and dust him one of these days. "You presume wrong. Huey's son was manning the news stand, and he claims Huey's out of commission for a while."

"What does 'out of commission' mean?"

"Darned if I know."

My breath caught in my throat. Then I burst out, "It was Huey!"

"What was Huey?" my irritating employer asked, slouching into his room, over to his desk, removing his coat and hat, and hanging them on the rack. I followed hot on his heels.

"The man I saw being murdered," I said in exasperation. "For heaven's sake, Ernie, it's the only scenario that makes sense!"

"Somebody murdering Huey doesn't make any sense at all," said Ernie, confound him. "Why would anybody murder Huey? He's just a newspaper guy. And a nice one."

"Oh, for heaven's sake. Charles Dickens might approve of coincidences in his works of fiction, but I don't."

Ernie eyed me as he picked up the neatly typed letter I'd laid out for him, slumped into his chair and slung his feet onto his desk, setting the newspaper aside for the nonce. "What's Charles Dickens have to do with anything."

"Bother!" said I, and returned to my desk.

He followed me shortly thereafter, the signed letter in his hand. "Can you see that this gets into the early mail?"

"I certainly will. It's nice to have work again."

"Yeah. It is kind of nice."

"What do you think happened to Gladys?"

Ernie shrugged. "How should I know?"

"Ernie! Don't you have any ideas at all?" He could be exasperating without half trying, could Ernie.

"Hell, Mrs. Hallowell called me over the weekend in tears. If she doesn't know what happened to her kid, how am I supposed to know?"

I gazed up at him unhappily. "Didn't she give you any clues at all? Did Gladys have an unsuitable gentleman friend? Do you think she was kidnapped? Did she run away from home because she was unhappy there?"

With an amazing show of energy, considering he was Ernie, he threw up his arms. "I don't have a notion in the world, and I won't have one until Mrs. Hallowell telephones, sets up an appointment, and I have an opportunity to talk to her."

Phooey.

Ernie returned to his office, and I licked a stamp, affixed it to the envelope, and left the office to take it to the reception desk. "Be right back," I said as I opened the front office door.

"Uh," said Ernie. Typical.

Lulu, filing her nails as usual, was pleased to see me. "Hey, Mercy. You don't usually show up before lunch."

"Believe it or not, we actually have a job prospect." I flapped the envelope at her. "This is a letter Ernie wrote to a potential client."

"Wow, that makes two jobs in only a couple of days!"

"Not to mention a murder."

"Well, yeah, but since nobody can find the body, I don't know if it counts as a job. Especially since nobody's hired Ernie to do anything about it, right?"

"You're right of course," I said, my posture slumping slightly. Curse that disappearing body!

When I returned to the office, I was surprised to see Ernie standing beside my desk, the *Los Angeles Times* in his hand and folded back to expose an article on the second page.

"You were right," said he.

"About what?" said I.

"About the body being Huey's."

"What? Are you serious? If you're playing some kind of joke—"

Ernie cut me off by thrusting the newspaper at me and saying, "Read this."

So I did. This is what the article said:

Body Discovered in Venice Canal.

That was only the headline, but it stopped me cold. I glanced up at Ernie. "Venice? How could the body of a Los Angeles newspaper vendor end up in a canal in Venice?" I figured he was making sport of me, and I was not amused.

"Venice, California, Mercy. Not Venice, Italy."

"Oh. I didn't know we had one."

"We do."

So I returned to the article, which continued:

The body of sixty-five-year-old Hugh Earl Davis was found Sunday evening in a Venice canal. The gruesome discovery was made by Mr. George Pettigrew, who was walking his dog at the time. Mr. Pettigrew's spaniel drew Mr. Pettigrew's attention to the body, which was floating in the canal. Identification found in the deceased man's pocket identified him as Mr. Hugh Earl Davis. Mr. Davis operated a newsstand on Hill Street in Los Angeles for many years.

Mr. Davis appeared to have been done to death by strangulation. When contacted, representatives of the Los Angeles Police Department were unable to give our reporter any details about the crime. This is only the most recent of a series of foul felonies committed in the City of Los Angeles, which appears to become more violent each day. This newspaper is putting out a call for the assistance of all citizens. We must be vigilant if we are to rid our fair city of the perpetrators of such atrocities. For some time, Los Angeles was spared the cruelest of the vicious deeds committed by bootleggers and their like, but as Prohibition lingers, crime has risen. Our police force has much to answer for.

"My goodness," I said when I'd finished the article. "The *Times* seems to be blaming the police for Mr. Davis's murder. That doesn't seem fair to me."

"Reporters. Can't do anything with 'em. They're like fleas on a dog."

Ew. Buttercup didn't have any nasty fleas. Since Ernie probably wouldn't care about Buttercup's condition, I asked a more pertinent question. "Do you think bootleggers were responsible for Mr. Davis's murder?"

"Don't know," said Ernie with another of his characteristic shrugs. I wanted to pop him one.

"Well, you can at least talk to his son, can't you? Maybe he has some idea if his father knew anyone who'd do such a dire deed."

After heaving a huge sigh, Ernie said, "Let the police do their job, Mercy. This is a criminal matter of murder. I'm not involved. You're not involved. Nobody's hired me to look in to Huey's murder. It's not my business."

He spoke the last sentence with a good deal of emphasis and conviction. Undeterred by his logic, I said, "Well, don't you *care*? I thought Mr. Davis was your friend."

"We weren't friends. I only bought a paper from him every

morning and we occasionally talked baseball scores. Now his son's manning the stand."

Something then struck me as rather odd. "Didn't his son mention anything about his father's murder when you bought your newspaper this morning?"

"Nope."

"Did he look sad, at least?"

"Didn't notice."

Good Lord. Ernie was only slightly less annoying than Mr. Davis's here-and-there-again corpse.

As he walked back to his own room, Ernie said over his shoulder, "The *L.A. Times* uses 'contact' as a verb, you'll notice."

He was right, curse him.

In spite of the *Los Angeles Times* and its poor taste in word usage, the rest of the day went rather well. After last week's dry spell, when absolutely nothing of interest happened in our office, Monday brought with it a slew of telephone calls. I added appointments to Ernie's calendar one after the other until I began to think my poor boss would be overwhelmed with work. As the secretary to a private investigator, I didn't ask too many questions of the folks who telephoned. Anyone who needs a P.I. wants his or her business kept as confidential as possible. I was dying to know what they all wanted with Ernie, though.

After I'd written in the fifth appointment for Tuesday, I decided to ask Ernie if I should continue to take appointments for Wednesday, Thursday and Friday. I mean, he might have to go out and do some sleuthing for a few of these cases, and he couldn't very well snoop into things if his entire week was filled with interviews with potential clients.

Hugging my desk calendar to my bosom, I strode into Ernie's office, where he was employed in shooting elastic bands at the waste-paper basket. Too bad nobody'd called last Friday, giving him something useful to do today. Ah, well.

"Ernie," said I, drawing his attention and making him miss the basket.

"Damn," he said. I don't think he was cursing me, but rather his loss of concentration. "Yeah?"

"I've already made five appointments for tomorrow. Shall I continue to fill up the rest of the week, or will you need some time to go out and do some investigating?"

He shrugged. "Don't know yet, do I?"

"Hmm. You have a point. Still, do you think I should leave some of your afternoons free in case you need to leave the building to investigate something?"

He tilted his head to one side for a couple of seconds, and then tilted it to the other side, pondering deeply, I presume. My nerves began to twitch, and I almost wished I had an elastic band to shoot at Ernie. Finally he answered me.

"Yeah. I guess so. Don't make any appointments after three tomorrow afternoon if you haven't already filled up the calendar." He leaned forward, at last appearing interested. "What time's my first appointment?"

"Nine a.m., with a Mr. Bellingham. He wouldn't discuss his problem with me."

"No reason he should," said Ernie.

My lips pinched, but I didn't respond to his crack. "At ten o'clock, a Miss Smith will come in."

"Miss Smith, my a—foot," said Ernie.

I frowned at him. "Then, at eleven, Mrs. Edwin Johnson has an appointment. At eleven forty-five—"

"Hey," he interrupted. "Don't I get lunch?"

"At eleven forty-five," I repeated, louder this time, "Mr. James McGill is coming in. He said he'll only need fifteen or twenty minutes of your time."

"He a salesman?"

"No, he is not! Darn you, Ernie, don't you think I know better than to sic a salesman on you? I made it plain to all of our callers you are only interested in appointments with potential clients."

Ernie shrugged. "Go on. I hope you left me time for lunch."

"Of course I did. At one-thirty, Mr. Clarence deLong—that's a small D and a capital L, and there's no separation between the de and the Long—"

Ernie muttered, "Good God."

"I believe it's important to get the correct spellings of these people's names right off the mark in case you need to write to them or…or report them to Phil Bigelow or anything of a like nature."

A grin quirked at the right corner of Ernie's mouth, but he didn't speak, which was probably a good thing.

"And the last appointment I took was for two-thirty, with a Mrs. Max Glenn."

"You did good, kiddo."

"Well," I mumbled.

With a laugh, Ernie said, "I just wanted to get a rise out of you, Miss Hoity-Toity Boston."

"I am not!"

"Calm down, Mercy. I'm only teasing."

"Well, I don't like it."

"Sorry, kiddo."

"And don't call me kiddo!"

Ernie lifted his hands, as if he were surrendering to the coppers. "All right. All right. Didn't realize how sensitive you were."

Now I felt stupid. However, I couldn't argue with Ernie over my sensitivity or lack thereof, because the outer office door opened, and I had to greet whoever had come through the door. Turning on my heel, I walked into the office from Ernie's room to find a strange gentleman standing in the doorway, holding a fine fedora hat in his hands and looking around with some interest. That is to say, I didn't know if the man was strange or not—or a gentleman, for that matter—I only mean I'd never seen him before he showed up.

I put on my brightest professional secretary's smile. "May I help you, sir?"

"As to that, I can't say," said the man.

Then he fell down, *plop*, on the floor.

SEVEN

"**E**rnie!" I shrieked. "A man just fainted out here!"

I heard Ernie's feet hit the floor as he rose from his chair, and then he was at my side. As for me, I fear I wasn't doing anything useful, like calling an ambulance or the police or a doctor. I only stood there like a statue, gaping at the fellow on the floor, praying he wasn't another murder victim.

Kneeling beside him, Ernie felt his pulse. "He's alive."

"Thank God." I relaxed a bit.

"Wh-wh-wha——" the gentleman said, his eyelids fluttering slightly.

"Take it easy, man. You passed out in my secretary's room. You probably need to stay down for a minute or two." Ernie glanced up at me. "Mercy, will you get this fellow a glass of water?"

"Certainly," said I, and I speedily set my calendar on my desk, reached into my side drawer where I kept a couple of glasses for hysterical clients, and rushed out of the office and to the ladies' room down the hall, where I filled the glass halfway. Didn't want to spill any water in my hurry. When I returned to the office, Ernie had guided the man to one of the chairs in front of my desk, where he sat, looking pale and shaky.

"Here you go. Do you think you need any help in drinking it?" I asked, only later thinking what an odd question it had been.

"Thank you. No, thank you. I don't believe I need any help."

His hand shook when he took the glass, however, and he dribbled a little water on his chin.

"Do you want me to telephone a doctor?" I asked solicitously. "There's one in this building. On the second floor. I'll be happy to telephone if you'd like me to."

"No, no," said the man, reaching into his suit-coat pocket and withdrawing a packet of what turned out to be tiny pills. He stuck two of them under his tongue. "Heart condition," he said. "I can't take too much excitement or exertion."

Oh, my! This sounded intriguing. "I'm so sorry," I said.

"Did you need to speak with me?" asked Ernie, shooting me a look telling me to shut up. Well! "Is that why you came here today?"

Setting the empty glass on my desk a trifle awkwardly, the man peered at Ernie. "That depends. Are you the private investigator?"

"Yes, I am. If you believe you're up to it, I can help you in to my office, and we can discuss any private matter you may wish to have investigated."

"Thank you," said the man. "Give me another minute or two, please."

"Of course. Do you need more water?"

"No, thank you. It only takes a minute or two for the pills to dissolve. Then I'll be fine."

Nitroglycerin tablets, thought I to myself. I'd read about them in certain mystery novels, but had never seen them used before. As the man recovered, I studied him. Not overtly, as I'm sure I need not say. Only I just did. Fudge. At any rate, I gave him a good once-over.

He wore an elegantly tailored gray suit, which, I could tell, had been made for him by a good tailor. With it he wore an expensive silk tie. I knew it was silk and expensive after having lived with Harvey Nash for several months. Chloe always made sure he wore only the best when it came to neckwear, and this man's tie was the match of any tie in Harvey's collection. His shoes were likewise expensive and well-made, perhaps in Italy.

Hmmm, if this guy turned out to be one of Ernie's clients, it looked as though he could easily pay Ernie's fees. This was encouraging. Provided, of course, his poor overburdened heart didn't give out before he could pay us.

And then the telephone rang, and I had to stop thinking and answer it. By golly, it was another potential client on the 'phone! I wondered what had happened over the weekend to cause so many people to seek assistance from a private investigator.

No answer occurred to me, so I made the first appointment for Wednesday with the ringee, and Ernie led the gray-faced, gray-clad potential client into his office.

The telephone rang twice before the fainting man exited Ernie's office, Ernie escorting him, probably to make sure he didn't faint again until he got to someplace where we couldn't be held responsible for him. One of the callers was Mrs. Swale, who was already our client, but the other was another potential new client. My goodness, but business had turned brisk all of a sudden.

As soon as the gray man had left and Ernie turned around, planning to return to his office without letting me know what the man had wanted, I spoke.

"What did he want?"

Ernie eyed me sourly.

Before he could tell me the man's business was none of mine, I said something I considered perfectly brilliant under the circumstances. "I am your private secretary, Ernest Templeton. That means I'm private secretary to a private investigator. In other words, I'm twice as private as you are. I am completely discreet and wouldn't blab under torture. It's unfair of you to keep *our* clients' business from me."

"You think you have it all figured out, don't you?"

"I don't have anything but my position in your firm figured out," said I smartly.

"Oh, what the hell." And darned if he didn't sit in the chair beside my desk and open his mouth! Boy, you never know what sound reasoning will get you, do you?

"Actually," said Ernie, propping one foot upon his other knee in a very Ernie-like pose of nonchalance, "it's kind of odd."

"Why so?"

"That, believe it or not, was Mr. Richard Swale."

I blinked. "The husband of the mastiff woman who bribed the judge?"

"The very one."

"They don't look as if they belong together," I observed. "In fact, while Mrs. Swale looks very much like one of her mastiffs, that guy looked kind of like a greyhound. Or maybe one of those fancier dogs. An Afghan or a Saluki maybe."

With a chuckle, Ernie said, "I don't know what kind of dog he resembles, but apparently he's some kind of hound, so you're right on that point."

"Oh, my!" I felt my eyes open wide.

"Yeah. With his heart condition, he probably shouldn't be straying too far from hearth and home. On the other hand, look at what he has to live with."

I felt my mouth prim up and endeavored to smooth it out. I was trying *so* hard to fit in here in the Wild West, but my strict Boston upbringing seemed forever to get in my way. Still, it sounded to me as if Ernie meant Mr. Swale had been wandering into pastures not his own, and I didn't approve. In spite of myself, I said, "He married her. He's obliged to keep his marital contract, if you ask me. I think it's deplorable for a man to run around on his wife with other women."

"And vice-versa." Ernie grinned an evil grin.

"Yes, of course, vice-versa." I scowled back at him.

"I almost hate to admit it, but I agree with you. However, agreement doesn't negate the fact that Mr. Swale is being blackmailed, too."

"Good heavens. By the same person who's blackmailing his wife?"

"I don't know at this point. He has yet to get any communication from the blackmailer other than this." He handed me a sheet of paper. The paper had been neatly folded at one time in its life, then crumpled up, and then smoothed out again, I suspected by Mr. Swale.

Five thousand dollars in a plain brown wrapper will keep your wife from knowing about Mrs. Guernsey. If you don't pay up, you'll be paying the piper for real.

My nose wrinkled. "What does 'you'll be paying the piper for real' mean? Did Mr. Swale tell you?"

"He's not sure, either, but I expect it means his philandering will be reported to his wife. After meeting Mrs. Swale, I can't see her putting up with a straying spouse. I expect one of them would be heading for Reno for a divorce right quick."

"Reno?"

"It's in Nevada. You can get easy divorces there. You can in Mexico, too, but Reno's legal."

For some reason, this news dismayed me. "Do very many people get divorced in Los Angeles?"

"Hell, Mercy, people get divorced everywhere. Most folks haven't been as sheltered as you've been, you know."

"Yes," I said, both irked and sad, "I know. It still makes me feel...I don't know. I can't imagine marrying someone I loved and having that love turn to indifference. Or hate."

"Not everyone shares your ideals," said Ernie. "Although I happen to agree with you."

He'd said as much before. I squinted at him. "For real?"

"For real. Surprised?"

"Well..." Yes, I was surprised. Ernie put up such a good front as a care-for-nobody; it was easy to forget he was, in reality, a man of principle. "I know you're a good man underneath, Ernie," I said at last.

"Underneath what?" He asked sardonically.

"Underneath your outer veneer of devil-may-care insouciance."

"Huh. Well, don't tell anyone else, okay?"

"Wouldn't dream of it. So what's going to happen now?"

With a shrug, Ernie said, "I don't know. I told Mr. Swale to get in touch with me—you'll notice I, unlike the *Los Angeles Times*, did not use 'contact' as a verb—when he hears from the blackmailer again."

We sat there for a few moments in the quiet room, Ernie slouched in the chair beside my desk, me with my chin cupped in my hands and my elbows on the desk. I don't know what Ernie was doing, but I was thinking. Finally I said, "If the marriage is so awful that Mrs. Swale spends all her time with mastiffs and Mr. Swale spends all his time with a woman other than she, maybe they *should* get divorced."

"Personally, I wouldn't have either one of them on a bet, but he doesn't want to get a divorce because she's the one with the money, and she'd also be the wronged party. So he'd lose big if she divorced him."

"I suppose his sweetie on the side isn't rich?"

"You suppose correctly."

"Shameful situation," said I.

"Yeah, I guess so," said Ernie.

"Why did Mr. Swale come to you? I mean why you instead of any other private detective in Los Angeles. Does he know that his wife is being blackmailed too?"

"I didn't ask him. Can't let on about his wife. If he tells me about her, then it's all right, but I can't tell him about her. Or her about him."

It took me a moment to figure out his explanation, but I did eventually. "It just seems odd they should both come to the same private investigator if they don't know each other's business."

"True."

"Perhaps your reputation as a good investigator is getting around," I said with more hope than assurance in my voice.

"Right. That must be it," said Ernie with a sardonic grin that told me he didn't believe it any more than I did. Then he creaked himself to his feet, stretched, and returned to his office where, I'm sure, he resumed shooting elastic bands at the waste-paper basket.

By the time the day ended, I'd made appointments for Ernie into Friday morning, leaving his afternoons free. This phenomenon hadn't happened in the entire history of my employment with him. Except that people only hired him when they were in trouble, this was a good sign. The more I thought about the matter, the more I decided perhaps Ernie's reputation as a first-class private eye actually *was* getting around, although I couldn't tell you why. He'd been furious with me when I'd placed an ad in the *Times* advertising our business. Well, who knew? Life was a constant mystery. At least it had been for me since the preceding Thursday.

Speaking of which, as Lulu, Caroline and I made our way to Angels Flight, I decided to do a little sleuthing on my own. What the heck. We always walked past Huey Davis's newsstand anyway. Maybe I'd buy a magazine and have a chat with Mr. Davis's son this afternoon. So what if the weather was foul and the wind blowing a gale?

For the record, the awful winds Los Angeles and vicinity get during the fall and winter months are called Santa Anas. I don't know why.

"Just a minute," I told my friends as we approached the newsstand. "I want to chat with this fellow for a moment."

Lulu and Caroline looked at me as if I'd lost my mind. "It's cold," said Lulu. "I just want to get home."

Bother. "Well, you two go along. I'll catch up or see you at home."

Hunched in her coat with a shawl-like woolen collar covering her nice woolen suit, Caroline said, "I hope you don't mind, but I'm going to walk on. I'm freezing."

"It's cold, all right," said Lulu, hugging her own coat, a raccoon number she'd managed to discover in Los Angeles's garment district a month or so prior, around her. I hoped it was warm because she then said, "But I think I'll stick with Mercy. She always has a reason for these odd turns, you know."

Odd turns? Those words didn't sound like the Lulu I knew. I glanced at her, and she shrugged, as if she didn't know where the expression had come from either.

As for me, I'd pulled my cloche hat far down on my shingled head, trying to cover my ears and not succeeding. However, my woolen coat, which I'd brought with me from Boston, was warm as toast, as were my woolen gloves. If my sister caught me in these duds, she'd probably pretend she didn't know me, but at least I was warm. Well, except for my nose and ears.

The newsstand proprietor, whom I assumed to be Mr. Huey Davis's son, sat huddled on his stool, his knees drawn up nearly to his chin. He wore a loud checked coat that reminded me of the one his father had worn on the day he died, and he had his cloth cap pulled down on his head in an attempt to keep warm. The gloves he wore had the fingers cut out of them, I guess so he could handle his merchandise with ease. They couldn't have provided him with much warmth.

As we approached his stand, he glanced up at us from what I saw was a racing form. Hmm. Perhaps he and his father shared the same vice. Maybe his father had bet on the ponies (or the gee-gees, as Ernie called them), and had run afoul of a book maker. It was certainly an idea worth pursuing.

"Help you ladies?" he asked when he realized we weren't going to walk on past his stand.

"Yes, if you please," I said. "Do you have the latest issue of the *Saturday Evening Post*?" I didn't want to grill him without buying something, because I thought that would have been rude.

"Sure thing. Right here." He reached out and plucked a magazine from a rack. I noticed he'd weighted down the newspapers with bricks. Smart, with the wind whipping things around as it was.

"Thank you," I said, handing him my dime.

"Welcome," he said, sticking the money in his cash belt.

Now what? How did one lead up to asking impertinent questions? I hadn't been around Ernie during enough interviews, I guess.

"Um, are you Mr. Hugh Davis's son?" I asked out of the blue. Subtlety clearly wasn't my strong suit.

He squinted up at me from his stool. "Yeah. I'm his son. What of it?"

"Nothing," I said hastily, detecting a note of hostility in his voice. "It's just…well, I work for Mr. Ernest Templeton, and—"

"You're Boston?" he asked, his hostility vanishing in a grin. "Ernie told me about you."

He had, had he? Before I could ask him what slanders Ernie had been perpetrating about me, Lulu stepped up to the bat (which is a term taken from baseball. I think).

"Mercy's Ernie's secretary," she said quickly, probably to prevent me from saying what I'd been going to say. "And we were real sorry to learn about your father."

Mr. Davis's son's face fell. "Yeah." He shook his head. "I don't know what happened. The old man just disappeared, and now they say he was strangled, and somebody dumped him in a canal somewhere."

"Venice," I muttered.

"Mercy saw it happen," Lulu blurted out.

The junior Mr. Davis gawped up at me. "You did what?"

I cleared my throat. "I was looking out the office window last Thursday morning, and I believe I saw your father being murdered."

His eyes went wide. "What?"

"I saw your father being murdered. It was…most unpleasant. Although," I hastened to add, "I'm sure his loss to you is even more painful than witnessing the crime was for me."

A gust of wind darned near blew the newsstand over, but Lulu and I grabbed on to a pole propping up same, Mr. Davis did like-wise, and it remained standing. We all three shivered.

"Say," said Mr. Davis after a catastrophe was averted, "have you told the coppers about this?"

"You bet I have. They didn't believe me at first because the body vanished from the alley before they got there. Then Lulu and I saw the body again on Saturday—"

"You *what?*"

"Oh, dear. I'm sorry. This must be very distressing for you. It was for me, and I didn't even know your father."

Mr. Davis stuffed his hands into his coat pockets. His fingers must have been icy by then. "I don't get it. You say you saw my old man get killed, and then you found him on *Saturday*? And then he was fished out of a canal in Venice. What's going on here?"

It did sound extraordinary when put that way. I endeavored to explain, Lulu adding bits of color along the way.

"Anyhow," I summarized, "that's all we know. The police weren't quick enough to catch the killers."

"Heck, they weren't quick enough to catch the body," muttered Lulu through her raccoon-fur collar, which she'd pulled up to cover her nose.

"Yes, that's true, too," I admitted. "I've been trying to get Ernie to investigate the crime, but he claims he can't because he has nothing to go on."

"Huh," said Mr. Davis. "He probably won't investigate because there's no money in it. I don't have no money, for sure. Damned coppers. Sorry, ladies."

"It's all right," said Lulu. "We feel the same way about 'em."

Lulu did, for sure. I wasn't yet ready to condemn the entire L.A.P.D., although most of the specimens therefrom whom I'd met hadn't impressed me favorably, Phil Bigelow being an exception.

"I'm going to see what I can do to persuade Ernie to look in to your father's case," I said. Then I had another one of my brilliant ideas. Before I could mull it over—sometimes ideas don't seem so brilliant if you look at them too closely—I said, "Say, I don't suppose you'd be willing to visit the two boarding houses directly behind the Figueroa building, would you? The crime happened right in the alleyway there, and those are the two closest buildings. I still think somebody in one of those boarding houses might know more than they're telling."

"Yeah?" Mr. Davis appeared interested.

"They only rent to men so, although Lulu and I visited one of them on the pretext of looking for a room for her brother, you might have better luck," I said.

"Let me think about it," said Mr. Davis. "You might just have an idea there."

It was an idea, all right. I noticed he didn't say it was a good one. "Yes. Please do think about it. We'll chat again tomorrow," I said.

"We'd better get going now," said Lulu, tugging at my sleeve. "I'm about to freeze to the sidewalk."

"Thanks for stopping by, ladies," said Mr. Davis. He seemed perkier than he had when Lulu and I first stopped at his stand. "Talk to you tomorrow."

And then Lulu and I fairly ran to Angels Flight, where we found Caroline hadn't stuck around and waited for us, but had used the wits God had given her and was probably home already.

EIGHT

"**D**o you think that guy will really help us?" asked Lulu as we huddled in the car called Olivet on our way up Bunker Hill to Olive. If it remained this cold, I might just have to drive us to work in my Roadster on the morrow. Heaven alone knew where I'd park it, the traffic situation in Los Angeles being what it was.

Anyway, Lulu and I discussed the case through chattering teeth as we made our way home. When we got there, Caroline and Sue both greeted us at the door.

"Did you learn anything from that fellow?" Caroline asked.

"I don't know," I said through lips that had probably turned blue long since. "I hope we will. It would be nice to have a man investigating with us, especially since we're kind of useless when it comes to those boarding houses."

"I think you ought to let the police work it out," said Caroline. Have I mentioned Caroline, while kind and considerate, was a very conventional girl? Well, she was.

"But they aren't working on it at all. At least not that I can tell," I said bitterly. "They don't seem to give a care."

"You don't know they don't care though really, do you, Mercy?"

asked Sue. "They didn't have a body before. Now they have a body."

"Hmm," said I, not wanting to give up my own investigation merely because of Sue's impeccable logic. Darn it, I wanted to solve the crime. I saw it committed with my own two eyes, it was awful, and…well, I wanted to be part of the solution to it.

"I suppose," said Lulu slowly, through lips that were probably blue under their layer of lip rouge, "it would be easier if we could figure out a motive for the murder."

"You're right," I said. "What can the motive for the murder of a newspaper sales person possibly have been?"

I think Lulu shrugged, although she was so bundled up in her raccoon-fur collar, it was hard to tell. "Who knows? Talk to Ernie about him. Get to know what he was like. Was he a secret boozer? Did he take drugs? Heck, maybe his drug connection killed him because he couldn't pay up. Or maybe he found out his son was taking drugs and confronted the people who got him started."

Merciful heavens, I hadn't realized Lulu possessed such an agile imagination. Perhaps she should be the one writing the mystery stories. Evidently she'd just begun to think, because she went on.

"Or maybe he bet on the gee-gees and couldn't pay his bookie. Or maybe he ran numbers and skimmed some of the profits from his take."

As I hung my woolen coat on the rack beside the door, Caroline, Sue and I all stared hard at Lulu, I in admiration. I'm not sure what Caroline and Sue thought, although it was Sue who spoke first.

"What's a gee-gee?"

"A racehorse," I answered for Lulu. "I actually thought about the horseracing angle, although the notion of liquor or drugs hadn't occurred to me. Good ideas, Lulu." Then, because I honestly wanted to know, I asked, "Um, what's running numbers?"

Lulu emerged from her fur collar to stare at me as if she thought I was joking.

"I'd like to know, too," said Sue.

"Me, too," said Caroline.

"Shoot, you guys are so innocent," said Lulu, who clearly believed herself to be more worldly wise than the rest of us. She was right, too, but that's only because she'd lived in Los Angeles for longer than we had. I, for one, was trying like thunder to undo my innocence.

That doesn't sound right. What I meant was, I was trying like mad to learn the ins and outs of the mean streets of Los Angeles and of the people who committed crimes on them. Preferably without getting hurt in the process, which is the excuse Ernie always gave me when he told me to butt out of his cases. Huh. As Lulu, too, hung her coat on the rack, she spoke.

"Well, let me see if I can explain it. You see, some guys like to bet on things like horses and ball games and who's going to win the Kentucky Derby and so on."

"What's the Kentucky Derby," asked Caroline.

Heck, even *I* knew what the Kentucky Derby was. My sense of self-worth crawled upward a fraction of an inch.

"It's a big horse race they have in Kentucky every year," said Lulu. "Anyhow, some guys like to bet on all sorts of stuff. But gambling is supposed to be illegal, so if you want to bet on the outcome of a ball game or a horse race, you have to either go to a bookie, or—"

"What's a bookie," asked Caroline.

I wanted to tell her to shut up because I wanted to know what numbers running was, but I'm a polite person and didn't.

Lulu, however, seemed a trifle exasperated when she said, "A bookie is a bookmaker. A bookmaker is a guy who takes people's money and then pays off when the horse race or the ball game is over. He'll pay winners based on odds." She saw Caroline's mouth open again, so she hurried on, "Odds are what the chances of a particular horse or team's winning is. Are. Whatever I mean. Anyhow, bookies and numbers runners can give you odds, like it'll be ten to one a certain horse will win a race or the Yankees will win a game on Sunday, or something of the sort."

"The Yankees?" said Caroline blankly.

"They're a baseball team in New York," I told her.

"Oh."

"Anyhow, numbers runners go around from place to place collecting bets from people, and then you'll either lose the money you bet on the game or the horse, or you'll take in winnings, depending on the odds. The higher the odds against a horse or a team winning, the higher your take will be if that horse or team wins."

It didn't look to me as though Caroline had been appreciably enlightened, but I comprehended Lulu's explanation. Then something occurred to me.

"Say," I said, mainly to Lulu, since she seemed to be the only one who understood these things, "I suppose it's possible Mr. Davis might have been the depository of people's bets. Maybe he was working for someone else, and he kept some of the betting money for himself."

"Good idea, Mercy."

"Do you suppose his son would know?" I asked no one in particular.

"If he does, and if his father was doing something illegal or cheating the big boss, he probably won't tell us," said Lulu.

I heaved a sigh I could actually see, it was so darned cold next to the front door. "Crumb, it's cold in the entryway. Let's go to the living room." So we did.

As the four of us walked through the archway into the warmth of the rest of the house, I told Lulu, "You're probably right. But however can we find out if Mr. Davis was up to something shady?"

"You'd probably better leave it to the police," said Caroline. So typical.

"But they're even behinder than *we* are!" cried I in language my mother would deplore. I kind of did, too, actually, but I'd never tell my overbearing mother. "Besides, they honestly don't seem to care."

"Now, Mercy," said Caroline. "Just because they don't let you know how their investigation is going doesn't mean they're not investigating."

"Good point." And one I didn't care for.

Either Mr. or Mrs. Buck had built a fire in the fireplace, which didn't see much service in usually sunny Los Angeles. But the four of us gathered in front of the welcome warmth and I briskly rubbed my hands, trying to get feeling back into them.

The house smelled of delicious dinner-makings when we entered the living room, and I sighed with appreciation, both of Mrs. Buck's cooking and the heat beginning to thaw me out. Buttercup had raced out to greet us as soon as the front door opened, so I'd picked her up, and carried her with me to stand in front of the fireplace.

There we all patted her and told her how lovely and intelligent and generally wonderful she was. Then, after we were sufficiently thawed, I carried Buttercup upstairs, and I changed out of my working garb into an everyday house dress.

"Say, Buttercup, I'm going to buy myself some of those pretty lounging pajamas like Chloe wears." And, I might add, in which she'd scandalized our mutual mother, which was another good reason to get some.

Buttercup wagged at me, and I presumed her wag meant she approved of my suggestion.

"Good. Then maybe Lulu and I can go to Chinatown over the weekend, and I'll buy some." I frowned. "I'm pretty sure you can get them in Chinatown, anyway. There are a couple of consignment shops there." After I'd hung up my working attire and decided what I was going to wear the next day—no scrambling around on a workday morning for me, thank you. I liked to be prepared— Buttercup and I walked down the upstairs hall to Lulu's suite of rooms, where I knocked politely.

"C'mon in," she said in her ever-casual way.

So we went in. I found Lulu, clad in eye-poppingly purple lounging pajamas, sprawled in an easy chair beside the fireplace reading *Photoplay*, a movie magazine. Without looking up, she said, "Did you know there's some lady who dresses all in black who visits Rudolph Valentino's tomb every Sunday and leaves a red rose there?"

"Who is she?" I asked, taking the matching chair across from Lulu.

"Nobody knows." She closed the magazine, keeping a finger in it to hold her place, and gave me a grimace. "I think that's kind of a creepy thing to do."

Tilting my head as I considered the matter, I said, "Well, Rudolph Valentino was about as beloved as a motion-picture star could be, and he died far too young."

I remembered the day his death was announced. The news had been delivered to me by another secretary in the Figueroa Building. She'd stood, swaying, in the door to my office, her face like white rice, stunned by the news. I had also been pretty stunned. In fact, the entire city of Los Angeles had practically screeched to a halt four months earlier when Rudolph Valentino's untimely demise had become known. The whole place took to mourning, draping its buildings in black bunting. I remember seeing people crying in clumps on street corners. Heck, you'd have thought the president had died or something.

Which gave me pause. Heck, movie stars were only people. All they did was entertain the rest of us. Should they be so important that women fainted and cried and spent money on red roses every week when one of them, however handsome, died?

But philosophy could wait. I nodded at Lulu's pajamas. "Where'd you get those? I just decided I want to get some lounging pajamas for myself." I glanced at my pretty, but hardly exotic and— even I had to admit, dull—house dress. "Chloe's right. Too many of my clothes are still dull and boring. I want to spiff up my image some more. I've done a little spiffing, but I need to do more of it."

"Ernie'd like it if you did," said Lulu, grinning at me.

I frowned. "He won't see me in lounging pajamas, Lulu."

"Just joking," she said, although I didn't believe her. Both Lulu and Chloe thought I liked Ernie more than I did.

"Hmm. Anyhow, where do you think I should go to get some, and do you want to come with me? I thought maybe we could go on a shopping spree on Saturday."

"Sure. I get paid on Friday, so a shopping spree'd be fun."

Inwardly, I winced. Every now and then I forgot my fellow housemates really, honest-to-goodness, had to work for their livings. Mind you, I didn't play at my job. In fact I did it to the best of my ability, but I didn't really need my job in order to live. It's a good thing Lulu was around to remind me of my good fortune.

"Great. Where do you think we should go?"

Without hesitation, Lulu said, "Chinatown. They have some really pretty pajamas in some of the shops there. And they're cheaper than any you'll find at the Broadway or another department store. You got a beautiful dress at a consignment shop there, don't forget."

"You're right, I did. I also discovered the gown I wore had originally been worn by Renee Adoree, in fact."

"How'd you find that out?" asked Lulu, agog.

"A fellow I met during Thanksgiving week is a costumer for a picture studio. He told me."

"Wow. I didn't know you met another genuine Hollywood costumer."

Lulu had said "another" Hollywood costumer because we both already knew one, at least slightly. In fact, Lulu's brother Rupert worked for Mr. Francis Easthope, the costumer in question and a fast friend of Chloe and Harvey's.

"Yes, I did. He was a nice fellow, too."

"Was he a friend of that spiritualist lady you met in Pasadena?"

"Yes. I believe they're great pals."

Lulu sighed. "How come everybody gets to know movie people but me?"

"That's not true, Lulu. You even had dinner with John Gilbert at the Ambassador Hotel!"

Her smile took on a dreamy quality. "True. And it's all because I met you. You never know what life's going to throw at you, do you?"

"I guess not," I said. Gesturing at her own vivid ensemble, I asked, "Where'd you get those?"

"The Broadway. But they're lots cheaper in Chinatown. If they weren't having a big sale, I never could have afforded these." She stroked her fabric-encased leg. "They aren't silk, but they feel kind of like it."

"They're really pretty," I said, blinking at the bright purple. I decided I'd like to get something in a soft green or blue. And if it had Chinese butterflies or flowers on it, so much the better.

Shortly thereafter, Lulu and I left her room, Buttercup pattering at our feet, and went down to the living room, where I picked up the newspaper. Unlike Ernie, I didn't buy my *Los Angeles Times* from a news stand, but had it delivered to my door every day. Since I was a working girl and didn't have time to read the paper in the morning, I chose the evening edition.

While Lulu, Caroline and Sue chatted amiably, I dove into the newspaper, hoping to find someone had discovered something more about poor Huey Davis and why he'd been strangled and eventually dumped in a Venice canal. And why in the name of glory was there a city in California called Venice, anyway? Who'd named it that and why? Did they have to dig the canals, or were they natural?

All of that is neither here nor there, however. Although I'd like to solve the mystery surrounding Mr. Huey Davis's murder—or have Ernie do it—even I, who am a basically optimistic person, knew there was precious little evidence to be had. For the sake of Mr. Davis and his family, I hoped somebody would solve his dastardly murder one of these days.

I scanned the *Times* from front to back and saw nothing at all printed about Mr. Hugh Davis or his murder. Nuts.

By the time Mrs. Buck called us in to dinner, I was feeling a little disgruntled. I perked up at the sight of roasted pork, buttered carrots, mashed potatoes and gravy and a cherry pie with ice cream for dessert.

"Where'd you find cherries in October?" the ever-practical Lulu asked.

"Out of a can," said Mrs. Buck.

"Delicious," I said, wondering what other marvels could be found in the canned-goods aisles of stores during these modern times.

"My mother always preserves apricots and peaches during the summer," Caroline volunteered. "And tomatoes. Lots and lots of tomatoes."

"Oh, yeah," said Lulu. "We used to preserve darned near everything in Oklahoma. Beans, tomatoes, peas, spinach, okra, peaches, pears...you name it, we preserved it. Came in handy during the winter. Of course, we actually *got* winter in Oklahoma."

"We did in Boston, too," I said, although it had never crossed my mind to wonder how the cook managed to prepare our meals during those cold and icy months. Talk about a sheltered upbringing! Shoot, I had *so many* disadvantages to overcome, the task seemed downright daunting sometimes.

But the meal was delicious, and I couldn't help having been born rich and pampered, so I didn't dwell on my shortcomings but enjoyed my food. Then I took Buttercup for a short trip to the back yard, where she obligingly did her doggly duty. After that we went upstairs, and I put in a good hour of typing, with occasional pauses for thought. The writing of books requires a *whole* lot of thought.

After that, I washed up, put on my nightgown, took my library copy of *The Annam Jewel*, by Patricia Wentworth, propped myself up on my bed with Buttercup at my feet, and read until my eyes got heavy. Then I laid my book aside, said a brief prayer that I might be able to write as well as Miss Wentworth one day, and went to sleep. I felt good to have had a relatively productive day.

It rained on Tuesday.

My three housemates and I gazed out the dining room window as we ate our breakfast. Lulu, although clad in a vivid and perky yellow ensemble, appeared as gloomy as the weather.

"I don't want to walk in the rain. It's coming down hard," said she.

"It's pouring," confirmed Sue.

"It's time for our galoshes and raincoats, I guess," said Caroline, as prosaic as ever.

"Why don't I drive us all to work today?" said I. "That way, we won't get too wet."

"Good idea, Mercy!" Lulu.

"Yes, thank you!" Sue.

"Oh, how kind." Caroline.

Therefore, I was the only one of us to get thoroughly soaked after I dropped off my friends and, after searching in vain for a parking place near the Figueroa Building, finally decided to park in the alley behind my place of work, even though doing so kind of gave me the willies. Fortunately for me, Lulu told Mr. Buck I was trying to find a parking place. Because he knew what the parking situation was around our building, he'd already unlocked the back door for me and held it open as I slogged to the building from my Roadster.

I straggled in, dripping and drooping, took off my rain hat and coat, and shook out my umbrella, thereby getting water all over the back entranceway. I looked at the puddle I'd made, dismayed. "I'm so sorry, Mr. Buck."

"Don't worry, Miss Mercy," he said. He brandished a mop and bucket at me. "I came prepared."

"This is so kind of you," I told him.

"Only doing my job, Miss Mercy," he said. What a nice man.

Anyway, taking my dripping outer garments with me, I then climbed the back stairs. Water had leaked from the collar of my raincoat inside to my blue suit, so I was thoroughly damp and miserable by the time I got to the office of Ernest Templeton, P.I., on the third floor of the Figueroa Building. I was surprised to find the door unlocked and even more surprised to step into the office and see my boss standing at my desk, reading something. He glanced up as I entered, still dripping.

He frowned. "You look like a drowned rat."

"Thank you *ever* so much," I said, irked. I hung my rain hat and coat on the rack beside the door, shook my umbrella one last time, and decided to leave it open and let it dry behind my desk. "Unlike you, I don't have a special parking space reserved for me by Mr. Buck. I didn't think I'd *ever* find a place to park my car."

"That's supposed to be bad luck, you know," said Ernie.

I sat and frowned up at him. "What's bad luck?"

"Opening an umbrella indoors."

"Bah."

"And humbug to you, too."

"What are you doing here so early," I muttered as I pulled off my rain boots. Rain had managed to get inside them, too, and my sensible shoes were cold and wet. Nuts. Try to do people a good turn, and this was what happened.

"Mrs. Hallowell's coming in at nine-thirty."

Those words caught my interest, and I tipped my head so I could see Ernie, towering over me like a lanky pine tree. "Gladys's mother?"

"The very one."

"Oh, my. I'll be interested to see a woman who's managed to lose a daughter."

"Hell, all you have to do is look at your own mother if you want to see one of those."

Thoroughly peeved, I said, "My mother hasn't lost her daughters. Her daughters have finally managed to escape from her clutches. Unfortunately, as you well know, she knows precisely where to find us."

Ernie chuckled. Then it was I realized what he'd been reading as he stood at my desk: perusing my book! I uttered a sharp screech. "Ernest Templeton! What are you doing, reading my book? Did you ask if you could read it? Did I *say* you could read it? No, I did not! I consider this a gross invasion of my privacy!"

"Calm down, kiddo—"

"And don't call me *kiddo*!"

Ernie rolled his eyes. If I weren't so self-disciplined, I'd have kicked him.

"It was in my desk drawer," I ranted on. "You had to rummage through my desk in order to find my manuscript! That's...that's..."

"That's life." Ernie shrugged. "And it's actually my desk. The whole office is mine, if you think about it."

"But it's *my* manuscript, and I didn't give you permission to read it!" I always brought the carbon copy of the work I did at home to the office to add to the pile. I figured it was better to have two copies of it in case one got lost or whatever.

"True, but I suspect you wrote most of it here at work. Which means you did it on my time."

"Did not! I wrote most of it at home!" I chewed my lip, wanting to scream some more, but Ernie'd stolen my ammunition. After a significant silence, I muttered, "Besides, there wasn't anything else to do."

"Absolutely. I don't mind if you want to occupy your time writing a mystery story when we don't have any work."

Blast it. Now he was being so reasonable, I couldn't even yell at him. "Thank you," I snarled. Opening my handbag, I took last night's carbon copies out and added them to the bottom of the pile Ernie had been perusing.

"You're welcome. It's pretty good, by the way."

I blinked at him. "What is?"

"Your book. You're a good writer. I like your story. Who's the villain? Have you decided yet?"

Feeling myself flush from my tiptoes to my scalp, I said, "Thank you. I think the villain is going to be Mr. MacDowell."

Frowning, Ernie thought for a minute. I held my breath. He liked my book. He *liked* my *book*! I could scarcely take it in.

After what seemed like several hours, Ernie shrugged. "Mac-Dowell will work."

And he went to his office. The usual sounds didn't follow this activity, since he'd already tossed his hat at the coat rack behind his desk and draped his coat over his chair's back. I did, however, hear his feet hit the desktop and then a snap as he opened the newspaper, which he'd continue reading until Mrs. Hallowell showed up.

He liked my book.

My heart glowed as if the manuscript had been bought by an editor at a publishing house.

NINE

I took an instant dislike to Mrs. Hallowell when she showed up, lost daughter or no lost daughter. She reminded me a good deal of Mrs. Swale, in that she was large and snooty and resembled a mastiff. I didn't blame Gladys for running away from home, although, to be fair, I did hope the girl was alive and well somewhere. I also hoped she'd run away and not been kidnapped or had anything horrid happen to her.

Mrs. Hallowell didn't remain in Ernie's company for long, and her eyes appeared a trifle red when he escorted her to the front entrance of the outer office. "I'll get on it right away, Mrs. Hallowell. You can expect daily reports."

"Thank you." She dabbed at her reddened eyes and left the office.

Ernie turned at the door and winked at me.

"What's that for?" I asked.

"What's what for?" he countered.

I heaved an exasperated sigh. "The wink. Why'd you wink at me? I didn't much care for the woman when she first came in, but she must be awfully worried about her daughter."

As usual, Ernie shrugged. "As to that, I can't say."

"What do you mean, you can't say?" Ernest Templeton was probably the most frustrating human male I'd ever met in my entire life, and I'm even including my father and my brother, who are merely unpleasant and stuffy. Before I could tell him so, he slumped into one of the chairs in front of my desk and yawned at me.

"I don't know. I guess I just don't buy her story."

"What do you mean, you don't buy it?"

"I don't believe her."

My eyes opened wide. "You think Mrs. Hallowell's lying about her daughter being missing?"

He frowned, his usual air of insouciance sloughing off him like the water from my rain gear earlier in the morning. "I don't know. But her story didn't make much sense."

Bravely daring—I never knew when Ernie would use that tired old "it's the client's business, not yours" trick with me—I said, "Why doesn't it make sense? What did she say?"

Still frowning, he said, "I'm not sure." And with that, he got up and went back to his office, leaving me fuming at my desk.

There wasn't time to sulk, however, the day being full of appointments and people entering and leaving the office. At a little past noon, as I was contemplating the various merits of braving the rain or going without any luncheon—I mean lunch—at all, Ernie came out of his office, hat on head, shrugging into an overcoat, and said, "Come on, kiddo—I mean Mercy. Let's go to lunch at Charley's. We can pick up Lulu on the way."

Although I loved Charley's, I didn't want to get soaked again. When I glanced at Ernie and noticed he held a huge black umbrella, I decided why not? "Sure. Thanks, Ernie. Let me get on my galoshes and raincoat and hat."

So, after collecting Lulu, we rushed outside to Ernie's dilapidated Studebaker, and he drove us the very few blocks to Chinatown. Luckily, perhaps because of the rain, there were lots of empty parking spaces near the noodle shop, so we didn't have to run too far in the drizzle to get to where the food was. As ever, the food was great.

Then we went back to the Figueroa Building and saw more

clients. I didn't get the opportunity to talk to Ernie for the rest of the day, so I wasn't able to ask him more probing questions about Mrs. Hallowell and why her story didn't ring true to him. Blast.

The rest of the week passed much as Monday had, except Ernie was away from the office for large chunks of time, investigating. Because the rain continued, I was just as glad I was a mere secretary and not a legitimate private investigator. I don't think I'd enjoy snooping around in other people's business in the pouring rain.

At last Thursday rolled around. I'd actually had several letters to type, and when I took them to Ernie's office for him to read and sign, I asked casually, "Are you still planning to meet with Mrs. Swale's blackmailer this evening?"

Eyeing me keenly, Ernie said, "Yes, I am. And no, you can't come with me."

I sniffed. "You already told me I couldn't go with you. I wasn't going to ask again."

"Huh." He went back to his stack of letters.

Irked, I said, "Don't you think Mrs. Swale and Mrs. Hallowell bear a striking resemblance to each other?"

He didn't even glance up. "No."

"They do, too! They both look like mastiffs!"

This comment earned me a chuckle but nothing else.

I fairly snatched the letters from his hand when he was through with them, I was so annoyed.

Naturally, Lulu and I were excited about going to the Melrose Hotel in the evening, although we didn't mention our errand to the other members of my household. For one thing, in case Caroline and/or Sue wanted to go with us, I thought it would be far more difficult to hide four people than two. For another, I just didn't want them involved. Lulu and I were buddies. I liked Caroline and Sue, but I wasn't ready to share an adventure with them.

Well...truth to tell, Caroline had been involved in something of an adventure a few months prior, but I didn't like to think about it.

Lucky for Lulu and me, both of the other girls had gone to their rooms by eight-thirty, when she and I set out. I don't know about Lulu, but I was inordinately glad the rain had stopped. I found driving in the rain nerve-wracking even in the daytime. I'd have been terrified if I'd had to maneuver through the pouring rain at night, trying to find a place I'd never been before.

We arrived at the Melrose Hotel early and, fortunately, the hotel provided a large parking area for its guests. And the rest of us, too.

"I'm glad we don't have to walk blocks," said Lulu.

"Me, too. I don't like walking in a strange neighborhood after dark."

"This neighborhood isn't so strange," Lulu said. "Heck, I go to the movie palace down here a lot."

"It's new to me," I told her unnecessarily.

"Everything is new to you," said Lulu.

With a sigh, I said, "Too true."

What's more, I'd been nervous driving to the Melrose, because the route took me out of my comfortable surroundings and thrust me onto strange streets I'd never driven on before. But Lulu guided me and did a good job navigating. We went to First Street and then to Beverly, and from Beverly to Virgil, where I turned right and then hung a left—I believe that's the proper term—onto Melrose.

"But you got us here."

"*You* got us here."

Lulu shrugged. "You drove."

"True. But without you, we'd never have made it. I think I'm not very good with directions. I get turned around easily."

"Well, there's no need to worry about it now. Let's go to the lobby and see where we can hide."

"We'd better start being careful now. Knowing Ernie, he'll be there already."

Lulu looked at me, and I looked back at her. We'd done our best to disguise ourselves without putting on tons of makeup or wearing odd clothing. We'd done that once before and been mistaken by a couple of officers from the Los Angeles Police Department as...well, as ladies who are no better than they should be. Although, truth to tell, I've never understood that expression. Still, we both wore dark clothing and hats, which we pulled down low on our heads. Since the weather, while not wet, remained cold, it was natural to bundle up. I'd persuaded Lulu to wear a scarf over her platinum locks, too, since her hair was her most distinguishing feature, even when she wore drab colors.

"I feel like a milkmaid," grumbled Lulu as we peeked into the Melrose's lobby, searching for signs of Ernie.

"Milkmaids wear little blue gowns and white pinafores," I said. "You don't look anything at all like a milkmaid."

"What do you know about milkmaids?"

"Nothing. Only what I read in books."

"Huh. Well, I still feel like a milkmaid."

"At least we don't stand out. Nobody's staring at us or anything."

"That's because we haven't gone inside the hotel yet."

She had a point. "I don't see Ernie anywhere. Let's go."

I believe both of us held our breath when we stepped inside the hotel. It was quite a fancy place without being gaudy, for which I was grateful. I didn't, after all, want to hide in a dive.

"Look," said Lulu softly. "There are some potted plants over there. We can hide behind them."

I glanced at the registration desk, where a proper-looking gentleman was eyeing us with disfavor. I smiled at him in order to make him think we were there on legitimate business. He didn't smile back. "I think the registration man thinks we're up to no good."

"To heck with him."

"I guess." I wasn't accustomed to people looking at me the way the registration-desk man was doing. "But maybe we'd better look as though we belong here while we wait."

"How can we do that and hide at the same time?"

Bother. Then I saw the elevators, two of them, in a hallway a short distance from the potted plants Lulu had pointed out. "Let's go to the elevators. We can pretend we're just here visiting someone. That man doesn't need to know any different, and he won't be able to see us after we get behind the plants."

"Good idea."

So we walked to the elevators. I didn't turn around to see if the registration fellow was watching us, but I did turn around at the elevators to discover, not only could he not see us, but we couldn't see him. I decided this was probably a good thing.

"Good. He won't know we didn't take the elevator up."

Lulu pushed the *up* button at the elevator.

"What are you doing?" I asked.

"He might not be able to see us, but he'll be able to hear, and if an elevator doesn't come to pick us up, he might get snoopy."

Hmm. It seemed to me that, so far, Lulu had a better handle on the investigation game than I did. This was a lowering reflection, but I told myself to learn from Lulu's example and not wallow in misery about my shortcomings. "Good idea," I muttered.

Sure enough, the elevator hit the lobby floor with considerable noise. It was operated by a young woman in a nice uniform, who smiled at us. We smiled back at her, and I didn't know what to do next.

It was a darned good thing I had Lulu with me. She said, "Third floor, please," and stepped onto the elevator. I must have looked panicky, because she whispered, "Be right back." Then the elevator operator shut the door, and Lulu vanished.

Well, now what?

I decided I might as well look through the potted plants to see if Ernie had reached the Melrose lobby yet. We still had about ten minutes until nine o'clock, but my heart nearly leapt from my chest when I peeked between a couple of branches and saw my boss, pacing in front of a chair not five feet in front of me. He looked angry already, and he didn't even know I was there. I hoped.

A minute or two later, Lulu joined me. I pointed at Ernie with one hand and put a finger to my lips with the other to clue Lulu in that we were no longer alone. Well, we hadn't been *alone* before but…Oh, you know what I mean.

Lulu nodded, and we both stood still and watched Ernie pace. Every now and then, he'd pull up his coat sleeve, glance at his wristwatch and frown some more. I guess he wasn't too keen on black-mailers. Well, I wasn't either, so I understood his annoyance.

Nine o'clock came and went, Lulu and I kept hiding behind the potted plants—I think they were ficus trees—and Ernie continued to pace.

About ten past nine, Lulu whispered in my ear, "Do you think the guy's going to show?"

"I don't know," I whispered back.

And then a very large man in a checked coat and a plaid cap walked in. I swallowed the gasp that tried to escape my throat, but I did grab on to Lulu's arm. Hard. I know it was hard, because she said, "Ow."

"Sorry," I whispered. "But I'm almost positive that's one of the men who killed Mr. Davis in the alley last week."

I saw Lulu's eyes get huge. "Honest?"

"Yes. But let's be quiet now. He's walking up to Ernie."

He did walk up to Ernie, and Ernie stopped pacing and scowled at him. "You here for something?" he growled. My goodness, I'd never heard him sound so cold and frightening before.

"Yeah. You got the mazuma?" the other man growled back in a voice that went well with the rest of him, being rough around the edges and kind of gravelly. Rusty. Harsh.

"How do I know you're the one I'm supposed to give it to?" said Ernie.

"You know it because I say so."

Ernie sneered a sneer of absolute perfection. Gee, I didn't know my boss was so talented. "Not good enough for me, bub. You got a better reason?"

"Yeah. I'm here for Gallagher."

Aha. Ernie had been waiting for the name, I guess. How smart of him. In my brain, I was taking notes about how the investigatorial game was played.

Ernie held out an envelope, but didn't give it up when the other man's enormous hand gripped it with fingers that looked like those big bratwurst sausages they sold at the Grand Central Market. "You tell Gallagher this is the end. If this doesn't satisfy him, my client will go to the coppers, scandal or no scandal."

"Yeah, yeah, yeah," said the other man. "Hand it over."

"Give Gallagher my message," demanded Ernie.

"Yeah, yeah. I'll give him your message."

Ernie surrendered the envelope and stood staring after the man as he left the Melrose Hotel's fancy lobby. I felt as though a nasty inky blot had been erased from the elegant hotel as the door closed behind that ugly checked coat.

And then Ernie turned toward the potted plants and said, "Get out here right now, Mercedes Louise Allcutt and Lucille Mullins LaBelle."

Caught! Dang. How had he spotted us?

Still and all, I was kind of glad of it, because I wouldn't have to wait until tomorrow, when I'd have had to confess to spying on him before revealing my news.

"How'd you know we were here?" asked Lulu. She didn't sound chagrined, but only curious.

"Oh, I expected Mercy to come," said Ernie, giving me a good hot glower. "I might have known she'd drag you along, too." He turned on me. "Don't you have any wits at all? Don't you know I was dealing with a very bad man? For cripes' sakes, Mercy, show a little sense every now and then, why don't you?" He tapped his head, as if showing me where my brain resided.

"Never mind scolding me," I said, deciding to save the question of whether or not I had any sense until later. "I already knew he was a very bad man. He was one of the men who killed Mr. Davis in the alleyway, Ernie!"

I heard a noise from the registration desk and turned to find the gentleman there staring at us with a shocked expression on his face.

Taking Lulu and me by an arm each, Ernie propelled us toward the Melrose's front door. "Let's get out of here. Next you'll be announcing our business over the hotel loud speaker."

"I won't either!" I cried, indignant. "Anyhow, does the hotel have a loud speaker?"

"Not if you leave," muttered Ernie.

"That's just mean!"

"Huh."

Once we were on the sidewalk, I opened my mouth to complain some more, but Ernie stopped me. "Don't talk anymore now, Mercy. Don't say another word until we get away from here."

Drat. He was being sensible. I hated when he went sensible on me when I was mad at him. Nevertheless, I didn't object when he more or less dragged Lulu and me to his battered old Studebaker and opened the front door. Lulu got in first, which meant I'd have to talk around her when Ernie took his place behind the steering wheel.

After a short spate of silence, during which I tried to organize my thoughts, Ernie spoke first. "All right. Now tell me why you think that's one of the guys who offed Huey?"

Offed. What an interesting term. I vowed to remember it to use in my novel. "I recognized the coat and hat," I said.

"You sure? Last Thursday you claimed you didn't see any of the men involved in the crime."

"I didn't see their faces. I saw their clothing, and I remembered the man's hat clashed hideously with his stupid checkered coat."

It was dark in the machine, but I'm pretty sure Ernie rolled his eyes. Before he could say anything, though, Lulu spoke.

"Yeah. You couldn't forget that combination any time soon, could you? It was really ugly."

This, from a woman who routinely wore blood-red fingernails with violent purple clothing. I didn't say that, but only smiled at Lulu. "Exactly." Then I said, "I didn't know your first name was Lucille."

"That's why I shortened it to Lulu," said she. "Lucille sounds so stuffy."

"So does Mercedes," I said.

"Shut up for a minute, will you?" said Ernie. We shut up. "I wonder if it's worth going to the police station with this information."

"I think you ought at least to tell Phil," I told him. "Heck, if the police were to arrive right away, they might catch the man."

"I doubt it," said Ernie, the eternal pessimist. "He probably got into a car right outside the lobby door. Probably had a driver ready to roar."

"I didn't hear a roar," I said.

"Figure of speech."

"Hmm. If he did have a driver waiting, I'd bet you anything it was the other man, the one who wielded the cord and strangled Mr. Davis." The memory made me shiver.

"You cold, Mercy?" Lulu asked solicitously.

"No. Just remembering the murder."

"You'd better hope the man I gave the money to didn't see the pair of you behind those damned trees," said Ernie. "If he did, you two might be next."

"Next?" I asked before the hideous implication of Ernie's dour words penetrated my foggy brain. Then I all but shrieked, "You can't be serious!"

"Can't I?"

"But we were hidden," said Lulu uncertainly. "He couldn't have seen us. Could he?"

"If I saw you, anybody else could have seen you, too."

"How did you see us?" I asked, truly curious, not to mention aghast at the notion the criminal might have spotted us, too.

"I already knew you'd be there, and behind those plants was the only place to hide."

"Aha! So you didn't actually see us!"

"Yes, I did. I knew it was you behind those damned trees."

"But that awful man wouldn't have known it was us," I insisted.

"I wouldn't bet on it."

I wouldn't bet on anything at all, but I knew it wasn't the proper time to tell Ernie about my aversion to gambling. I slumped in the front seat of his Studebaker, wishing I hadn't gone to the Melrose at all.

"Shoot. I hope you're wrong, Ernie," said Lulu.

"Me, too," said I.

"Me, too," said Ernie. "But I think it's time to pay a call on Phil Bigelow."

"Good idea. My Roadster is parked in the lot."

"I know. I saw it there."

"So *that's* how you knew we were there! How dare you try to frighten us, Ernest Templeton? That checkered man has no idea what kind of machine I drive!"

"Maybe not, but if he and his partner were staking out the hotel, he might have noticed the two of you. I'm sure you were acting furtive. Weren't you?"

I could feel his penetrating stare even in the dark automobile. In a small voice, Lulu said, "But…Were we acting furtive, Mercy?"

"No," I said with more vehemence than I felt. "We were not. Anyway, we're all bundled up. Nobody'd ever recognize us if they saw us in our normal clothes."

Actually, while this might be true of Lulu, who looked more or less like an exotically plumed bird on the average day, I might be another story, in my sensible working ensembles. Nuts. I just hated it when Ernie was right. I also didn't like the idea that Checkers and his murderous crony might be able to recognize Lulu and me if they saw us again. Not, of course, that they'd know we'd been at the Melrose to spy on Ernie, but still….

"I'll drive you to your car, and you can follow me to Phil's," said Ernie as if he didn't expect an argument from either one of us.

He didn't get one.

TEN

Following Ernie was no trouble. He made sure I was right behind him the whole way to Phil's house. Lulu and I were quiet for a good few minutes after we got into the Roadster. I don't know about Lulu, but I was feeling more than a trifle stupid.

"I don't know about you," said Lulu, breaking the silence at last, "but I feel kind of dumb."

Two minds running in the same rut. Too bad they weren't brilliant minds running in the same perceptive and thoughtful rut.

"Me, too," I admitted. "In fact, I was thinking the same thing." After another minute or so of silence, I added, "But, to give us credit, we didn't know the man who would show up to take the blackmail money would turn out to be our murderer."

"He's not *my* murderer," grumbled Lulu.

"Well, no," I acknowledged. "Although, technically, he's not my murderer either. He wasn't the one with the cord. He's the one who held Mr. Davis while the other man murdered him."

"Somehow that doesn't make me feel a whole lot better," said Lulu.

"No." I heaved a big sigh. "Me, neither."

On the bright side, at least I'd get to see where Phil lived. I'd wondered about him before. You know, if he lived in a cheap apartment, or if he was married and had a wife and kids and stuff like that. Ordinary curiosity about the people one meets in life. As he was Ernie's best friend, I hoped he had a happy home life. If he bucked the forces of evil every day, as Ernie claimed, he deserved one.

I was surprised when Ernie led us through the downtown area toward where my own lovely home was located. Before we got to Bunker Hill, however, he turned onto Grand Avenue and then turned right onto a short, one block-long street. Almost instantly thereafter, he pulled to a stop in front of a comfortable little bungalow and got out of his Studebaker. He walked back to where I was attempting to get as close to the curb as I could without driving up onto somebody's front lawn. Los Angeles could use a few more streetlights in some places. Not to mention curbs and street signs. I didn't even know the name of this street.

Without waiting for Ernie to open the door for me, I climbed out of the Roadster. Shooting me a pretty fair frown, Ernie turned abruptly and opened Lulu's door for her. That was okay by me. I was totally fascinated to find out Phil Bigelow, detective, lived on this cunning little street.

"What's the name of this street, Ernie? It's darling."

"I'm sure Phil will appreciate your approval. This is Temple Place. One block long, and close to everything, including the station where Phil works."

"First Street Station, right?" I asked, peering around. All the houses on the little street appeared well cared-for, although it was too dark for me to tell for sure.

"Yeah. Phil works at First," growled Ernie. "Now you two be quiet. I'm going to have to wake the poor man up from his well-deserved rest.

"We didn't have to come here," I pointed out, peeved. "We could have gone to the police station and avoided waking Phil up."

"Nuts. I want Phil to know I just handed over blackmail money to a murderer. The beat coppers don't know anything about the murder. At least I can give Phil a description of one of the culprits now." It sounded as if he thought I'd been deliberately withholding information about the man in the checkered coat for some fell purpose.

"Well, so can *I* now," I said snappishly. "I didn't see his face on the day of the murder. Only that ugly coat and hat."

"Huh."

Disgruntled, I followed Ernie up a paved walkway to a large front porch, Lulu beside me. I don't think she felt as disgruntled as I. The porch held one of those glider things, and I could imagine Phil out there on a sunny Saturday morning, reading the *Los Angeles Times* and relaxing with his feet on the porch railing. It made me feel good to know he had some means of relaxation, given the stressful nature of his job.

Ernie gave two quick raps on the door, and we waited. Just as he was lifting his fist to knock again, the door opened slightly. It was held a few inches open by one of those chain-lock gadgets. It occurred to me I probably should get a couple of those for my own house as a safety measure. Trust a policeman to know how to protect his own.

"Who is it?" a woman asked, sounding as if she'd just awakened from a sound sleep. Naturally, this made me feel guilty.

"Sorry to wake you up, Pauline. It's Ernie, and I need to talk to Phil."

"Ernie Templeton, sometimes you're more trouble than you're worth," the woman said. But she had a smile in her voice.

She shut the door, and I heard the chain lock slipping back and the chain falling. Then she opened the door wide, and I beheld a truly stunning woman. She wore no makeup, and she'd wrapped her hair in a net, wore an oldish-looking chenille robe and sloppy slippers. Gee, if I greeted anyone clad the same way, I sure wouldn't be stunning. But Pauline Bigelow was. Lucky Phil. I wondered if they had any children. She appeared surprised when Lulu and I straggled into her home after Ernie.

"Really sorry about this, Pauline. Let me introduce you to my pain-in-the-neck secretary, Mercy Allcutt, and the Figueroa Building's receptionist, Lulu LaBelle."

Under any other circumstances, I would have given my irritating boss a stinging rebuke, but I felt uncomfortable having just barged in on this woman. I settled for giving him a frown before shaking hands with Pauline Bigelow. "Don't pay any attention to Ernie. I'm a good secretary, really."

She laughed. She had a pretty laugh. Dang. She had everything.

"How do," said Lulu, shaking Pauline's hand next. She seemed as intimidated as I felt.

"I'll get Phil. He's hard to wake up sometimes."

"I'm really sorry about this, Pauline, but it has to do with the murder Mercy witnessed last week."

"Oh, my, so you're the one who saw that poor man being strangled!" Pauline gazed at me with renewed interest. "I should have remembered your name. Goodness knows Phil has spoken of you more than once. And so has Ernie."

I'll just bet they had.

"It must have been awful for you," she went on, sounding sympathetic, which was a lot more than either Phil or Ernie ever had.

"It was awful. Thank you."

"Have a seat. I'll get Phil. And then I'll...I don't know. Bring you some cookies and make a pot of tea or something."

"Please don't go to any bother on our account," I hastened to say to her back as she left the room. "We've already caused you too much trouble."

"Speak for yourself," snarled Ernie. "Pauline makes the best cookies I've ever eaten."

"You come here often?" I asked, for some reason feeling wistful. It must be nice to have friends to visit and take tea with. And Pauline could cook, too. Cooking was yet one more thing I hadn't learned how to do in what seemed to me just then to have been an utterly wasted life.

"Yeah. I have meals here a lot. They're nice to invite me," said Ernie. "Pauline's a really good cook."

I sighed. "I want Mrs. Buck to teach me how to cook." I decided then and there I would invite Ernie to dinner. And maybe Phil and Pauline, too.

"Yeah? I don't like to cook," said Lulu.

"I might not like it, either, but I'd at least like to know how."

"Why? You have servants to do everything for you," said Ernie. I heard the sneer in his voice, curse him.

I decided not to take the bait, but only asked, "Do Phil and Pauline have any children?"

"A little girl. She's about five, I think. Name of Rose."

Aw. A little girl named Rose. How nice it must be. "I never pictured Phil as a husband and a father. I only always thought of him as a detective."

"Yeah," said Lulu in a grumpy tone. "Me, too." I doubted Lulu would ever forgive Phil for arresting Rupert.

I wouldn't mind if someone arrested my own brother. He was such a pill, getting arrested might turn him human.

Naw. Probably not.

Lulu, Ernie and I fell silent for a while, and I glanced around the room in which Pauline had left us. I guess it was the living room, and it was comfortably furnished with a couple of overstuffed chairs in addition to the sofa upon which the three of us perched. None of the furniture appeared expensive or new, but taken as a whole, the room exuded a kind of cozy charm. An upright piano stood against the far wall, and several sheets of music sat propped on the music stand.

Out of curiosity, I got up and moseyed over to the piano, where I saw the sheet music for "Tea for Two" and "California, Here I Come." Since it was difficult for me to imagine Phil playing the piano, I assumed Pauline was the piano-player in the family. Then again, what did I know? Heck, I'd never pictured Phil as a family man, either.

All of a sudden, however, I could picture Phil, Pauline and their little daughter, Rose, gathered around the piano of an evening and singing while Pauline played. It occurred to me I should get myself a piano. I'd taken piano lessons for years, after all. And if I'd been reluctant to do so at the time, I could now envision how much pleasure playing a piano and singing could bring to a household. I wondered if Lulu, Caroline and Sue could sing. My own voice was fair. Not operatic, by any means, but fair.

"What the devil are you doing here at this time of night?" came a gravelly voice from a door at the other end of the living room. Startled out of my domestic thoughts, I turned to see Phil in a striped bathrobe, rubbing his eyes. "Don't I have to deal with the job all day long? How come you had to bring it to my home in the middle of the night?"

Ernie peeked at his watch. "It's only a little after ten, Phil. For cripes' sake, what time do you and Pauline hit the hay?"

"As early as possible. I have a tough job, and Pauline cooks and cleans and takes care of Rose all day long." Phil saw Lulu and me and said, "Oh. H'lo Mercy, Miss LaBelle."

"Sorry about this, Phil," I said. "Ernie said we had to wake you up."

Lulu merely nodded.

"Cripes," muttered Phil as he came the rest of the way into the living room and plopped onto one of the overstuffed chairs.

"It's important, Phil. I truly am sorry to wake you up, but you need to know this," said Ernie. He didn't look sorry. In fact, he grinned at his friend as if he'd caught him doing something naughty.

"Huh. Well, what is it?" Phil didn't return Ernie's grin. Rather, he glowered.

"I just handed over a blackmail payment to one of the men Mercy saw killing Huey Davis last Thursday."

Phil sat up straighter in his chair. "You what?"

"You heard me."

"Somebody was blackmailing you?"

"No, no, no. The blackmail was for one of my clients. The guy who came to the Melrose Hotel to pick it up was one of the killers. Mercy recognized him." Ernie shot me an unpleasant glance. "At last."

"That's not fair! I didn't see his face last Thursday. The only reason I knew he was one of the murderers tonight was because he was wearing the same loathsome coat and hat."

"How come you and Miss LaBelle were there for a blackmail handoff, anyhow?" asked Phil. He would.

"They crashed the party," said Ernie, frowning at Lulu and me.

"Huh," said Phil, once again rubbing his eyes and then his stubbly chin. "That might be dangerous, you know, Mercy. If that goon saw you—"

"He wouldn't know me from Adam," I interrupted. "Or Eve."

"Huh." Phil sounded very much like Ernie just then. Then he added, "I don't know how much this will help."

"It'll help if this mug has a criminal history. Mercy, Lulu and I could all identify a picture of him now."

"Huh," said Phil again. He didn't continue.

"Well?" Ernie demanded. "He's a local crook, and he's evidently got his fingers in both murder and blackmail. I suspect Huey's murder happened because Huey ran afoul of some criminal outfit tonight's guy is associated with. Maybe numbers running or bookmaking or something."

I jumped a little when Ernie mentioned numbers running. I hadn't realized he'd actually been thinking about the murder until this minute. My attitude toward my annoying employer softened minimally.

"We've got tabs on a couple of gangs of numbers runners," Phil said slowly. "And we know a whole lot of bookies."

I wanted to ask him why, if the L.A.P.D. knew about such creatures, they were allowed to continue their criminous careers, but I didn't. There was a whole lot I didn't understand about the world at this point. I had, however, been made to understand, and clearly, that while the police might suspect people of doing any number of dastardly deeds, they needed proof in order to convict criminals of committing crimes. Rumors didn't cut it. And many of the people who availed themselves of the services of those shady characters didn't want their names associated with same.

"You take Kodaks of local bimbos when you arrest them, don't you?" Ernie asked.

"Yeah..."

"Well, why don't we all go down to the station and look through some of them?"

"Now?" asked Phil, sounding as if he didn't like the idea one bit.

"Not now. But Mercy, Lulu and I can come down tomorrow. You can get some police mugs of local bums together, and we can run through them. Maybe after work?" The last question was directed at Lulu and me.

By this time I'd made my way back to the sofa and sat next to Lulu. "What's a police mug?" I asked.

Ernie heaved a sigh. Gee whiz! I was only wondering, was all.

"A mug is a photograph of a crook. They've been taking front-on head shots and profiles since the late eighteen hundreds. The coppers call 'em mug shots."

"Oh. Thank you."

"Well?" demanded Ernie, "Will you two come to the station after work and look at mugs or not?"

Lulu and I looked at each other, and Lulu shrugged. "Why not?" she said. "Can't hurt. Might help."

"True." I turned to Phil. "What happens if we find the man's photograph among the ones you show us? I mean, you'll need more than our identification to arrest him, won't you?"

"You bet we will, but we can bring him to the station and sweat him a little."

I didn't care for the image his sentence brought to my mind, but it did prompt my next question. "Do you use the third degree in Los Angeles? Or is that strictly a New York interrogation technique?" I might not know much from personal experience, but I read a lot.

Ernie, as might have been expected, rolled his eyes. Phil grinned at me. "Naw. We don't go in for rubber hoses and bright lights here in L.A. We're very polite when we interrogate our suspects."

"Huh," said Lulu.

Irked, I said, "I just wondered."

Pauline entered the room at that point, carrying what looked like a heavy tray, and Ernie rose from the sofa and walked over to take it from her.

"Thanks, Ernie. I have some of your favorite shortbread for you."

"You're too nice to a bunch of house-breakers, Pauline," said Ernie.

"You can say that again," muttered Phil. I got the feeling he wasn't joking.

But at least his wife was nice to us. And the shortbread was delicious.

We left the Bigelow home shortly after taking cookies and tea, and Ernie drove to his apartment, wherever it was. I managed to find my way to Bunker Hill from Temple Place, mainly because Lulu was quite familiar with downtown Los Angeles.

"What did you think of Mrs. Bigelow?" I asked Lulu as I drove the Roadster north on Olive.

"I like her a lot better than her husband."

"I know you have a grudge against Phil, but he's really not a bad person. Rupert was just in the wrong place at the wrong time."

"Nuts to that. Your detective friend just wanted to pin the murder on the person he could find easiest."

I sighed. "Maybe you're right. But you have to admit being a policeman can't be easy. Look at all the bad people you have to deal with all the time."

"Rupert's not a bad person."

"I know it. But the fellow we saw tonight sure is. Why, he not only collected blackmail money, but I saw him abet a murderer only a week ago."

"Yeah. I'll give you that. But if they don't want to deal with crooks, why do they become policemen?"

"To serve their fellow men and make the world a better place?" I said, knowing it sounded highfalutin. Still, it might be true. Maybe.

"I guess," said Lulu grudgingly. "The job seems to turn them bad, though. Even Ernie says so."

"I guess."

We arrived home shortly thereafter, and both Lulu and I trudged to our rooms, an ecstatic Buttercup frolicking at our feet. She frolicked so much, in fact, she nearly tumbled me down the stairs. I picked her up and didn't scold, understanding she didn't like being deserted at night. Not that she'd been alone, since the Bucks and Caroline and Sue were still around, but I was her special person, and I'd left her behind to go snooping at the Melrose.

My suite of rooms was at the top of the staircase. I opened the door and said to Lulu, "Night, Lulu."

"Night, Mercy."

And that was that. All in all, it had been a productive evening. Sort of. We hadn't managed to sneak our presence past the perceptive Ernie, but we had seen, rather too closely for my pleasure, one of the men who murdered Huey Davis.

I only hoped the man hadn't seen me back.

ELEVEN

The next day, Friday, I told Sue and Caroline that Lulu and I had an appointment at the police station after work, so they should go directly home after their own work days and not wait for us.

"The police station?" said Caroline, clearly appalled. "Why do you have to go to the police station?"

All of us girls were sitting at the breakfast table finishing up the nice breakfast Mrs. Buck had prepared for us. I glanced at Lulu and shook my head, just in case she wanted to spill the beans about where we'd gone, why, and what we'd done the prior evening. But Lulu only gave me a grimace, so I knew she'd already caught on.

Anyhow, I'd already thought of an excuse that was pretty close to the truth. "We're going to look through police mug books to see if we can identify either of the men who killed Mr. Davis last week."

"What's a police mug book?" asked Caroline.

With what was probably undue pride, I told her what a police mug shot was and that the authorities collected mug shots in mug books.

"I thought you didn't see either of their faces," said Sue, who had an unfortunately good memory.

"And Lulu wasn't even there, was she?" added Caroline.

Nuts. "No, Lulu wasn't there. This is just a wild stab on the part of the police. There might be something about the photographs I recognize. Lulu very kindly agreed to accompany me to the police station, since I didn't want to go alone." There. Let them make what they would of that.

They didn't make anything of it. Sue merely shrugged, and Caroline said, "I don't envy you."

Shortly thereafter, we all left my home and a disconsolate Butter-cup—who probably wouldn't be disconsolate for long, since Mrs. Buck was in the kitchen and liked giving her treats—and walked to Angels Flight. There we paid the conductor our respective nickels and whizzed down the hill. From the bottom of Angels Flight we trudged our normal paths to our various places of employment.

The morning being cold and overcast, both Lulu and I had bundled up, Lulu in her raccoon coat, and I in one of my Boston wool coats. Everyone we passed appeared as hunched over and uncomfortable as Lulu and I were.

"I wish it would stop being so darned cold," Lulu said.

"I wish it, too. I'd always heard Los Angeles was the land of milk and honey where the weather always smiled down upon its inhabitants."

Lulu snorted. "Got that off a postcard, did you?"

"No, but Chloe wrote me lots of letters."

I'd never admit it to Lulu or the rest of my tenants, but I missed seeing my sister every day. Chloe and I were extremely close. We still wrote letters, and every time Harvey and Chloe went to a big first-night celebration at one of the picture palaces in downtown L.A., we got together. Still, seeing each other every now and then, while better than when she was in Los Angeles and I in Boston, wasn't as much fun as living together in the same house.

Perhaps I sighed, because Lulu asked, "What's wrong, Mercy? Don't you want to go to the police station this afternoon?"

"What? Oh, no. I mean, yes, I do. I was thinking about Chloe."

"You miss her, don't you?"

"Yes, I do. She and Harvey asked if I wanted to move to Beverly Hills with them, but I wanted to stay on Bunker Hill and keep working for Ernie."

"Well, you can always use the telephone," said Lulu philosophically. "Rupert and I stay in touch on the telephone, although we live closer to each other than you and Chloe do."

"True. The connection to Beverly Hills is sometimes pretty scratchy, though."

"It'll get better. People are inventing new stuff all the time."

And wasn't that the truth! Shoot, pretty soon, according to Harvey, the moving pictures were going to have sound, and we'd get to hear the actors and actresses actually speak their lines and not have to read them in subtitles. Hope the ones I liked had decent voices. I suppose listening to people talk in the flickers would put a lot of theatrical organists out of a job, but you couldn't stop progress.

My chain of thought suffered a sudden, staggering shift when Lulu and I approached the late Mr. Davis's newspaper stand, and I saw his son.

Both Lulu and I stopped short and stared at the late Mr. Hugh Davis's son, whose name I didn't know. He was bundled up in warm clothes, but he also sported a face that looked as though someone heavy had tap-danced on it, and an arm in a cast and a sling. A crutch leaned against the news stand.

"Good heavens, Mr. Davis! Whatever happened to you?"

Through eyes black and almost swollen shut, he squinted at Lulu and me. He said, "H'lo, Boston. I got roughed up some."

"*Some*! I should say you got roughed up a whole lot."

"Yeah," he agreed unhappily.

"But at least you got medical attention." I motioned to his crutch and his sling and cast.

"Yeah."

"Do you know who did it?"

Mr. Davis shook his head and then winced. "I don't know. A couple big bruisers."

Lulu and I exchanged a significant glance or two. "Did one of them wear a checked coat and a plaid cloth cap?"

"Why'd they pick on you?" asked Lulu at the same time.

"I didn't notice their clothes," he said, "and I think they picked on me 'cause of my old man. They said they wanted the money. But I don't know about no money. Hell—pardon me, ladies. Heck, if I'd'a known where the money was they was talking about, I'd'a give it to them."

"Good gracious," I said, appalled. "Did you tell the police?"

"I don't like the coppers," said Mr. Davis, sounding grumpy about it.

"Oh, but if the attack on you has something to do with your father's murder, you *must* talk to them!" I said, horrified that he'd not reported a violent crime against his person.

"I don't know..."

"Truly, Mr. Davis. This is important. If those ruffians did this to you, they might just kill you as they did your father."

He winced again. "Yeah. I thought about that possibility, too."

"I'll telephone the police as soon as I get to the office," I told him. "And when you see Mr. Templeton, please tell him what you told me."

"Yeah. I was gonna talk to Ernie about it anyway. I don't know about the coppers, though."

"You *must* talk to them. You need to give them descriptions of the men who beat you up. The more information the police have about those men, the sooner they'll be able to solve your father's murder."

It sounded to me as though Mr. Davis said, "Uh," but as he turned to assist a customer just then, I'm not sure. Lulu and I walked on to the Figueroa Building.

"Oh, boy," said Lulu. "Now I *really* hope that bum didn't see us last night."

A spike of fear shot through me at the thought, but I only said, "Me, too."

It turned out I telephoned Phil Bigelow even sooner than I'd planned to, because as soon as I unlocked the outer office door, hung up my hat and coat, and put my gloves and handbag in my desk drawer and began dusting the office, who should walk into the office but Ernie and the younger Mr. Davis. I turned when I heard the door open and gasped. Mr. Davis looked absolutely *awful.*

"Oh, Mr. Davis! You look even worse now than when I saw you a couple of minutes ago!"

"Thanks," he said, sounding ungracious. Couldn't blame him, really. My comment had been tactless. I could almost hear my mother screech at me from Pasadena.

"We're going to telephone Phil and have him come here and get information about the men who beat up Louie."

Huey and Louie. All righty. Why not? "Good. The police need to catch those vicious men before they hurt anybody else."

"Uh," said Louie.

"Who's watching your newspaper stand?" I asked as Ernie opened the door to his room. I hadn't yet had a chance to dust in there, but it probably hadn't collected much dust overnight.

"I asked Mr. Buck to watch over it while Louie here talks to Phil and me," said Ernie.

"Mr. Buck is really useful," I said. Then, hoping like mad, I said, "Want me to take notes as you and Phil interrogate Mr. Davis?"

"Interrogate me?"

"She likes to use big words," said Ernie. Then, squinting at me, Ernie frowned for a couple of seconds and said, "Yeah, I guess so. It'll be good to have a record, I suppose."

"Yes, it will!" I said happily.

"Call Phil, will you, Mercy? Ask him to come here as soon as he can, and tell him why."

"Yes, sir."

Both men grunted as they entered Ernie's room. Exasperating creatures, men.

Nevertheless, I telephoned the Los Angeles Police Station on First Street, asked for Detective Bigelow, and was connected to his telephone.

The 'phone on his end rang once, and then I heard a gruff, "Bigelow here."

"Good morning, Phil. It's Mercy. It was lovely meeting your wife last night."

A pause preceded Phil's, "Yeah. Pauline was glad to meet you, too."

Very well, I guess it really wasn't the time for idle chitchat. "Ernie would like you to come to his office as soon as possible, Phil. Louie Davis, son of the man who was murdered in the alley, was beaten up last night. He looks terrible."

"Who beat him up?"

"He claims not to know."

"Do you believe him?"

Did I? Maybe it was naïve of me, but I couldn't imagine why Mr. Davis would fib about not knowing who beat him up. "Um, yes, I did. Why would he lie?"

"Don't know. Please tell Ernie I'll be there as soon as I can."

"Thank you."

"Yeah." And he hung up the telephone on his end of the wire. I stared at the receiver in my hand for a couple of seconds and then replaced it on its cradle. All business this morning, Detective Phil Bigelow.

Oh, well, who cared? I got one of my secretarial pads and three sharpened pencils and went into Ernie's office. Poor Mr. Davis sat in a chair before Ernie's desk. Unlike me, he appeared quite unhappy, which made sense.

"Can I get you anything, Mr. Davis?" I asked solicitously before taking the chair in a corner of the room where the men's backs would be to me. It's my theory, unsubstantiated by anything concrete, that people are more likely to tell all if they weren't reminded constantly that their words were being taken down by an efficient secretary.

"Got any whiskey?" Mr. Davis croaked.

It was silly of me to be shocked, wasn't it? I didn't let on. "No, but I can fetch a glass of water and some aspirin tablets."

"No laudanum?" he asked plaintively.

"I'm sorry. I don't have any of that, either."

"Then skip it," he said.

"Is Phil on his way?" asked Ernie, probably trying to steer the conversation in a useful direction, although I'd only meant to offer aid and assistance to a man who was clearly in a good deal of pain.

"Yes, he said he'll be here as soon as he can be."

"Good." Ernie squinted at me for a second then said, "You know, it's not a bad idea to get poor Louie something for his pain. Is that doctor still on the second floor of the building?"

"Yes. Doctor Vernon Piper." Ernie had been to see him a few months earlier after he, too, had sustained injuries on the job. His own job; not Mr. Davis's, I mean. "Would you like me to telephone his office?"

"Yeah. Ask if they have anything that might help a man who's been beaten to a pulp."

"Very well. I'll just leave my pad and pencils here and telephone from my desk."

"Good idea," said Ernie, hunching over his desk and pretty much blocking access to the telephone thereon.

So I went to my own desk, but I left Ernie's door open so they couldn't have any secret conversations while I wasn't there. I didn't altogether trust Ernie not to renege on his promise to let me take notes.

Dr. Piper's receptionist—or maybe she was his nurse—said the doctor couldn't prescribe any pain medications unless he saw the patient for himself. Because I doubted either Ernie or Mr. Davis would settle for this answer without some kind of fight, I said, "The man can hardly move. He was beaten up last night. He has two black eyes, a broken arm, and has difficulty walking. You may speak to Mr. Templeton if you'd like to."

"Please hold the line for a moment, Miss Allcutt"—we knew each other's names by this time—"I'll ask Dr. Piper. Is the man one of Mr. Templeton's clients?"

Was he? I didn't know. Therefore I lied. "Yes, he is. He's the son of the man who was murdered behind this building last week."

"All right. Please hold the wire." Gee, she didn't even sound surprised.

So I held the wire. Well, I held the telephone receiver, which amounts to the same thing, while Miss Crumpland—not her fault—discussed Mr. Davis with Dr. Piper. Miss Crumpland didn't keep me waiting long.

"Miss Allcutt?"

"Yes?"

"Dr. Piper asked that you come to our office to pick up the medication. He doesn't like handing out pain medication without seeing the patient first, but he said he knows you and Mr. Templeton, and he trusts the both of you. Please bring the patient's name and address, so I can add it to the book. We have to keep records of whom we give these medications to. The doctor will have you sign for the medicine, since it is a compound made from opium."

Opium! That sounded sinister. My brain instantly conjured images of smoke-filled rooms with people sprawled here and there, smoking themselves into drug-induced dreams or oblivion. However, I called it to attention at once and said, "Yes. I'll be happy to pick it up. Thank you."

"You're welcome."

We each hung up our telephone receivers, and I went to the door of Ernie's office and told him where I was off to.

"Thanks, Mercy. You mean Doc Piper will actually part with some pain medication without seeing Louie first?" His eyebrows lifted in what looked like surprise to me.

"If you didn't think he'd do it, why'd you have me call?" I regretted my curt question as soon as I'd asked it. It wasn't a good policy to talk back to one's boss, especially in front of a client. If Mr. Davis was a client.

Ernie only grinned at me and said, "Better you than me if the doctor got mad at us for asking. Besides, you're cuter than I am."

Beast! "I see. I'll go down to his office now. I'll have to sign for the medication because it's derived from opium."

"Amen, sister!" said Mr. Davis, sounding happier than I'd yet heard him.

"The doctor's office needs your name and address, Mr. Davis. They evidently have to keep track of the people to whom they give these medications."

"Speaking of giving stuff," said Ernie, "did they tell you how much this medicine will cost?"

"No, and I didn't think to ask." Shame, Mercy Allcutt! Just because I wasn't accustomed to asking about the prices of things I bought was no reason to forget the rest of the world wasn't as fortunate as I. "Would you like me to call them back and ask?"

"Naw. That's okay. Here, take this." Ernie reached into his trousers pocket and pulled out a wad of cash. He peeled off a five-dollar bill. "Shouldn't take more than this."

"I hope you're right," said Mr. Davis. "I don't have much money to pay you back with. Used all my money on getting patched up."

"Don't worry about it yet," Ernie told him. "We'll send you a bill."

We would, would we? Well, maybe we would. At any rate, I noted Mr. Davis's personal details—he lived in a boarding house not far from the Figueroa Building—and left the office, took the stairs, and went to Dr. Vernon Piper's office.

There I traded Mr. Davis's information for a small bottle. Before she handed it to me, Miss Crumpland had me sign my own name and personal statistics in a large book. I noticed on the spine of same, the word POISONS was written in India ink.

Merciful heavens. I didn't know doctors considered opium a poison, although I don't know why I was surprised. People had been using opium to kill other people for centuries. Millennia, even, maybe. These days it probably wasn't as common as arsenic, but it did the job.

It occurred to me I might want to poison someone in the book I was writing, but I didn't allow the thought to distract me from my purpose. I trotted back up the staircase and, because Miss Crumpland had told me Mr. Davis would need to drink water after taking a capful of the medicine, I retrieved the glass from my desk drawer, trod down the hallway to the ladies' room, and filled the glass.

Mr. Davis almost cried when he took the small bottle I handed him when I returned to Ernie's office. Poor guy. I felt sorry for him.

TWELVE

Ernie had to take the bottle from Mr. Davis and open it for him, because Mr. Davis's hands were in such bad shape. Then he— Ernie, I mean—filled the medicine cap with the vile-looking concoction within the bottle.

"I don't think you can handle this on your own, can you?" he asked Mr. Davis.

"Just dump it down my throat, okay?" said Mr. Davis, sounding desperate.

"He has to take a drink of water after he swallows the medicine," I reminded both men, holding out the glass filled with water.

"Huh. Guess I can dump the stuff down your throat and then hold the glass to your lips," said Ernie to Mr. Davis.

"Thank you."

I saw tears in the poor fellow's eyes. He must have been in terrible pain. After he swallowed the syrupy concoction, he grimaced eloquently and gulped down almost all the water in the glass Ernie held to his lips. He spilled some of it down his chin and onto his shirt front. Undaunted, Ernie opened up a desk drawer and pulled out a clean handkerchief. He kept several clean hankies in there because it wasn't unusual for prospective clients to cry at him. That's what he called it: crying at him.

Poor Mr. Davis suffered a coughing fit after trying to swallow all the water at once, and I knew each cough jarred his poor wounded body. I wished I could do something useful, but I didn't know what. Therefore, I stood at Ernie's side, recapped the medicine bottle, wiped up some water spilled on the desk, and went back to the chair I aimed to sit in.

By the time Phil arrived, Mr. Davis had stopped coughing, but he didn't appear appreciably less wracked by pain than he'd been before he took his medicine. Probably all that coughing had disturbed his many injuries.

Ernie and I heard the outer office door open and he signaled for me to see who'd entered. I'd forgotten to look at my desk calendar to check if we had any appointments that morning. And here I prided myself on my secretarial efficiency. Well, I'd look now.

"Good morning again, Phil," I said, glad to see the detective and not someone whose appointment I'd neglected to notice.

"Hey, Mercy. They in there?" He jerked his head at Ernie's room.

"Yes. Please go in. I have to check my calendar, and then I'll join you." Because I didn't want the party to start without me, I said, "Ernie wants me to take notes."

"Right. Thanks, Mercy."

I think he was grinning when he disappeared into Ernie's room. He knew how much I wanted to be a P.I.'s assistant. He also knew how much Ernie didn't need or want me to be his assistant. Huh. I'd show them.

But there wasn't time to fuss about my position in life. I snatched the calendar on my desk, turned it around and saw Ernie had an appointment with Mrs. Swale, the mastiff lady and blackmailee, at nine-thirty that morning. As I placed the calendar back on my desk, I glanced at the clock. Eight-thirty. I hoped an hour would be enough time for Ernie and Phil to interrogate Mr. Davis.

When I returned to Ernie's office and sat on the chair in the corner, the men were chatting about nothing in particular. I cleared my throat to catch Ernie's attention. He looked up. "Yeah?"

Yeah? Sometimes I despaired of my ever-nonchalant employer. But there was no time to fret about his lack of professionalism. "You have an appointment with Mrs. Swale at nine-thirty this morning."

"Swale?" Ernie looked blank.

"The mastiff woman. Blackmail?" Was that giving away too much to a client and a copper. Nothing I could do about it now.

"Ah. Yes. Thanks." To the other two men in his room, he said, "Okay, we'll have to make this quick. Can you describe the men who beat you up, Louie?"

"All I know is they was big. And they kept asking me for money. Said my dad owed them money, but they didn't say for what."

"You sure about them not telling you why your dad owed them money?" asked a clearly skeptical Phil.

"Yeah. Come on, Louie, you know your old man had a little side business going on." To illustrate his point, Ernie held up his right hand and rubbed his fingers with his thumb to show what he meant.

Because his back was to me, I couldn't see Louie's face, but I did see his shoulders slump slightly. Maybe the medicine was taking effect. Or maybe he was reluctant to divulge his father's illegal goings-on.

"Unless you're involved in the under-the-table stuff, too," said Phil, "you might as well tell us about it. If the mugs who beat you up come back and still want the money, they might not stop at a beating."

After a significant hesitation, Mr. Davis sighed. Then he sat mute.

Ernie pressed on. "Come on, Louie. I know you miss your dad, and you don't want to squeal on him, but telling us what he was doing might save your life. We can't help you if you don't help us."

Another spate of silence preceded another sigh from Mr. Davis. "Aw, shit. All right, I'll tell you. But I don't know where Dad kept the money! I can't hand over money I don't have."

"True," said Phil. "But did they give you any idea when they'll be back to pick up the money they want? We can set a watch on your stand."

"They got me as I was walking home," said Mr. Davis, sounding unhappy. "I don't know where they came from. I was just about home—boarding house near this building—when they mugged me. Came right out of the alley and dragged me in. They kept saying, 'Where's the dough? Where's the dough?' I didn't know what dough they was talking about."

"Your father was keeper of the numbers, wasn't he?" said Ernie.

I glanced up from my notebook, a little surprised to hear about *numbers* again. I was *so* glad Ernie had let me take notes!

Still, Mr. Davis didn't speak.

Finally, Ernie said, "Louie, if you don't tell us what's going on, we can't help you. Phil here doesn't give a rap if your father made a little money on the side, but he'll care a whole lot if your father's illegal business gets you killed, too. He's got enough to do with one murder investigation, especially since there's so precious little to go on."

I saw Mr. Davis bow his head. "I know," he said. "I know. I don't want to die, either. I miss my dad."

"Do you know who he worked for?" asked Phil, clearly losing patience. "If you can give us a name, maybe we can do something."

"I don't *know!*" insisted Mr. Davis. "I don't think he worked *for* anybody. He just took a few bets. Pa never mentioned names. He never had any trouble with anybody. I don't know where he kept the money, either. I don't want 'em to kill me because I don't *know.*"

His voice had taken on an edge of desperation, and I felt kind of sorry for him. Operating a news stand probably didn't provide a huge income, so making a little money on the side had perhaps sounded like a good idea. Until someone got mad and killed you.

"Huey never said he was having any trouble with anyone?" asked Ernie.

"Well…Yeah. In the past week or so, he said a couple of thugs had started pressuring him to let them run the business. You know, my dad was just a small-time operator. He didn't take in much money. He…he performed a neighborhood service. He was small potatoes. I got the feeling the guys who'd been pestering him wanted him to go big-time, and Dad didn't want to go big, because he figured it would only lead to trouble. He just had a little side business going on. For nickels and dimes. Like that."

"Right. A neighborhood service," said a sarcastic Phil, evidently no more enchanted with small-time crooks than he was with their larger cousins.

"It's the truth," said Mr. Davis, although without much heat. I think the injured fellow was wearing out.

"Listen, Louie, I think one of the mugs who killed your father picked up some blackmail money from one of my clients last night. I was the intermediary," said Ernie.

"The what?" Mr. Davis sounded confused. Guess he didn't have a large vocabulary.

"The intermediary. That means I was the guy who handed over the blackmail money for my client. If you can give us a name, it would really help. Does the name Gallagher ring any bells?"

Oh, my! I'd forgotten all about someone named Gallagher sending the horrid checked-coated man to pick up the blackmail money at the Melrose Hotel!

"Gallagher?" said Mr. Davis. "Gallagher. You know, the name does ring a bell. I think my dad said something about somebody wanting to push in on his business. Dad's business, I mean. Name might'a been Gallagher."

"You know anything about this Gallagher bum, Ernie?" asked Phil.

"Not a thing, except he sent a goon to pick up money from me at the Melrose Hotel." He shook his head. "Stupidest thing I ever heard of. Evidently Gallagher blackmailed one of my clients in connection with a dog show."

"A dog show? How'd he do that?" asked Phil.

Ernie shook his head. "Your guess is as good as mine."

"It's kind of a stretch to go from a dog show to a numbers racket, isn't it?" Phil again.

"You'd think so, wouldn't you?"

"A dog show?" Mr. Davis sounded confused. Made sense to me. "You mean like the greyhound races?"

"No, I mean like fancy dogs in a show ring. Kind of like a bathing beauty contest for dogs."

"Huh," said Mr. Davis. "Never heard of such a thing."

Ernie lifted his arm, shook down his sleeve and glanced at his wristwatch. "Listen, Louie, I think you should shut down the news stand for a day or so. Or at least until we figure out who killed your father."

"But I've gotta keep the place open," Mr. Davis protested. "It's my living."

"If you keep running the thing, it's more likely to be your death than your living," Ernie pointed out.

Shaking his head slowly, Mr. Davis muttered, "Shit." I'm sure he wouldn't have used such a word if he'd remembered my presence in the room. See how important it was for the stenographer to sit in a corner?

Phil leaned slightly closer to Mr. Davis. "What did you do before your dad was killed?"

"Had another news stand on Temple and Hill. Near the court-house. Me and my dad, we had two stands."

"Did you take numbers, too?" asked Phil.

"No. I didn't want to get mixed up in anything illegal. Wish my dad hadn't."

"Me, too," said Ernie. "How are you going to keep both stands open now?"

Shaking his head again, Mr. Davis said, "Beats me. A pal of mine is working the courthouse stand today, but I don't know how long he'll want to do it. He's got business of his own."

"What we're going to do is this," said Phil decisively. "I'm going to put a man at the stand on this street. Can your pal keep the other stand open for the time being? You probably should take some time off to heal anyway."

"But—"

Ernie cut him off. "But nothing, Louie. You need to heal, and

Phil here needs to find a murderer. He'd rather do it before your father's murderers kill you, too."

"But—"

"Forget it, Davis. I'm putting a man at your stand, and another one to watch for who comes and goes. You claim not to know much about your father's numbers-running racket, but not knowing isn't going to protect you. You must have already figured out that the crooks didn't believe you when you told them you didn't know where the money was." Phil made a gesture that pretty much included the entirety of poor Louie Davis's mangled self.

After a couple of seconds filled with tension and silence, Mr. Davis said, "Aw, hell. All right. Now I have this medicine, I can probably sleep some. Hurt too much last night. Didn't get any sleep at all." He shook his head. "I don't know how I'm gonna pay any more doctor bills, if I have to see him again."

"I'm sure we can work something out," said Ernie. I wondered if he meant it. Probably. Ernie might occasionally stretch the truth a bit, but he wasn't much of a liar.

"Yeah," said Phil, not sounding as if he cared a whole lot. "Maybe if you find your father's stash, you can pay the doctor from that."

"Not if the guys who won in last week's pool come by wanting their take," grumbled Mr. Davis.

"Well, don't worry about it right now. You won't be at your father's stand for a few days." Phil glanced at Ernie, who nodded.

"Do you want me to walk you to your boarding house?" asked Ernie. Then he caught my eye and remembered Mrs. Swale. "Crumb. No, I can't do that. Phil, can you escort Louie home? I'd like to keep him alive if possible. He lives near this building, so he might live right next to the murderers. Mercy says she saw his father being killed when she was looking out of this window." He lifted an arm and tapped on the glass behind him with a knuckle or two.

"I can get a guy to see you home," said Phil. "Let me use your telephone, Ernie."

So Ernie let Phil use his telephone, and Phil called for someone to transport the battered Mr. Davis from the Figueroa Building to his boarding house.

In the meantime, my brain whirled with possibilities. I'd bet pretty much anything, if I did things as silly as betting, the murderers' base of operation was one of those boarding houses behind the Figueroa Building.

But which one?

This might be a time for Lulu to call her brother into action. Rupert wasn't a large, muscular fellow, but at least he might get past the first floor of those stupid boarding houses and look around for us.

I decided not to tell Ernie about my plans because he'd only complain.

THIRTEEN

$\mathbf{M}$r. Davis, along with his police escort, had barely exited Ernie's office, leaving Ernie and Phil to chat some more, when the front door opened. Looking up, prepared to smile at the unpleasant Mrs. Swale, instead I gasped in astonishment. Maybe horror.

Yeah. It was horror.

Two of the largest animals I'd ever seen in my life thumped into the room. Before I could scream or hide under the desk—which wouldn't have done me any good at all—I noticed Mrs. Swale behind the two canines, holding them by leashes so slender, they wouldn't have stopped either one of the dogs from attacking and eating me for luncheon.

Aha. Mastiffs. The huge animals were mastiffs. I'd seen pictures of mastiffs. Saints preserve us.

"M-my goodness, Mrs. Swale," I said after swallowing the lump of terror that had lodged in my throat. "Th-those are your dogs? M-mastiffs?" I pressed a hand to my thundering heart.

Frowning at me in unconcealed disapprobation, Mrs. Swale said, "Yes. There's no need to be frightened, Miss Allcutt. My dogs are perfectly trained for obedience to my commands."

"I see." Thank God.

"Unless I give them a signal, they are two of the most docile canines in the world."

"Oh." I decided never to give Mrs. Swale a reason to dislike me. At least, any more than she already seemed to dislike me. Because I didn't know what I'd done to offend her, unless she just didn't care for underlings as a breed, I wasn't sure what to do to get and stay on her good side, if she had one. "They're...um, quite large. For dogs."

"They're massive," said Mrs. Swale, giving her two dogs a loving look. "They're bred from the original English mastiffs, you know."

"Um, no. I didn't know that."

"My, yes. The forebears of these two handsome fellows used to function as guard dogs and were trained to hunt down and savage anyone who trespassed upon their owner's property."

"Oh." My voice had gone slightly higher than normal.

"Breeders in Great Britain and members of the American Kennel Club have been attempting to breed the aggressive tendencies out of them, but they're still formidable if given a reason to be." Gazing adoringly at her pets and with a definite note of haughtiness in her tone, she went on, "Caesar and Augustus here are sweethearts unless called upon to chase an intruder or protect me. They'd never allow anyone to hurt me. If anyone tried, he'd lose. These dogs weigh two hundred pounds each. Well, Augustus weighs about two hundred fifteen pounds. They can take down pretty much anyone or anything."

"I imagine they can." Yet another octave. If those dogs remained in my room much longer, I might turn into a soprano.

With an impressive sneer, she said, "There's no reason to be afraid, young woman. I already told you my dogs have been trained. Beautifully trained. Unless given the signal, they're happy, friendly dogs. Are you not accustomed to being around dogs?" Her sneer turned into a frown, convincing me she did not approve of people who didn't surround themselves with dogs.

Hoping to appease her, I said, "I love dogs. I have a perfectly wonderful toy poodle. Her name is Buttercup, because she's a blonde." Thank goodness, my voice had returned to its normal pitch.

"Poodles." Mrs. Swale might as well have spat on the floor as say the word. "I suppose at least *standard* poodles serve a purpose. I have no use for toy breeds."

"I love my Buttercup."

"Frivolous," scoffed Mrs. Swale.

Thinking of an incident in the not-too-distant past, I said, "Buttercup saved several people and me by attacking a man who was holding us at gunpoint. That was only a few months ago." I attempted to speak in a resolute voice. I only achieved an almost-firm aspic, but it was better than high and squeaky.

"Hmm. Your dog has more gumption than I'd have thought any inconsequential toy breed to possess."

"Buttercup is quite brave," I said stoutly and without a single quiver.

"Hmm. I still have no use for toy breeds. Mastiffs, however... well, mastiffs are superior canines. Why, did you know that Julius Caesar was so impressed by English mastiffs when his army invaded Great Britain, he took some of the dogs back with him to Rome? Many of his soldiers were routed out and killed by the mastiffs used against them by the British, and Caesar decided he needed some of them in his army."

"I...didn't know that. Fascinating." I even kind of meant it. I also figured her statement had been the truth. If the English mastiffs Caesar's poor men encountered had been anything like these two monster dogs, I had no doubt the wretched soldiers had died bloody and painful deaths. On the other hand, they had no business invading somebody else's country, but still...

Besides, as in most military conflicts, the soldiers had no say in what they were asked and/or forced to do. I personally think the people who start wars ought to fight them, but my mother calls my thoughts on the subject radical and socialistic.

Once I stopped quaking with fear, I noticed the dogs didn't seem interested in attacking me. Rather, they just stood there, peering at me as if I were a not-too-engrossing neutral object. They looked as though they wore black masks, but the rest of their fur was a buff color. All in all, I'd take Buttercup. Buttercup and these guys looked as if they belonged to entirely different species.

"But enough of this. Is Mr. Templeton available?"

"Yes. He is. Um…he has someone with him right now, but he's ready for your appointment." Crumb. I'm the one who should get up and tap on Ernie's door to let him know his nine-thirty appointment had arrived. With outriders.

"Well, go and get him, young woman! Why are you dilly-dallying?"

Because those two gargantuan dogs terrified me? I couldn't admit such a thing, even if it was the truth. I feared if I moved, they might object. If they objected, I'd be dead.

"Oh, for heaven's sake, you're afraid of my puppies, aren't you?"

Puppies? Dear Lord.

"Um…" I wanted to deny her assertion, but I couldn't do it. "They're just so…big. I've never seen such big dogs."

"I'm sure that's true. Mastiffs aren't as popular as some of the frothier breeds." Her words were meant as another insult to Buttercup. Nasty woman. "But come here and see for yourself."

"Um, do what?" There went my voice, climbing up the octaves again.

"Get out from behind that desk and make friends with Caesar and Augustus! They're as friendly as can be." I still hesitated, and I saw her eyebrows lower. "Come here at once, young woman. You're being ridiculous."

"Very well." Cautiously, I stood from my chair. Neither Caesar nor Augustus objected, although they watched me closely. Then I pushed my chair back and walked to the edge of my desk. One or the other of the dogs—I didn't know which was which, and I couldn't tell them apart anyway—tilted its head to observe my movements.

And then, bravely daring and silently praying I'd survive to go home after work and tell Buttercup what a wonderful, gorgeous, precious pet she was, I slowly approached the dogs. They snuffled a bit, and I saw they were both slobbering. Ew. I wouldn't want a slobbering dog. Buttercup never slobbered. When I was about three feet away from the dogs, I stopped and stood still.

"This is nonsensical," said Mrs. Swale, clearly telling me she thought me a stupid, cowardly member of the human species. "Caesar!" she said, making me start slightly. "Shake hands with Miss Allcutt."

Darned if one of those monsters didn't sit on its butt and lift a paw to me. I'd have been charmed if the dog had carried about a hundred seventy-five fewer pounds. Nevertheless, I girded my loins—I have no idea how to do that—and held out a hand to the biggest canine paw I'd ever encountered.

"Step closer, Miss Allcutt. Caesar can't reach you from there."

Which was just the way I liked it. But no. I decided I was being as nonsensical and cowardly as Mrs. Swale considered me, so I stepped boldly forth and shook Caesar's paw. My hand didn't fit around it, but Caesar didn't seem to mind. He just drooled on my hand a little and slapped his foot to the office floor.

"Good boy, Caesar. Augustus, shake Miss Allcutt's hand."

And darned if her other dog didn't follow its companion's lead, plopping its bottom on the floor—actually, he plopped it on the cunning throw rug I'd bought in Chinatown—and hold out one of *his* paws. Understanding the routine now, I took his paw—my hand didn't reach around that one, either—and said, "Happy to meet you, Augustus." Suddenly frightened lest Caesar might object not to have been spoken to by me, I said, "And you, too, Caesar."

"There now," said Mrs. Swale. "Aren't they sweet?"

"Yes indeed," I said.

"Good. Now go get Mr. Templeton. We have an appointment, and he's late."

Glancing at the darling little clock I'd hung on the wall, I saw the woman was correct. The time was now nine-thirty-three. "Yes. I'm sorry. He had an earlier appointment, and is consulting with Detective Philip Bigelow of the L.A.P.D., but I'll tap on his door and let him know you're here."

"Please do," said she, her voice back to being imperious. When she'd spoken to her dogs, she'd sounded almost nice.

So I dared turn my back on the hounds from hell—no, that's not fair. They weren't hounds, although they might do a good job guarding the gates of hell if Cerberus ever decided to take a holiday—and walked to Ernie's door. I tapped thereon then turned the knob.

Phil and Ernie had been talking, heads almost touching over Ernie's desk. Both men looked up and frowned at me. Well! Of all the nerve! So much for them. "Mrs. Swale is here for her scheduled appointment, Mr. Templeton," I said in a sugary voice. Let him find out about the dogs for himself. Oh, and I always called Ernie "Mr. Templeton" when there were clients around.

"Oh, yeah. Thanks. I'll see her," said Ernie. He rose from his chair, snatched his coat jacket off its back and shrugged into same. Phil did likewise. Well, except for the coat part. "Tell me what you find out, Phil, and I'll do likewise."

The rats had been discussing the case without me! It was just like them.

"Will do. Thanks, Ernie. Thanks, Mercy," said Phil.

He started for Ernie's door and I stepped aside, smiling sweetly. As soon as he saw the three parties cluttering up my room, he said, "*Cripes!*" and staggered backwards.

"What's the matter?" Ernie asked, alarmed.

I maintained my sweet smile. Ernie charged to the door, saw what awaited him, and he skidded to a halt. "Holy suffering cats!"

Ever helpful, I said (still sweetly), "Mrs. Swale brought Caesar and Augustus with her today, Mr. Templeton." Peering into Ernie's office to find Phil staring, bug-eyed, at the open door, I told him, "It's perfectly all right, Detective Bigelow. Mrs. Swale brought her dogs with her today. They won't attack anyone unless Mrs. Swale tells them to."

"Those things are *dogs*?" Phil's voice had gone a little high, too. Guess terror can do that to anyone and not just me.

"Mastiffs," I told him. "English mastiffs."

He muttered, "Shit," under his voice.

I suppose Mrs. Swale didn't hear him, because she didn't sic either Caesar or Augustus on him.

"You men are being perfectly ridiculous," announced Mrs. Swale. "Come along, Caesar and Augustus. Mr. Templeton, please tell your friend to vacate your office so we may have our appointment. Our *scheduled* appointment."

"Yes, ma'am," said Ernie, recovering his composure far more quickly than I thought proper.

As for Phil, he walked to the door, took in a lungful of air, and sidled around the two massive dogs and the one massive woman. I do believe I heard him run down the hallway to the elevator.

"Do you need me to take notes?" I asked Ernie, hoping.

"No, thanks," he said, drat him. "I just need to tell Mrs. Swale about my meeting last night at the Melrose."

"Very well." I didn't flinch as the trio of giants walked past me and into Ernie's office. I did, however, sink gratefully into the chair behind my desk, fold my arms and rest my head upon same for a moment or two.

The jangling of the telephone on my desk startled me so much, I nearly yelped. I sat straight up in my chair, grabbed the mouthpiece and said in a voice firm as cement, "Mr. Templeton's office. Miss Allcutt speaking."

"Oh, Mercy!" Lulu, and she sounded scared.

Instantly, all thoughts about canine and human monsters fled, and I spoke into the receiver. "Whatever is the matter, Lulu? Can you talk? Is someone holding a gun on you or something?"

Oh, Lord. Well, If Lulu *was* being held at gunpoint by some raving lunatic, at least Phil would enter the lobby soon and see what was going on. He was a policeman. Surely, he could save poor Lulu. Or even Caesar and Augustus! If Mrs. Swale considered Lulu worth saving.

"Huh? What are you talking about? Who has a gun?"

"Nobody. I mean, I don't know. You sounded scared, and I was worried about you."

"Naw. I'm fine, but a few minutes ago I saw that woman and those two…whatever-they-weres. I knew they were going up to your office, and *I* was worried about *you*. Are you and Ernie all right,

Mercy? I wanted to call sooner, but people came coming to the desk and yapping at me."

I let out a deep breath. "Oh. Mrs. Swale and Caesar and Augustus."

"Huh?"

"The woman is Mrs. Swale, Ernie's client. She brought her two mastiffs with her today. Their names are Caesar and Augustus."

"You mean she's the lady who bribed the dog-show judge, and those things are *dogs*?"

To my way of thinking, Lulu's astonishment was perfectly reasonable. I'd had the same reaction, after all. "Yes. They're mastiffs. Well, she said their ancestors were English mastiffs. When Caesar invaded England, he liked them so much because they were so savage, he took some of them back to Rome with him."

The telephone line crackled softly as Lulu digested the history lesson I'd just imparted.

"Holy Moses," Lulu said at last.

"Yup. A little later than Moses, though."

"Huh?"

"Never mind."

"Say, Mercy, you want to go to the diner across the street for lunch today? It's so darned cold and miserable, and those...dogs?"

"Yes. Dogs."

"They scared me so much, I don't want to stay here for lunch. Anyhow, I just brought a bacon sandwich from home, and I'd rather get a bowl of hot soup."

"Sounds like a great idea to me. Noon?"

"Noon it is. You can tell me more about those...dogs...over lunch."

Clearly, Lulu still had her doubts as to the correct species into which Caesar and Augustus fitted.

Seemed logical to me.

FOURTEEN

As we sat in the diner across the street from the Figueroa Building waiting for our lunches to be set before us, Lulu frowned slightly. We'd run the topic of Caesar and Augustus into the ground, and I steered the conversation toward discovering the murderer of Mr. Huey Davis.

I thought the plan I'd just rendered unto Lulu was peachy. Lulu, however, appeared troubled. "I dunno, Mercy. Rupert's no match for the guy we saw last night. Or that Baker woman, if she's involved. She's almost as big as her house. She's even bigger than the dog woman."

"True. But at least Mrs. Baker might allow him to see available rooms. Maybe he'll spot something."

"Like what?"

"Like…I don't know. Like, maybe Mrs. Baker has a couple of sons who are big bruisers. Rupert wouldn't have to fight them or anything. He could just report back to us."

"Us?"

The waitress set two bowls of soup in front of Lulu and me. Vegetable with beef is what the chalked letters on the board behind her claimed the soup to be. When I peered into my bowl, I thought

I saw some carrots and celery in it. Maybe a piece of meat. Didn't look precisely delicious.

Lulu dipped her spoon into her own bowl and took a tentative sip. "I'm getting too used to eating Mrs. Buck's cooking, I think. I ate this same soup last year when the weather was cold and it tasted better than it does today."

"I guess we're spoiled," I said, thinking the same thing about the relative merits of this soup and Mrs. Buck's cooking skills.

"Yeah. Oh, well, at least this is hot."

"True, and it's a cold, cold day." So said the young woman who grew up in Boston, Massachusetts, where we got snowed upon every single winter. It hadn't taken me long to adjust to sunny California's milder weather.

"Yeah. It gets lots colder than this in Oklahoma, but I've been in L.A. for three years now."

"I was thinking the same thing about Boston, and I've only lived here for six months or so. Still, I wish we could bring Mrs. Buck with us to work. She could fix lunch for the whole building." But Mrs. Buck was at present in my home on Bunker Hill, unless she'd gone down to the Grand Central Market to shop for something, so we were stuck with the diner's chow.

"She could open a diner of her own," said Lulu. "She'd probably make a fortune."

"Yeah, but who'd cook for us?"

With a sigh, Lulu took another sip of soup. After she swallowed she said, "Yeah. There's that."

"Anyway, what do you think of my suggestion? Do you think Rupert would mind checking out a couple of those boarding houses for us?"

"I think Rupert doesn't need to get involved with any more murders," said Lulu frankly. "Besides, now Ernie's copper pal is involved, you don't need to think about the case any longer. Let the coppers do their jobs for once."

"Those same coppers arrested Rupert for murder a couple of months back, even though a blithering idiot would know he couldn't have done the deed."

"Yeah," grumbled Lulu. I doubted she'd ever forgive Phil Bigelow for that one, even though she had liked his wife.

We chewed and sipped in silence for a few minutes. Along with our bowls of soup, we each had also ordered a toasted cheese sandwich. Not a bad lunch for fifteen cents. It would have been better if Mrs. Buck had made the soup, but you couldn't have everything.

"Ernie's been busy lately," observed Lulu, delicately patting her lips with the napkin provided by the diner. She didn't want to smear her vivid red lip rouge.

"Yes. He has been. I'm glad. For a couple of weeks there, I feared he'd have to fire me because we had so little work to do. Then things picked up all of a sudden."

"You mean starting with the woman who looks like her bulldogs?"

"Mastiffs. Yes. She's the one who gave Ernie the money to pay off the thug last night."

"Why'd she pay a blackmailer? She could have just had one of her dogs eat him."

"True. They used to be used as guard dogs and to keep poachers off people's property."

"What's a poacher?"

Peering at Lulu from the tail of my eye, I saw she seemed honestly curious. "A poacher is someone who steals somebody else's chickens or a deer in the king's forest and stuff like that. Mostly in the Middle Ages, I think. According to Mrs. Swale, mastiffs aren't aggressive anymore, but they used to be ferocious. I guess the king's gamekeeper used to have a few mastiffs to scare poachers off the king's land."

"Figures. Sic a huge, mean dog on a poor guy who's only trying to feed his family. What's a king need with all those deer?"

She had me there. "I don't know. I've only read about poachers in books set in England."

"Huh."

"Anyway, after Mrs. Swale hired Ernie, several more people called, so we've been busy for about a week now. I hope it doesn't let up. We need the business."

"You don't need the business," said Lulu.

"That's not my fault," I said.

"I know. I didn't mean to tease."

"Huh."

The door to the diner opened, bringing in a draft of frigid air. Frigid for Los Angeles, I mean. Lulu and I hunched over our soup bowls to keep warm. I glanced at the door and my mouth didn't drop open, but that's only because I had a chunk of sandwich in it. I nudged Lulu's elbow with mine and as soon as I'd swallowed, I whispered, "Don't look at the door."

As soon as she swallowed what she'd been eating, Lulu said, "I'm not. Why?"

"Wait until we get out of here."

With a shrug, Lulu said, "I guess I'm pretty much finished."

"Me, too, but don't get up yet." Cautiously I turned my head slightly to see where the huge man in the checkered coat and the ugly plaid cap was in relation to the counter and Lulu and me. I saw he'd taken a booth on the other side of the diner. He had a companion with him: a man as big and ugly as he, and clad in a cheap sack suit. A shiver having nothing to do with the weather chased another shiver up my spine and back down again. "Okay," I whispered. "It's safe. Let's go."

"I've gotta get change for a buck," said Lulu.

"Forget it," I told her, carefully placing a half-dollar on the counter, making sure it didn't clatter. The waitress was passing as I did so, and she smiled happily at me. Guess she wasn't used to getting big tips.

"But—"

Through gritted teeth, I said, "Come *on*, Lulu. Now."

So she did. As soon as we stepped out of the diner, the wind hit us and we both caught our breath. I didn't give Lulu a chance to adjust the violet-colored scarf she'd wound around her neck under her raccoon coat, but grabbed an arm and marched her with me as I threaded through the traffic to get across the street. My spinal shivers hadn't abated by the time we made it to the other side.

"Mercy!"

"Shh." Pushing open the door to the Figueroa Building, I shoved Lulu inside.

As soon as the door closed behind us, I let out a huge breath and sagged against the wall. "My Lord, Lulu, did you see that man?"

"What man? You told me not to look at anything. I owe you for lunch."

"Forget about lunch! The man who came into the diner right before we left is the man from last night! My God, Lulu, the murderer is right there, inside the diner where we ate our lunch!"

Lulu's mouth dropped open. She shut it with a clack of teeth and screeched, "*What?*"

"You heard me. Call the police, Lulu. They might be able to get him now. He's with the man who actually garroted Mr. Davis. If they act fast, they can get them both!"

"Call the…Oh, yes! Okay. I'll call the police." She hurried to her chair behind the receptionist's desk, plucked the receiver from the cradle of her candlestick telephone, and dialed O on the rotary pad.

Only then did I recall the policemen Phil had said he'd post at the late Huey Davis's news stand. Bracing myself for another blast of cold air, I left Lulu to the telephone and dashed for the door of the building.

"Mercy!" Lulu bellowed after me.

"There should be cops right down the street!" I bellowed back as I pushed the door open.

Lordy, the wind nearly blew me back inside the building. I snugged my cloche hat closer to my head, held the lapels of my woolen coat to my neck, and started walking quickly down the street.

But what was this? No policeman stood at the news stand. Rather, a shivering Mr. Emerald Buck, custodian of the Figueroa Building, hunched on the tall stool formerly occupied by the late Mr. Huey Davis and then his son, Louie.

"Mr. Buck!" I cried. "What are you doing here?"

"Working the news stand, Miss Mercy. Mr. Ernie asked me to take over for the poor man who got beat up."

"But the police were supposed to station a fellow here to take over for you! They haven't appeared yet?"

"Not yet," said the miserable Mr. Buck.

"Drat Phil Bigelow to perdition," I spat out. What good was the only honest cop in Los Angeles if he didn't keep his word?

Desperately, I peered up and down the sidewalk, hoping to spot a uniform. Then I realized that, if Phil *had* kept his word, the coppers he sent would probably be wearing street clothes and not uniforms. Still and all, one of them was supposed to have already taken over this stupid news stand from Mr. Buck. Blast and heck!

This wasn't fair. "Can you fold up this thing, Mr. Buck? You can't stay here in the freezing cold any longer. You're liable to catch your death. I'll help you."

"But—"

"But nothing. You're freezing to death out here, and Detective Bigelow was supposed to send someone to take over for you hours ago."

"Well…"

"Come on, Mr. Buck. I'm your employer, and I need you well and healthy."

"Thank you, Miss Mercy. I'd kinda like that, too. But I'm not sure what to do with all this truck. I think there's some boxes tucked away under the kiosk to store the papers and magazines that haven't been sold."

Aha! Kiosk. That's the word that had been eluding me ever since I heard about Mr. Davis and his news stand. Not that it matters.

"Let me look," I said. And I did. Mr. Buck joined me on the dirty sidewalk, and we unearthed two big containers that looked like steamer trunks. He and I started loading the magazines and news-papers into the trunks.

Then somebody said, "Hey! What are you doing there?"

I peered up to see a man wearing an overcoat frowning down at Mr. Buck and me. "We're packing up these things so Mr. Buck can go indoors. He's been taking care of this kiosk for hours as a favor to someone else, and it's not fair. He was supposed to be relieved long before now by somebody from the police."

"That person would be me," said the suited man.

"Well, you jolly well took your time!" I said, indignant on Mr. Buck's behalf.

After glancing up and down the sidewalk himself, the policeman knelt beside us. "I was sent here by Detective Phil Bigelow to watch this stand. Put those mags and papers back."

I stood and huffed out a cloud of steam into the chilly air. "*You* put them back! You were supposed to be here two or three hours ago!"

"Now listen here, lady—"

"Nuts to that. *You* listen! I was in the meeting with Detective Bigelow and Mr. Templeton when Detective Bigelow said he'd post men here. That was before nine-thirty this morning, and it's now almost one o'clock! Mr. Buck and I are returning to the Figueroa Building right this very minute. If you have any complaints, take them up with Detective Bigelow."

I sensed Mr. Buck was about to register an objection to my peremptory command. Being a black man and all, I'm sure he was worried the policeman might beat him to a pulp for disobeying him. I, however, am from Boston and my mother's daughter, not to mention his and his wife's employer, so he didn't quite dare. And that made me mad, too.

Therefore, I went on. "In fact, I aim to telephone the police department as soon as I get back to my office and ask why it took them so long to get a man here!"

The policeman frowned, but he didn't fuss anymore, either. Although it pains me to admit it, my privileged upbringing occasionally came in handy, if only whilst dealing with serfs.

Then I remembered why I'd rushed to the stupid kiosk in the first place. "And aside from all that, I saw both of the men who murdered Mr. Huey Davis! They're in the diner straight across the street from the Figueroa Building not five minutes ago!"

"Miss Mercy!" said Mr. Buck, aghast.

"Huh?" said the copper. Not the brightest penny in the collection plate, I gathered.

"The men who murdered Mr. Davis," I said, speaking slowly and concisely, "are at this very minute sitting in the diner across the street from the Figueroa Building. They're sitting in a booth in the—" I squinted up the street. "They're sitting in a booth in the Figueroa Street Diner. One of them is wearing a hideous checked suit and an ugly plaid cap, and the other one—he's the one who used the cord to strangle Mr. Davis—is wearing an ugly sack suit."

"How do you—"

"Because I saw them do the deed!" I roared before the oafish policeman could finish his question. Turning to Mr. Buck, I took his arm—which felt like an icicle even under his fairly heavy jacket—and said, "Let's get back to the building, Mr. Buck. Maybe we can send somebody for coffee to warm you up."

The policeman tried again. "But—"

The fierceness of my scowl actually sent him staggering backward a step or two. Ha! Every now and then my mother comes in handy. Only from a distance, but still...

Tugging to get him started, I preceded Mr. Buck up the street. He let out a huge breath when we entered the Figueroa Building, the air in which must have been forty or fifty degrees warmer than the air outside.

Perhaps that's an exaggeration, but I'll bet it didn't feel like one to Mr. Buck. He still shivered.

And Lulu was still on the telephone. "I tell you, they're right across the street! Listen, you! My friend saw those two men murder that man behind this building last week!"

So. The police were giving Lulu a hard time, too, were they? When Mr. Buck and I reached her reception desk, Lulu looked helplessly at me. I held out my hand, and she gave me the mouthpiece.

"Who is this?" I demanded.

Silence on the other end of the wire.

I repeated, "Who is this? The woman with whom you were arguing and I just saw two murderers sitting at a booth in the Figueroa

Street Diner. You and your cronies have wasted so much time, they've probably eaten their lunches and left the diner already. If they have, it's your fault. Connect my call to Detective Phil Bigelow this instant."

Spluttering issued from the police end of the wire.

"This *instant*. Detective Phil Bigelow. *Now*."

I heard some clicking noises and then a ring. Then I heard, "Bigelow" over the wire. I nearly collapsed from relief.

"Phil! Why didn't you send anyone to relieve Mr. Buck? He's frozen nearly to death, and in the meantime your precious Los Angeles police officers haven't bothered to go across the street from this building to catch the two murderers who were sitting in a booth in the diner there. It's the Figueroa Street Diner, and they were both in there not ten minutes ago! The police have wasted so much time, they're probably long gone by now!"

"Mercy? Is that you?"

"*Yes!*" Very well, it probably wasn't nice of me to screech, but I was really annoyed, and the prior several minutes had been stressful.

"You saw the men who murdered Davis?"

"Yes! In the diner across the street from here! And if Mr. Buck catches pneumonia, the Los Angeles Police Department will pay his doctor bills! I'll make sure of it!"

"Calm down, Mercy, I—"

"I *won't* calm down! I told the idiot who finally showed up at the news kiosk about the murderers and where they were, but I haven't seen a squad of uniformed policemen storm the diner or anything. Why aren't the police ever around when you need them?"

"Okay, Mercy. Take it easy."

"Bother! *You* take it easy! I told you where to find the murderers. If you dawdle and they get away, it won't be my fault."

And I hung up on him. I felt kind of bad about that later, but not a whole lot.

FIFTEEN

"Cripes, Mercy, will you sit down and quit yelling?"

I stood, quivering, in Ernie's office and had just explained the chain of events leading to Mr. Buck contracting pneumonia and me slamming the receiver into the telephone cradle and rupturing Phil Bigelow's eardrum.

Wanting to yell some more, but knowing none of this was Ernie's fault, I sat. I also stopped screeching. My body felt as if it had been dipped in starch, however. Tense. I was tense. All over. Not only had I been starched, but I also felt as though I were an elastic band stretched slightly past its breaking point.

"You say you saw the thug from last night in the diner across the street?"

"Isn't that what I just said?"

"Yeah, but it seems like kind of a stretch to me that he'd just pop into the diner while you're there, too."

"You're treading on thin ice, Mr. Ernest Templeton, P.I. I saw the man you met last night in the diner across the street. He met up with the man who actually committed the murder, and they're sitting together in a booth! Neither one of them saw me."

"Okay. You told Phil this?"

"Yes. And why didn't he send someone to relieve poor Mr. Buck? Mr. Buck was doing you a favor, yet you left him in the freezing cold and wind for *hours!*"

"I didn't do a damned thing."

"You're the one who asked him to take over the news stand, aren't you?"

"Well, yeah, but Phil was supposed—"

"But Phil didn't," I said, interrupting him. Then I inhaled a deep breath and tried to calm my rattled nerves. It wasn't wise to interrupt one's employer. It probably wasn't wise to bellow at him, either. I swallowed and said, "I'm sorry for interrupting you. And for yelling."

My ever-casual boss just shrugged and said, "I'm used to it."

I was about to shriek at him that he wasn't being fair and I'd been provoked past bearing, but the door to the outer office opened, and I rose from my chair to see who had come to call. I hadn't looked at the calendar on my desk when I stomped upstairs from the lobby, so I might have missed noticing an appointment I'd made for Ernie.

When I saw who stood at the door, I stopped stomping and said, "Phil. Did you get them?"

Taking his hat off, Phil sighed and said, "No such luck."

I felt my lips squinch up, smoothed them out again and said, "Oh. What a shame." Then I continued to my desk and sat in my chair. There I looked at the calendar. Thank heaven we had no appointments scheduled until three o'clock.

"Listen, Mercy," said Phil, walking over to my desk and sitting in one of the chairs in front of it. Guess he didn't dare sit at the one I'd positioned beside the desk. After all, I might have reached out and whacked him with the ruler I kept in my middle drawer.

"I'm listening."

"Tread carefully, Phil," came Ernie's voice from his office. "She's on a rampage today."

"Rampage, my foot! Darn you both!"

"Better come in here, Phil. She might strike."

"I'll strike, all right," I muttered. Then, because I didn't want to be left out of any more discussions, I followed Phil into Ernie's office.

"Mercy, you should be manning the secretarial desk," Ernie said mildly.

"You don't have an appointment until three o'clock, and I don't want you to lose any more threads. The police could have had both of those men if they'd only acted in a timely manner."

Ernie rolled his eyes. Probably Phil did, too, but I didn't see him do it. That's because I noticed Ernie's hat on the floor, where it had probably landed when he'd flung it at the hat rack. Stiffly I walked over to the hat and was about to do my boss a favor and pick it up when I happened to glance out of the window, and all thoughts of hat-picking-up fled my brain.

"There they are again!" I hollered. "They're right there! Right *there*!" I emphasized my point by stabbing the window glass several times, thereby leaving smudgy fingerprints.

"What?" Phil, who had just sat, got up again.

Unfortunately, he stepped on Ernie's hat when he hurried over to stand behind me. Served them both right.

Swiveling his desk chair so he, too, could look out the window, Ernie said, "I'll be damned." He glanced at Phil. "Can you get some men here fast?"

"I don't know. Dial the station for me, will you?"

"Sure." Ernie picked up the receiver on his telephone and used the rotary dial to call Station Number One.

Phil loped out of Ernie's room, through mine, and down the hall. I heard his big cop's shoes thunder down the hall toward the elevator.

As I stared out the window at the two killers, who didn't appear to be in a hurry, they ambled down the alley chatting amiably with each other. "Those guys must live in one of those boarding houses," I said to Ernie.

Ernie evidently didn't hear me. "Hey, who stepped on my hat?"

Turning, I saw him pick up his headgear and slap it against his desk to get the wrinkles out. Frowning at me he said, "Did you stomp on my hat?"

"No. I did *not* stomp on your hat, you miserable oaf!" Oh, dear. I *know* it's unwise to call one's boss an oaf. I attempted a placatory tone when I explained, "I saw it on the floor and came back here to pick it up, but before I could do so, I saw those two men in the alley. Phil's the one who squashed your hat."

"You sure? You were pretty mad. I know how you get when you're riled."

"I do not damage other people's property, even when I'm riled, as you well know, Ernie Templeton. I am not a vandal."

"Yeah. I know. Dammit. I'll have to take it to the hatter. You're not heavy enough to make these creases."

"Thank you *so* much." As we talked, I kept peering out the window. At one point, Checkered Jacket peered up, and I could have sworn he looked directly at me. I hastily stepped away from the window.

But I was being silly. He couldn't see me from way down there. Could he?

Shoot. I didn't know. I hoped to heck he couldn't.

Just then the two men swirled around, looked at each other, then turned again and started running.

"There's the police!" I hollered delightedly at Ernie, who was still mourning his crumpled hat.

My words galvanized him, however, and he rose from his chair to stare out the window with me. Forgetting about perhaps having been seen by a couple of extremely large, homicidal men, I all but pressed my nose to the window to watch the action. The police contingent was in an automobile bumping crazily over the ruts and potholes of the unpaved alleyway from the north. I checked to the south and was disappointed not to see a police car coming from that direction, too.

I tell you, if *I* were in charge of things, I'd have ordered two patrol cars to trap those killers in the alley. Unfortunately, I wasn't in charge. By the time Ernie and I watched the police car bounce to the spot directly beneath us, the two murderers had run off somewhere.

"Where could they have gone?" I asked Ernie, not expecting much of an answer.

"Don't know. In between a couple of buildings, I guess."

"They're too big to fit through one of those tiny spaces," I objected.

"Maybe they pulled their tummies in." At his most sarcastic now, my boss.

I felt crabby myself, so I understood. "Why didn't Phil send two cars? They could have trapped the men in the alley."

"Maybe, but they might still have slithered in between a couple of those buildings."

"They *must* live around here. Phil should have his men canvass the neighborhood again."

"I'm sure he will."

"I'm not. He seems to be as inept as all those other crooked coppers you keep telling me about."

"Phil is neither corrupt nor inept," Ernie said heatedly. "You don't know what it's like out there on the streets. Hell, half the coppers on the force are on the take. In fact, I wouldn't be surprised if the big boss, Gallagher, is a cop."

Shocked, I stood still and gazed up at my boss's face. I had to tilt my head back in order to do it, as Ernie was a whole lot taller than I. "Are you serious?"

"Yes, I'm serious," Ernie said, again picking up his hat and frowning at it. "Damn it. I don't think I can get the creases out of this blasted thing."

"There's a haberdasher down the street. I see it as I walk to work every day. Want me to take your hat to the haberdasher's and see if they can fix it?"

"When did you say my next appointment is scheduled?"

"Three o'clock."

"Crumb. No. I'll go after my three o'clock. Any other appointments after that one?"

"No."

"Who's coming at three?"

"Mr. Swale again."

"Ah, hell. What's he want now?"

"I have no idea. Have you dealt with the blackmailers who were harassing him?"

"Not yet. Haven't had time. Well, I spoke with the woman, but haven't had time to do anything else or report to Swale. The woman said she's not going to push the matter, but he'll probably fire me anyway, dammit."

"I'll leave you to curse alone, Mr. Templeton," I said. Then I turned on my heel and headed to my own desk, wishing I could take a ruler to the backs of Ernie's hands. He cursed too much for my taste. Which was silly. Ernie was Ernie, and I…liked him a lot.

As I sat at my desk, contemplating the nature of things, I considered asking Lulu and Rupert to go with Buttercup and me to take another survey of the boarding houses across the alley from the Figueroa Building. Now that I knew the two men who had killed Mr. Davis seemed to have remained in the neighborhood, I figured there couldn't be too many places for them to hide out. In fact, they didn't even seem to want to hide. It didn't occur to me to wonder why that was, although it probably should have.

The events of the morning and early afternoon had plum worn me out. When Mr. Swale arrived at the office at three o'clock on the dot, I barely managed a smile for him. I did, however, like the good secretary I was, rise from my chair and tap at Ernie's door.

I needn't have bothered. The door opened as I tapped, and my second tap landed on Ernie's chest. He frowned down at me.

"Mr. Swale is here for his appointment," I said needlessly. The two men could see each other.

Stupid day.

"Thanks," Ernie said anyway. He stepped aside to allow Mr. Swale to enter his office. I still couldn't picture the dapper, handsome if middle-aged Mr. Swale married to the mastiff-like Mrs. Swale. Oh, well. Mine was not to wonder why, as somebody wrote once, and which has always struck me as redundant. If you're wondering about something, you're already contemplating the why of the thing, aren't you? Oh, but wait. I think the correct citation is, "Ours is not to *reason* why."

Never mind. Stupid quotation anyway. Mine darned well *wasn't* to do and die, blast it.

"Say, Miss Allcutt."

So lost had I become in profitless musings, I gave a start of surprise when Ernie spoke to me. I turned to find him grinning down at me.

"Solving all the crimes in Los Angeles in your head, are you?"

"Actually, no. I was thinking about how we use the English language."

He shook his head. "Sometimes I wonder about you, Miss Allcutt. But you mentioned a haberdasher down the street, and I changed my mind. Do you mind taking my hat there to see if it can be redeemed?"

Standing pertly, I said, "I shall be happy to see if your hat can be rescued, Mr. Templeton. You'll have to take any incoming telephone calls while I'm away from my desk. Do you mind answering the 'phone?"

"I've been answering telephones my whole life, Miss Allcutt." Sometimes I thought Ernie's middle name should be Irreverence.

"Very well, then. I'll take your hand. Hat! I mean, I'll take your *hat* to the haberdashers." Bother. *Such* a stupid day.

"Thanks, kiddo." Seeing my smile vanish, he said, "I mean, Miss Allcutt."

"You're welcome." I snatched the hat from his hand and sat again. I didn't look at him for fear my cheeks might be pink, but opened my drawer and withdrew my hat and handbag.

"There's no rush," Ernie said at my back.

His comment made my nerves twitch, and I *did* turn to look at him. What was he up to now?

Evidently having learned to read my mind, he held his hands in an "I surrender" gesture and said, "I won't do anything to which you'll object while you're out of the office, and I'll tell you all about it when you get back. And I won't go anywhere. Promise."

"Hmmm."

"Promise. For one thing, I won't have a hat to wear."

"As if that's ever mattered to you."

"It does today. It's cold outside."

"Yes, it is." He had a point. Therefore, as he returned to his room and shut the door once more, I also grabbed my scarf and wrapped it around my neck before fetching my heavy Boston coat from the rack and buttoning it up. I even put on gloves.

SIXTEEN

A s I opened the door leading from the staircase and started walking across the lobby, I saw Lulu and Mr. Buck chatting. Mr. Buck had stopped shivering, I was glad to see, although he didn't look terribly happy.

"How are you, Mr. Buck?" I asked solicitously as I approached the reception desk. "Thawed out yet?"

"Yes, thank you, Miss Mercy. It's mighty cold out there, though." He eyed me with concern. "You going somewhere?"

"Ernie asked me to take his hat to the haberdasher down the street to see if they can get the creases out." I held out the squashed object for his and Lulu's inspection.

"Shoot, what did you do, Mercy?" asked Lulu. "Did you get so mad at Ernie, you jumped up and down on his hat?"

"No!" But I grinned. "I saw the two murderers who'd been in the diner across the street. They were walking down the alley behind this building. It was just like the other day when they murdered Mr. Davis, only they didn't kill anyone today. Detective Bigelow was the one who stepped on Ernie's hat, when he came to look out the window with me."

All three of us had a good laugh. Then I sighed. "I offered to

take this thing to the hat shop while Ernie's in with his latest client."
I again waved the crushed hat at my two companions.

"You're going outside alone?" Lulu asked, alarm sounding in her voice.

"Well, yes. Those guys aren't out front any longer."

"How do you know?" asked Lulu. "Did you see where they went? Or did the police pick them up?"

Good questions. "Um...I guess I don't know where they are. And no. Phil sent a squad car to pick them up in the alley, but he only sent one. He *needed* to send two, so the cars could have trapped the men in the alley."

"It's probably not easy to get instant results when a fellow's on those police radios asking for coppers to show up in a hurry," opined Mr. Buck. I'm surprised he was giving the Los Angeles Police Department any slack at all, given what his son had gone through not long back.

"I still don't think you should go out there alone, Mercy." Lulu seemed honestly concerned.

"I agree with Miss Lulu." Mr. Buck sounded as concerned as Lulu.

And, after thinking the matter over for a second or three, I decided they had an excellent point, especially if Checked Coat had seen me looking out the window when he glanced up. "Maybe you're right. But I told Ernie I'd take his hat to the hat shop."

"I'll go with you, Miss Mercy. Just wait until I get my hat and coat. This time I'll take my scarf, too."

"Thank you, Mr. Buck," I said, feeling humble in the presence of true goodness—I'm talking Lulu and Mr. Buck here—and happy to have these people as friends.

Mr. Buck returned with a warm woolen cap pulled down over his curly salt-and-pepper hair and a red scarf wrapped around his neck. He'd also donned a warmer overcoat to wear over the one he'd had on whilst guarding the news kiosk. Poor fellow. Ernie should be ashamed of himself for not remembering he'd left Mr. Buck out there in the freezing cold. Semi-freezing cold. Extremely chilly air, anyhow.

As he held the door open for me to pass through before him, Mr. Buck said, "I know the owner of the haberdasher. Name's Gallagher. Henry Gallagher."

After nearly stumbling over my sensibly shod feet, I stared at my companion. Not wanting to let any beans out of any sacks, I said merely, "Oh? Is he a nice fellow, this Mr. Gallagher?"

I saw Mr. Buck shrug. "He's always been polite to me." He glanced down at my upturned face. "Not everybody's polite to us people of color, you know, Miss Mercy. Not everyone's as nice as you are."

After pondering this sad truth for a second or two, I said, "I'm sorry."

"Not your fault. You're one of the good guys." His teeth showed against his dark face in a big grin. "You and Mr. Ernie. And Miss Lulu. She's a kick, isn't she, Miss Lulu?"

"She is that, all right," I said with a grin of my own.

But a fellow named Gallagher owned the haberdashery! This couldn't be a mere coincidence. Well, I suppose it *could* be, but it seemed a stretch that one Gallagher should own the haberdashery, and another Gallagher should be behind a numbers-running racket in the same neighborhood in which the two big, ugly murderers lived, or at least hung out. Unless, of course, they were brothers or—like the Davis men—father and son. But it didn't matter a whit if they were related or not. They were still tied to this neighborhood somehow. Hmmm.

On the other hand, I didn't know for certain Mr. Gallagher was behind anything except the judge-bribing incident at a dog show. Well, and Mr. Louie Davis said he thought his father had said something about a Gallagher. Unless it was the men who beat him up who'd mentioned Gallagher. I'd have to go over my notes again.

Thinking hard, I asked, "How long has Mr. Gallagher owned the haberdasher's shop? Do you know?"

"How long? No, Miss Mercy, I don't know. He's been there for a long time, though."

"Ah. Interesting."

I felt a tug on my arm as Mr. Buck took my elbow. I stopped walking and looked up at him.

He frowned. "Hold on a minute, Miss Mercy. What are you thinking about? If you know something about Mr. Gallagher, maybe you should tell me. Better yet, tell Mr. Ernie and have him take his own hat into the shop."

Fiddlesticks. "I don't know a thing about Mr. Gallagher, Mr. Buck. Truly, I don't." Should I say anything else? I glanced around. The sidewalks teemed with people, and automobiles clogged Figueroa Street. Lowering my voice and gesturing for him to bend down so I didn't have to yell, I said, "A person named Gallagher might be involved in the murder of Mr. Davis and a blackmail scheme Ernie got involved in. Well, not involved in, as such, but the blackmail of a client. I mean, Gallagher is a name that has come up in both cases. If you see what I mean." Bah. For someone who wanted to write novels, I could sure ball up the language, couldn't I?

After pondering my explanation for several seconds as people surged around us because we were blocking foot traffic, Mr. Buck said, "Then I think I should take Mr. Ernie's hat in to the shop, Miss Mercy. You don't need to meet another bad guy."

Slightly miffed, I demanded, "What do you mean, 'another bad guy'? What bad guys have I met recently?"

Mr. Buck tilted his head, his warm brown eyes assessing me, and I recalled a few of the people I'd met since moving to Los Angeles, and backtracked a bit: "Well..."

"I think I should take Mr. Ernie's hat into the shop, Miss Mercy."

"But if you and Lulu are correct, I'm not even safe alone here on the sidewalk."

"Hmm. That's true," said Mr. Buck.

It was? Good Lord, I didn't think taking Ernie's hat to the hat shop was all *that* dangerous. Maybe it was. Scary thought.

"All right. We'll both take the hat, but I'll do the talking. That all right with you, Miss Mercy?"

"Yes. Thank you, Mr. Buck. Do you really think it's unsafe for me to be outside alone? Really?" I remembered the instant a few hours ago when one of the murderers seemed to stare straight at me from the alley, and said, "Never mind. I think you're right. Thank you very much, Mr. Buck." I handed him Ernie's hat.

Taking it from me, he said, "You're more than welcome, Miss Mercy."

So we continued on our way to the haberdashers, which was called McConnell's Haberdashery. So how'd Mr. Gallagher get involved in the place? If he owned it, why wasn't it Gallagher's Haberdashery? Mysteries piled on mysteries.

The place didn't look as if it was the most profitable haberdashery in the City of Angels, but it seemed a nice shop, if small. A stout gentleman sat on a stool behind the counter, looking through a skinny newspaper. He glanced up when the door opened and smiled at Mr. Buck and me.

"Good afternoon, Mr. Buck."

"Good afternoon to you, Mr. Gallagher."

Gracious sakes! This was Mr. Gallagher! Was he a dirty, rotten criminal? I tried to get a good look at him without actually staring at the man. Hmmm. He looked nice and friendly.

Heck, maybe he was. There must be more than one man named Gallagher in Los Angeles, right?

"What can I do for you today, Mr. Buck?"

I liked it that he called Mr. Buck Mr. Buck. As Mr. Buck had mentioned, many white people didn't bother being polite to people of his color.

"Got me a hat needs tendin'," said Mr. Buck, setting Ernie's pitiful fedora on the counter.

Aha. The skinny newspaper was a racing form. Truth to tell, I didn't have a firm grasp of precisely what racing forms were, but because the paper resting on the counter bore the title *The Daily Racing Form* in fancy letters, I thought I was safe in deducing it was, indeed, a racing form. And, if this fellow was involved in horse racing, it wasn't too much of a stretch to think he might be involved in other forms of gambling, was it?

I wasn't sure, actually, but I'd ask both Mr. Buck and Ernie about it if Mr. Buck and I managed to make it back to the

Figueroa Building in one piece. Two pieces. Oh, you know what I mean.

"Holy cow, Mr. Buck, what happened to this poor fedora?"

"Somebody accidently stepped on it," said Mr. Buck, grinning.

"I'd say so." Mr. Gallagher nodded and glanced from the hat to Mr. Buck. "Do you want me to steam and press it back into shape?"

"If you can do that, please, yes. Thank you." Mr. Buck was ever so polite. At least to white people. Naw. He was nice and polite to everyone, near as I could tell.

Mr. Gallagher fingered the tattered hat band. "Want me to replace this, too? Looks like it could use a new one."

"That would be mighty nice of you, Mr. Gallagher."

"Sure. No problem. Is this your hat, Mr. Buck?"

Pulling at his woolen cap, Mr. Buck smiled and said, "No, sir. It belongs to a gentleman who has an office in the Figueroa Building."

"Ah. When would the gentleman like his hat back? I can do it now, if you want to wait. We aren't exactly doing a brisk business today. Probably because it's so brisk outside."

Mr. Gallagher chuckled. I attempted to define evil intent in his chuckle, but couldn't. Nuts. I needed to work on my detectival skills.

Turning to me, Mr. Buck said, "Do we have time to wait, Miss Mercy?"

"Sure," I said back, wishing he hadn't used my name, although I'm not sure why.

"Excellent. This won't take long," said Mr. Gallagher. He turned and pushed open a door behind him.

I nearly fainted when I observed a huge man in a cheap sack suit working at some kind of machine in the back room of the shop. I turned my head away so fast, I nearly gave myself whiplash. Then I tottered over to a display of hats on the other side of the room, trying my very best to stay out of sight range of the back-room door.

Sensing I was troubled—probably because I gasped, turned and all but ran across the room—Mr. Buck joined me at the hat display. "What's wrong, Miss Mercy?" he whispered.

"One of the murderers is right there in the back room," I whispered back. My heart thundered. Lordy, lordy, why did I tell Ernie I'd take his hat to the haberdasher?

Because I was an idiot? Melancholy notion.

"Don't look surprised," advised Mr. Buck. He picked a hat off the shelf. "What do you think about this one, Miss Mercy? Do you think Mr. Ernest would like this one? He's going to have to replace that fedora one of these days. He's worn that same hat for years now."

Good ploy! Wish I'd thought of it. I really needed a lot more practice experience before I could become a private detective's assistant, drat it.

"Yes. I'll tell him about it. He'll probably have to come in and try it on. I don't know what size hat he takes."

"I looked on the inside of that old fedora, and the size is worn away. Couldn't tell what size it was," said Mr. Buck, chuckling.

I chuckled, too. It was a feeble gesture, but I tried. "Of course, pretty soon it will warm up again. He'll probably need a new straw hat. I noticed his old one was kind of ragged the last time I saw it."

"True, true," said Mr. Buck. "I like this. It's sporty. Think Mr. Ernest would like a sporty straw hat?"

"I'm sure he would," I said, no longer pretending. As long as it was informal, Ernie would love it, whatever it was.

We stood with our backs to the counter chatting about nothing for what seemed like a century and a half, but which probably wasn't more than fifteen or twenty minutes. I could have slapped myself silly for jumping like a scalded cat when Mr. Gallagher said, "All right, Mr. Buck. Here you go. Good as new. Well, almost."

We turned, and I saw Mr. Gallagher looking straight at me. I wanted to melt into the floor.

"Didn't mean to startle you, ma'am," said he with a sly smile.

Oh, all right, so it probably wasn't a sly smile. It looked like one to me, but that's because I'd become incredibly nervous since I spotted that big, ugly killer in the back room.

I waved away his apology. "No. I'm sorry. Mr. Buck and I were so involved in discussing hats, you startled me, was all."

Shut up, Mercy Allcutt.

"I see," said Mr. Gallagher. He switched his attention to Mr. Buck. "Well, here you go, Mr. Buck. "We did our best for this poor thing, but the man who owns it will probably need to replace it one of these days." When he smiled, I saw the glint of gold in his mouth. Don't know why that made me so much more nervous than I already was, but it did.

"I'll tell him so," said Mr. Buck. "How much do we owe you?"

I'd forgotten all about money. Curse me and my sheltered upbringing! I should have had Ernie give me some money to pay for his stupid hat! I swear, I aimed to give myself a good hard lecture if we got out of this shop alive.

"Fifty cents for today's repairs," said Gallagher.

"I have it," I piped up, squeaking slightly. "Mr.... Uh, Mr. Ernest gave me a dollar bill. He wasn't sure how much it would cost."

"Thank you, ma'am," said Mr. Gallagher, taking the bill from my hand, which did *not* tremble.

"You're welcome." Gallagher strolled to the cash register, rang up the sale, and held out a half-dollar to me.

I took it with another, "Thank you," and a nod. Even worked up a smile.

"Want me to put this in a sack for you, Mr. Buck?" asked Gallagher.

"No need. Thank you kindly, sir."

"You're more than welcome," said Gallagher. As Mr. Buck and I got to the door, and Mr. Buck turned the knob, he said to our backs, "Come back soon."

Not in a hundred thousand million years!

SEVENTEEN

Ernie telephoned Phil the instant I told him about Mr. Buck's and my experience in McConnell's Haberdashery.

"I'm taking you and Lulu home tonight," he told me after he'd hung the receiver on its cradle.

"What about Caroline? She works at the Broadway. She meets Lulu and me here, and we always walk home together."

"I'll take Caroline, too," said Ernie, rolling his eyes.

"And we generally collect Sue along the way."

With a heavy sigh, Ernie said, "I'll take Sue, too."

"Thank you." I felt like crying but didn't. I hated feeling scared every time I turned around.

"And I'll pick you all up tomorrow morning, too."

"But Caroline has to be at work promptly at eight."

"I'll make an effort." Ernie frowned at me.

"It isn't my fault Gallagher works at a place called McConnell's or that a murderer works in the back room there," I said defensively since Ernie seemed peeved with me. *Me*, of all people! *I* hadn't murdered anyone!

"I know it's not your fault," he barked. "I just don't like this whole situation. The damned murderers keep showing up all over the place, and why the police can't find them is more than I'll ever know. Cripes, every time you turn around, *you* see them. They're like a colony of ants on this section of Figueroa Street."

"Exactly. They're exactly like ants. Maybe cockroaches." Ew. We didn't have cockroaches at Mercy Manor. Mr. and Mrs. Buck made sure of it.

"Yeah. Cockroaches describe them better, I guess."

I plunked myself down on the chair in front of Ernie's desk. I should have gone back to my own room and sat in my own chair, but I was still suffering from a fit of nerves, and Ernie made me feel safe.

Ernie eyed me without favor. "No work?" he asked.

"I don't think so. I think Mr. Swale was your last appointment. I was so rattled when Mr. Buck and I got back to the building, I forgot to look at my calendar."

"Why don't you look at it now," Ernie suggested. Only it wasn't really a suggestion.

"Yes, sir."

Boy, as soon as I looked at my calendar, I was glad Ernie had forced me to do so. "Yeeps! You have an appointment at four! Did you make this one? Looks like your handwriting."

"Yes, Miss Allcutt. While you were out getting my hat repaired by the local criminal gangland boss, I actually answered the telephone and made an appointment all by myself."

"Who's this Miss Padgett, and what does she want?"

"Don't know yet."

"Oh. Did your appointment with Mr. Swale go well?"

"Fine and dandy."

I pinned him with a death stare, and he elaborated. "He said the woman threatening to blackmail him got scared when I spoke with her. She's afraid to get involved with the police. After all, she's married, too. She said her husband would kill her or, worse, divorce her, if he found out."

"Divorce is worse than death?"

"Divorce would cut off her money supply."

I chuffed with disgust.

Ernie only grinned at me. "Anyhow, Swale was satisfied with my services. He gave me a check. I'd ask you to deposit it, but you'd probably get kidnapped and murdered on your way to the bank."

"Thanks for being such an uplifting employer, Ernie."

"No problem, kid—Mercy."

I sighed. Maybe I'd always be *kiddo* to Ernie. I hoped not.

When the time came for our last appointment of the day, I was surprised we hadn't had a visit from Phil Bigelow. I'd sort of expected him to come in and question me about my jaunt to McConnell's Haberdashery. Mind you, Ernie had done a swell job explaining what I'd seen and done there, but still…

At four o'clock on the dot, the front office door opened, and a young (I think) woman entered with a dog. It was perhaps the tallest dog I'd ever seen. It wouldn't precisely have dwarfed Mrs. Swale's mastiffs, but it would have towered over them, and it was relatively well-muscled. It didn't look menacing, as did Mrs. Swale's mastiffs, but it didn't seem at first glance to be sweet and cuddly, either.

I must have looked alarmed, because the woman with the dog said, "No need to be nervous around this dog. Bevan is an Irish wolfhound, and you'll never meet a sweeter dog."

"Oh," I said brilliantly. Recovering my composure, I went on to say, "It certainly is a big boy…girl…uh, dog."

The woman bestowed a benevolent smile upon me. "Bevan is a male's name, and yes, he is. Irish wolfhounds are the tallest dogs in the entire dog world according to the AKC."

"The AKC?"

"The American Kennel Club."

"Of course. I should have known. Someone else spoke to Mr. Templeton and me about the AKC recently." I shook my head to clear it of irrelevancies. "You're Miss Padgett?"

"I am. Here to see Mr. Templeton. I had to bring Bevan along with me." Her smile tipped upside down. "I don't dare leave him alone. Bevan's life has been threatened."

"No! How terrible!"

"Terrible is the correct word."

Ernie opened his office door and peeked out. Guess he'd heard us. Spying Bevan with Miss Padgett, he gave a deep, soulful sigh. I'm pretty sure he hadn't anticipated any more than I that we'd have to deal with another dog and dog-person in one day.

Standing, as I should have done already, I said, "Miss Padgett, this is Mr. Ernest Templeton. He will help you."

"Thank you very much, Miss…" Miss Padgett glanced at the name plaque on my desk. "Miss Allcutt."

"You're more than welcome." I sent a pleading look Ernie's way.

"Will you please come in and take notes, Miss Allcutt?"

"Of course," I replied in my most efficient secretarial voice, silently blessing Ernie's heart. If he had one. Then I grabbed my pad and several pencils and followed Ernie, Miss Padgett and Bevan into Ernie's room. Again I sat in my note-taking corner, *so* glad Ernie had read the pleading look in my eye. Or maybe he was only afraid to leave me on my own because he feared for my life. Disheartening thought.

However, either way worked for me. I wanted to know how and why anyone would threaten the life of a dog. I guess some dogs are taught to be savage like those old English mastiffs that used to tear poachers into bloody strips. But this extremely tall and shaggy Irish wolfhound, at least according to Miss Padgett, was no threat to anyone or anything. Except maybe a wolf. Perhaps that's how they got their name. Oh, who cares?

The way I see it is this: people can be awful and do awful things to each other, and I can even understand why some people might want an awful person to die. I can't imagine why *any*one would want to do away with a dog.

But that's not the point. We all sat in Ernie's office, Ernie looking quizzically at Miss Padgett, Miss Padgett with her arm around Bevan, and I with my pencil poised. My pencil *did* have a point.

I'm sorry.

"Now, what can I do for you, Miss Padgett?" Ernie asked, sounding as if he cared. I don't think he did especially, but she was a client and good for a few bucks.

Oh, my, those words sound callous. I hadn't meant them to.

Nevertheless, the fact remained that Ernie had to earn a living, and I wanted to keep my job.

After hesitating for a moment, as if pondering how to present her problem, Miss Padgett finally exclaimed, "A woman named Mrs. Richard Swale has threatened to kill my dogs, Boris and Bevan! This is my darling Bevan."

Not sure about Ernie, but I gave a start of surprise and opened my mouth. Before I could blurt out anything, I shut it again. Perhaps I was as trainable as a purebred dog. Probably not.

Unflappable, Ernie merely said, "Mrs. Swale? Lillian Swale? Has mastiffs?" He was already well-trained.

"Yes."

I heard a snuffle, and Miss Padgett fished in her handbag for a handkerchief, which she held to her eyes.

"Has she threatened your dog in person?" asked Ernie.

"You mean, has she come up to me and said she's going to kill my Bevan? No, she hasn't. But I know it's her."

Grammar, grammar. I wrote steadily on my pad.

"You've received threatening letters or something?"

"Notes. I've received notes. I *know* Mrs. Swale is the one writing them, because someone saw her do it. But the notes make no sense. I don't know why she's doing this!"

Miss Padgett broke down and sobbed. Ernie and I shared a speaking glance over her heaving shoulders. Poor thing.

"Miss Padgett?" I asked softly. Ernie frowned at me, but I didn't care. Much.

"I-I-I'm s-s-s-sorry," sobbed she.

"Please don't be sorry. Let me get you a glass of water, and I believe Mr. Templeton has an extra handkerchief or two."

"Th-thank you."

So, leaving my writing implements on my chair, I rushed out to my desk, got my client glass from the drawer, and hurried down the hall to fetch some water for the poor woman whose dogs had been threatened by a *beast* of a woman. I'd take three Irish wolfhounds over one Mrs. Swale any day of the week. Maybe even four or five.

167

By the way, I washed my client glass in between uses, in case you wondered.

But why in the name of heaven was Mrs. Swale threatening to murder Bevan and whatever the other dog's name was? I hoped Miss Padgett would stop crying long enough for me to find out. But not until she drank the water I was fetching for her. I didn't want her to blab while I was out of the office.

By the time I returned to the office, Miss Padgett had stopped sobbing and begun hiccupping. Ernie, looking bored but trying not to, dangled a handkerchief from his fingers, and it looked to me as if the woman had already wept through one of his extras. I'd have to take all the used ones home to be laundered. Providing there were any. For all I knew, his crying clients took his hankies home with him. He glanced up with relief when I reentered the office.

Taking the glass to Miss Padgett, I said, "Here you go," in the softest, sweetest voice I could summon, which was pretty darned soft and sweet. I wanted the woman to feel better and tell Ernie and me about the awful Mrs. Swale.

"Th-thank you, Miss Allcutt." Miss Padgett grabbed so eagerly at the glass, some of the water spilled on Bevan. All he did was lick a tear from her face. That's when I fell in love with him.

"What a sweet dog," I said.

"Bevan is a gentleman of the first order," said Miss Padgett, her voice a trifle stronger.

I'm sure Buttercup would lick my tears if she had an opportunity to do so. I hoped she never would.

"May I pet him?" I asked cautiously. Sure, Bevan seemed like a sweetie-pie, but he was twice as tall as I—or he would be if he stood on his hind legs—and I'd already had too many upsets in one day.

"Of course. Bevan is a love bug as well as a gentleman."

So I gingerly petted the shaggy head of the dog. It felt kind of like petting slender strands of sewing thread. Maybe softish straw. Therefore, even though I loved Bevan, I decided I'd stick with the soft and silky Buttercups of the world, at least for the time being.

"Are you feeling better now, Miss Padgett?" said Ernie. I could tell his words had oozed out between clenched teeth. Therefore, I resumed my note-taking chair.

"Yes. Thank you."

"You say Mrs. Swale has sent you notes? Have you kept them?"

"Oh, yes. I brought them with me. I'm absolutely terrified for Boris and Bevan! And I don't know why she's threatening them! We've met on the dog-show circuit, but her horrid mastiffs are in the working group, and my Boris and Bevan are in the sporting group! They aren't even in competition with each other. Well, they would be if one of each of our dogs won best of breed in the same show, but other than that they never compete! Why is she threatening my darling dogs?"

"I don't know," said Ernie, echoing my own thoughts on the matter. "What do you mean about mastiffs and Irish wolfhounds and whatever Boris is being in different groups?" he asked as Miss Padgett excavated further in her handbag.

"Dogs are separated into different groups. There are the working dogs, like…oh, Saint Bernard's and mastiffs—although they perform different jobs. But they still belong to one group called the working group. The sporting group includes dogs like spaniels, pointers and all the hounds. They're talking about moving hounds from the sporting group into a group of their own, as they did with terriers. I think it's a good idea."

Again Ernie and I exchanged glances. This time both glances expressed puzzlement. What *was* the woman talking about? I cleared my throat, but Ernie held up a hand to dissuade me from speaking. Therefore, I didn't speak.

"Miss Padgett, I'm not sure I quite understand all the permutations extant in the dog world. I'm sure the American Kennel Club performs an admirable service—"

"Oh, yes! It does. It does!"

Nice to know.

"Good. However, perhaps if I could see the notes you brought with you, I might more fully understand your problem. Situation. That is to say, the threat posed to your dogs."

"Of course. Here." She plopped a short pile of notes onto

Ernie's desk. I itched to look at those notes, but I stayed in my chair like a good little girl and allowed Ernie to reach for them, which he did.

He read one, put it aside and read another. The more notes he read, the more his puzzled expression deepened. I scowled ferociously at him, but he didn't see me so I might as well have saved my face from potential wrinkles. I decided I needed to cultivate patience, which was probably my least prominent personality trait.

Finally, holding a note in each hand, Ernie glanced up and spoke to Miss Padgett. "I still don't quite understand why these notes are worded as they are."

"I don't, *either*," squealed Miss Padgett, again making use of a hankie. Not sure whose it was.

His eyebrows lowering into a V over his nose, Ernie read one note aloud. "This one says, 'If you don't stop, your dogs will pay the price.' " Lifting his shoulders, he said, "What are you supposed to stop?"

"I don't *know!*" wailed Miss Padgett. "That's why I'm so upset. If I've done something to harm Mrs. Swale in any way whatsoever, I can't imagine what it might be! She has mastiffs. I have my darlings, Boris and Bevan. We have competed in various shows, like at the Pasadena Kennel Club Show and the Santa Barbara K.C. Show and the Los Angeles Kennel Club Show, but our dogs don't compete against each other, as I said. Unless they both win best of group, and that's never happened yet." She sniffed. "Although Bevan has taken best in group twice, and I don't believe any of the horrid Swale woman's dogs have ever achieved such heights."

"All right. So you're basically not in direct competition with each other. Correct?"

"Yes."

"Then I don't understand. This note says, 'What you're doing is evil, you tramp.'" He eyed the most definitely *not* tramp-like Miss Padgett and shook his head in seeming bewilderment. "Do you have any idea what she was talking about in this note?"

"No!"

"You're sure these are from Mrs. Swale?" Ernie tried, I guess hoping for some kind of clarification. I wouldn't mind a little myself.

"Yes. I know they're from her because Mr. Neville Fleister told me he saw her slip a note into my handbag during the Santa Barbara show. I get a new note every time I attend a show in which either Boris or Bevan is entered. It's...it's...It's just *terrible*! My nerves are *shattered*."

Good thing for her Bevan seemed to be a relaxed kind of dog. He just licked another tear off her face and resumed staring at Ernie. I think I saw his shoulders lift in a sigh. Bevan's shoulders, not Ernie's.

EIGHTEEN

"May I keep these notes, Miss Padgett? I'll return them to you after I've done some investigating."

Sniffling into yet another of Ernie's handkerchiefs, Miss Padgett nodded. After she'd composed herself slightly, she said, "Yes. Please do, but I would like them back. Oh, I *hope* you can stop the ghastly woman from threatening my darling dogs! If anything happens to either of them, I'll just *die*."

Very well, she might not be a tramp, but she definitely had a dramatic side. Still, I knew how she felt. If anyone did anything bad to my precious Buttercup, I'd be crushed.

Eventually, Ernie eased her out of the office. His shoulders sagged when he shut the door behind her.

He and I gazed at each other for a second or two. "Good God," he said.

"Indeed," I said.

Lifting his arm and flapping his coat sleeve down, Ernie squinted at his wristwatch. "Damn, it's past five. I hope Lulu hasn't left the building yet."

"I don't think she'd leave without me," I said, praying I was correct, although I doubted Lulu was in danger.

The front office door opened, and Lulu stood there with her coat on, looking troubled. "Oh, good. You're still here. I wondered what was going on. And then I saw the lady with that huge dog and worried the dog had eaten you or something."

"The woman was Miss Padgett, and the dog was Bevan," I told her. "He's an Irish wolfhound. Her appointment took a little longer than usual because she kept crying. Miss Padgett, not Bevan."

"Oh," said Lulu, who didn't seem appreciably enlightened but no longer looked apprehensive.

"I'll get my hat and coat and stuff. Has Caroline come in yet?"

"Not yet."

"I'm taking you three home in my Studebaker," Ernie announced as he went back into his room to fetch his hat.

"You are?" said Lulu. "How come?"

"He's worried about us. We saw those two murderers three or four times today."

"I didn't," said Lulu. "You did. And Mr. Buck."

"I'll take him home, too," said Ernie.

"He's already gone. Your detective friend drove off with him about a quarter of an hour ago." Lulu sniffed.

"Phil did *what?* Good Lord!" I turned on Ernie like a fury. "Is Phil Bigelow an absolute *idiot?* Does he think Mr. *Buck* belongs to that gang of murderers?"

"Calm down, Mercy. I suspect Phil drove Mr. Buck to your place in order to question him."

"Really?" I stared squinty-eyed at Ernie for a second, searching for any sign of subterfuge or misdirection on his face. Naturally, I saw nothing but Ernie's face. How come people in novels are always reading things in people's eyes or facial expressions? Unless someone is actively angry or laughing, I can never tell what they're thinking. Did this bespeak a lack of detectival ability on my part? Well, I'd work on it.

"I think Ernie's right, Mercy," said Lulu, who had no love for Phil Bigelow, as I believe I've explained already. "I heard him—the detective—say something about not wanting him—Mr. Buck—to expose himself to danger."

"Oh," I said. "Good for Phil."

"All right, then. May we leave now?" asked Ernie.

"I thought we were supposed to look at mug shots at the police department," I said, glancing at Ernie.

"They can wait. I want to get you home in one piece. That's the most important thing right now. Anyway, Phil saw the two thugs himself, so he can identify them as well as you can now. So can I, for that matter."

"As long as Caroline is downstairs," I told him. "If she isn't, we'll need to wait for her."

"She might not come by," said Lulu, "because we said we'd be going to the police station after work."

"Bother. That's right. Well," said I, "let's go see if she comes to the Figueroa Building before heading home. If she does, Ernie can take her, too."

After heaving an aggrieved sigh, Ernie said, "Yeah, yeah."

The three of us walked down the hall and, because Ernie and Lulu were with me, I agreed to take the elevator to the lobby. As soon as we hit the bottom and the door opened, we saw Caroline standing before the reception desk, peering around in a bewildered fashion.

"We're here!" I called to her.

She whirled around and smiled at us. "I'm so glad. I got a little worried when I didn't find you or Lulu in the lobby. Then I remembered you said you were going to the police station, so I was about to leave again."

"Ernie—Mr. Templeton, I mean—is going to drive us home," I told her.

"How kind of you, Mr. Templeton." Caroline was such a sweet girl.

"Not a problem," grunted Ernie. He opened the front door, but before Caroline could walk outside, he said, "I'll go first. Just a precaution."

Stepping back a pace, Caroline appeared surprised and a trifle disapproving.

"I'll tell you about it after we get home," I promised.

"Very well."

So Caroline and Lulu sat in the ratty back seat of Ernie's ratty car, and I sat in the ratty front passenger seat. It didn't take long for Ernie's disreputable Studebaker to pick Sue up at her dentist's office and make it to my house on Bunker Hill. Sure enough, a police car sat in the drive. I sighed. "Guess you were right about Phil taking Mr. Buck home."

"Figured that's what he'd do," said my boss, turning into the driveway.

"Thank you for the lift, Mr. Templeton," said Caroline, who didn't know him as well as Lulu and I did. She didn't use people's first names until she'd known them for seven or eight years. After she rented rooms in my house, I didn't think she'd *ever* stop calling me "Miss Allcutt."

"Yes," said Sue. "Thank you."

"Thanks, Ernie," said Lulu.

"Yes. Thank you, Ernie. Do you want to come and see Phil? Heck, want to stay for dinner?"

Pulling to a stop behind the police car, Ernie exited the Studebaker. He opened the back door first, so I opened my own door. Caroline appeared a wee bit shocked. Poor thing didn't have an unconventional bone in her body. I just smiled at her.

Buttercup met all five of us at the door, wagging her precious fluffy tail. I scooped her up. "I'm *so* glad you're not a mastiff or an Irish wolfhound," I whispered in her ear as she kissed my cheek.

This time Caroline looked at me as if she thought I'd lost my mind.

With a smile for her, I said, "You'll learn about it soon. Just go on up and change, or whatever you usually do."

"Very well," she said, and walked through the tiled entryway, into the living room and up the stairs.

Ernie, Lulu, Sue and I followed her into the living room.

"Where is everyone?" I asked no one in particular.

"Beats me," said Lulu. "If the cop car's here, that detective should be here, too."

"Maybe they're on the sun porch or in the kitchen," said Ernie, heading toward the dining room, which would lead him into the butler's pantry and eventually the kitchen.

Sure enough, when Lulu and I followed him thither we heard soft voices in the kitchen. Ernie shoved the door open and stared inside. Lulu and I each looked over a shoulder. Phil and Mr. Buck sat at the kitchen table, and Mrs. Buck was doing her best to dodge around them as she attempted to prepare dinner for my tenants and me.

"What the heck are you sitting in here for, Phil?" asked Ernie.

"Yeah," I said. "You're in Mrs. Buck's way. Come out to the living room."

I saw the glance the Bucks shared. They weren't accustomed to being treated like human beings by white people. I didn't approve of people treating other people poorly because of the color of their skin.

"Mr. Buck and the policeman can go to the sun porch, Miss Mercy," suggested Mrs. Buck.

"No. Just use the living room."

Phil must have noticed the flash of anger in my eyes, because he instantly rose and said, "Thank you, Mercy. We'll do that."

"Yes. Mrs. Buck has enough to do without having to avoid the two of you. Not only that, but you're taking up the whole kitchen table. She probably needs the table to put stuff on." I had no idea if this was true or not. My cooking skills were even less advanced than my detectival ones. And that notion was so depressing, I decided to stop thinking for the rest of the evening.

Phil and Mr. Buck meekly followed Lulu as Ernie held the door for them to pass through. He lifted an eyebrow at me, and I said, "I'll be there in a minute." He shrugged and followed everyone else, and I said, "Mrs. Buck, the kitchen is your realm. You don't have to put up with men clogging it up. You can just tell them to get out of your way any time you want to."

Looking at me doubtfully, Mrs. Buck said, "I'd just as soon not make a policeman mad, Miss Mercy."

So there we had it. "I'm sorry," I said, because I was. "But it's all right with me if you tell people to get out of your kitchen. I just want you to know that."

With a gentle smile, Mrs. Buck said, "I do know it, Miss Mercy. Thank you."

I didn't want to get mushy, so I asked, "What are you going to feed us for dinner tonight? It smells good." I spoke only the truth.

"We're having fried chicken, green beans, mashed potatoes and gravy, and biscuits. I've got an applesauce spice cake for dessert."

"Oh, I love your fried chicken," said I. "Um...I don't want to cause you any more trouble, but will there be enough for Ernie if he stays here?"

"Of course," said she. "There's always enough food for Mr. Ernie. Not sure about that policeman, though."

"Don't worry. He can go home to his wife. Poor Ernie's all alone in the world."

After maybe half a second, we both burst out laughing. Therefore, I left the kitchen feeling better than I had when I entered it, which was a good thing.

When I returned to the living room, Phil and Mr. Buck were sitting on a couple of chairs in a corner of the room. Ernie and Lulu had plopped themselves on another couple of chairs, so I sat on a nearby sofa. Buttercup jumped up into my lap, and I lavished pets upon her.

As Ernie and Lulu pinned their gazes on me, I said, "Mrs. Buck's making fried chicken for dinner and you're invited, Ernie."

"Oh, glory!" said Lulu. "She makes the *best* fried chicken! It's a lot better than my grandma's ever was."

"Thanks, Mercy," said Ernie. "That's right nice of you."

"It's nice of Mrs. Buck. She's the cook. And I'd never eaten a piece of fried chicken in my life until I moved to Los Angeles. Back east, we boil our chickens. Fricasseed chicken and dumplings, is what we had."

"I don't recall fried chicken in Chicago, either," said Ernie. "Although we had every other kind of food known to man."

"Yeah?" Lulu lifted an enquiring eyebrow.

"Yeah. Chicago has all these ethnic neighborhoods. Poles live in one section, Germans in another, Spaniards in another, Greeks in another. Chicago is just like that." He shrugged.

"Really," I said. "How interesting. Sounds much more interesting than Boston. The only thing I miss about Boston is getting all the fresh lobster and crab and stuff like that. Fried clam stands. I love fried clams. Seafood in general."

"You can get fish here," said Lulu. "I think."

"Yes, you can, but probably not fresh lobsters," said Ernie. "If you order that stuff in a restaurant, it costs a bundle."

I pondered the seafood question for a moment. "We should be able to get good fish here. Los Angeles is darned near *on* the Pacific Ocean."

"You can," said Ernie.

"Bet Mrs. Buck can get fresh fish for us at the Grand Central Market," I opined.

"I like catfish," said Lulu. "We had catfish a lot in Oklahoma. Caught it in streams and rivers and what-not."

"I've never eaten catfish," said I, unsurprised. I hadn't tasted a whole lot of foodstuffs available in the world.

The three of us were so involved in our fishy conversation, we jumped when Phil suddenly loomed up behind Ernie and Lulu and said, "Thanks, Mercy. I think Mr. Buck told me pretty much what went on in McConnell's Haberdashery today. Anything you'd like to add?"

"Have a seat," I told him. I looked around for Mr. Buck, but he'd vanished already. Probably didn't feel comfortable hanging out with all the white folks in the living room. I tell you, I sometimes despaired of the world. Often, in fact.

"Thanks." Phil sat on the other end of the sofa I occupied. He flipped open the notebook he carried and said, "All right, Mr. Buck said a man named Gallagher either owns or runs the hat shop, and you told him you saw one of the people you think killed Mr. Davis in the back room."

"I *did* see one of the people I *saw* kill Mr. Davis in the back room. Not the checked-suit guy, but the cheap sack-suit guy."

"Right," said Phil, jotting on his pad.

"They *must* live around there, Phil," said Ernie.

"Yes, they must," I agreed. "And at least one of them works around there. And so does Mr. Gallagher, who's probably the same Gallagher the checked-suit man talked to Ernie about at the Melrose."

Sharing a black look between Lulu and me, Phil said, "That's right. You went to the Melrose to watch Ernie deal with the blackmailer."

"Yes," I agreed.

Still looking peeved, Phil said, "Are you two *trying* to get yourselves killed?"

"No!" Lulu and I said in a fierce duet.

I went on, "We just wanted to see what a blackmail pay-off looked like. We were hiding. The bad man didn't see us."

"You hope," snarled Ernie.

"You hope," snarled Phil.

"Oh, very well. We hope," I agreed.

"The guy in the checked suit looked directly at you today when you pointed out him and the other guy in the alleyway," Ernie reminded me.

"You don't know that. For all you know, the sun was shining on the window, and all he saw was a glare."

"You hope," said Phil.

"Anyway, I'm picking up Mercy, Lulu and that other girl and taking them to work from now on," said Ernie. "And taking them home again until those guys are arrested and charged."

I suddenly thought of another person who might be in jeopardy. Or not. None of us knew anything for sure at the time. "What about Mr. Buck. He has to get there early to open the building. I guess he can wait and go in with us. Can't he, Ernie?"

"It's all right by me, but I doubt Buck will go for it. He works for the building's managers, don't forget. He has specific working hours."

"Oh," I said. "Now I'm really worried about him." I turned to Phil. "You can give him police protection, can't you?"

"I...What?"

179

"You can get a patrol car to pick him up and take him to the Figueroa Building. You can do that, can't you?

"Um…" Phil appeared confused for a moment.

"Yes, he can," Ernie said suddenly. "Can't you, Phil?" He spoke the last three words slowly and distinctly and tilted his head in my direction. "If you don't, neither one of us will ever hear the end of it."

"You're darned right you won't. And I'll write a letter to the *Los Angeles Times*, too, telling everyone the corrupt Los Angeles Police Department only cares about its white citizens."

"Now wait just a minute!" Phil said.

I said, "I will."

Ernie said, "She will."

Lulu said, "I will, too."

"Aw, hell," said Phil. "All right." He got up from the sofa, plopped his hat on his head and said, "I'm going home to see my family. I'm tired of today."

With a chuckle, Ernie said, "You're not the only one."

When Phil walked past the staircase, he tipped his hat to Caroline as she descended same.

All things considered, I counted the evening a success. It got even better when we stuffed ourselves with Mrs. Buck's spectacular fried chicken.

NINETEEN

The next morning, Mrs. Buck prepared waffles, sausages and fresh orange juice. Breakfast was *so* good.

"Thank you, Mrs. Buck," Caroline said.

"Yes," said Sue, looking at her plate with awe and admiration. "You usually save waffles for weekends."

Lulu didn't speak. She wasn't what people call a "morning person." But she dug into her waffles and sausages like a starving child.

"And this, after your spectacular fried chicken last night. Mrs. Buck," I said, "you're a wonder."

"I just appreciate you and Mr. Ernie so much, Miss Mercy. A police car showed up in your drive at six-thirty this morning to take Mr. Buck to work. If you and Mr. Ernie hadn't bossed that detective around, Mr. Buck would have had to walk to work. And I don't want him walkin' to work with murderers all around us."

Sue dropped a spoon, which clattered in her saucer. "M-murderers?"

Lulu squinted at her. "We told you about all the fun yesterday."

"The fun?" said Caroline, who was a literal-minded young woman.

"Lulu's just teasing, Caroline."

"Yeah. It wasn't any fun."

"I should say not." Sue stared at the table in horrified fascination. "I'd be afraid to step foot out of the house if I knew there were murderers around."

I didn't point out that there *were* murderers around, whether she knew about them or not. "You don't need to worry. Neither one of the killers has seen you. I'm not sure they know I witnessed their crime."

"And the guy you met at the haberdasher's is a blackmailer, unless he's behind the numbers-running racket and the murder." Lulu took a sip of coffee. "Actually, he's probably all of those things."

"Good heavens," said Caroline. "I knew you'd witnessed a murder, Mercy, but I had no idea the murderers know you saw them."

"We're not sure they do," I said, hoping to calm both Sue and Caroline. "Anyhow, Ernie's going to take us all to work today, so nobody has to walk."

Ernie's rackety car pulled into my driveway at twenty minutes to eight that morning, and Lulu, Caroline, Sue and I were all waiting for him. I'd introduced Sue to him the night before.

"This is very kind of you, Mr. Templeton," said Caroline.

"Not a problem," Ernie growled. I don't think he could be described as a "morning person," either.

Sue had opened her mouth, probably to thank him, too, but she shut it again. Guess she didn't want to be growled at.

"Who gets dropped off first?" asked Ernie.

"Miss Terry works at the Broadway, and Miss Krekeler works at Dr. Philby's office on Fifth and Hill," I told him.

"Gotcha. Miss Krekeler first, then Miss Terry, and then the three of us leftovers."

"Right," I said.

Silence reigned for the rest of our ride to work.

As usual, Mr. Buck had made certain no one had parked his or her car in front of the Figueroa Building before Ernie arrived.

Lulu and I managed to get out of the car with the help of Mr. Buck, who opened our doors for us before Ernie had got the beast to stop shuddering—the beast being his old Studebaker. He shook his head as he thumped the thing on its hood and walked around it to join Lulu, Mr. Buck and me on the sidewalk.

"Looks like you might need a little tune-up, Mr. Ernie," said Mr. Buck kindly.

"Tune-up, hell. I need a new car," grumbled Ernie.

"I wouldn't mind having a car of my own," said Lulu wistfully.

"They're handy to have, all right," said Mr. Buck, who also had no automobile.

I remained mute and suppressed the urge to tell my friends I'd be happy to buy Ernie, Lulu and the Bucks a brand-new car each. Having money is nice, but shoving one's good fortune at other people isn't a helpful thing to do. Ernie had taught me this valuable lesson when I started renting out rooms in my home.

"Ah," said Ernie when Mr. Buck handed him a copy of the *Los Angeles Times*. "Thank you. Is Louie back yet, or is the stand still being run by coppers?"

"Can't rightly tell you the answer to that one, Mr. Ernie," said Mr. Buck as he opened the front door of the Figueroa Building for us. "I didn't recognize the gentleman at the stand this morning."

"Well, hell, if a gentleman is manning the place, it's neither Louie *nor* the coppers," grunted Ernie.

Lulu and I snickered. Mr. Buck smiled appreciatively.

Ernie and I left Lulu at the receptionist's desk, and we made our way to the elevator. I hesitated for a second, but Ernie took my arm. "I'm not climbing three flights of stairs this early in the morning, Mercy. Ned's in prison and the elevator works fine, so you don't need to fear it any longer."

For the record, Ned is the person I shoved down the elevator shaft. He was trying to kill me at the time; pushing him wasn't a frivolous impulse on my part.

"You're right," I said, gingerly stepping into the elevator cage while Ernie held the door for me. "It just brings back memories, is all."

"Yeah, yeah."

In an attempt to wake him up, I said, "Do you know what you're going to do about Mrs. Swale threatening Miss Padgett?"

"Yeah, I think so."

I waited. And waited.

"Would you care to share?" I asked eventually.

"Yeah. Later. Let me read the paper. I've got to get some coffee, too."

"I'd offer to go across the street and get some from the diner, but—"

"You're not stepping foot out of the office unless someone else is with you until we figure out what the hell's going on around here."

Guess that told me. I said merely, "Very well." Then, because his foul attitude wasn't my fault and I didn't think I should have to bear the brunt of it, I said, "Why are you in such an all-fired bad mood this morning?"

"Don't like getting up early. I was up late last night, working on how to stop people from killing you." He frowned at me.

Oh. Well, that put his lousy mood in a different light, I reckoned. Therefore, I said, "Thank you."

"You're welcome."

"Did you come up with a way to do it?"

"No."

I sighed.

"But I will."

"Thank you."

"Don't thank me yet."

"I appreciate you trying to figure it out."

"Huh."

Okey-dokey. The elevator stopped at the third floor, and Ernie pulled the handle to open the door. I made sure the cage was flush with the floor before stepping into the hall. As soon as I stepped out, I stepped back in again, bumping into Ernie, who said, "Whuh!"

I pointed down the hallway toward Ernie's office. I'm sure my eyes were as huge as pie plates. A dog almost as tall as Miss Padgett's Bevan, turned at Ernie's office door, spied us, and then galloped down the hallway toward us. Thinking quickly, Ernie pulled the cage door shut. The dog's nose hit the mesh of the cage, the dog jumped back and gave a pained, "Yip!"

"Boris!" a voice called. "Boris, shame on you!"

That's when I noticed Miss Padgett running down the hallway toward the elevator. Aha. So this was her Boris. Boris was shaped more or less like Bevan, but he had long, wavy hair, a longer and pointier nose and was...well, beautiful. Or probably would be when he wasn't bounding after Ernie and me as if we were breakfast.

"Boris, you bad dog!" said Miss Padgett, finally reaching the elevator and picking up the leash Boris had evidently yanked from her grip. "I'm so sorry, Miss Allcutt and Mr. Templeton. Boris loves people, and sometimes he...well, gets away from me. He's usually very well behaved. I fear I wasn't paying as much attention to him as I ought."

"That's okay," said Ernie. "Is it safe to open the elevator?"

I still had a hand pressed to my thundering heart and couldn't speak. Staring at Boris in fascination, I wondered what he would have done if he'd reached us before Ernie closed the cage. Miss Padgett said he loved people. I presume she didn't mean he loved eating them.

"Oh, yes." Miss Padgett tugged Boris's lead and said, "Boris, sit."

Boris sat.

I stopped Ernie from opening the elevator cage by slapping his hand away from the handle. Oh. I guess that's where the word "handle" comes from.

Never mind.

"Are you sure he won't try to bite us?" I asked Miss Padgett. "I've never been run at by a dog that large."

"I'm so sorry, Miss Allcutt. He won't bite. He might try to lick you, but I have him under control now. He's a good deal younger than Bevan and hasn't had as much obedience training. But he's learning quickly." She knelt beside her giant dog and said, "Aren't you, Boris?" In the silly, high-pitched voice people use with dogs.

I'm not disapproving of her. I do the same thing with Buttercup, who allows the indignity in spite of being a purebred poodle.

Boris's silky tail swept the hallway runner, and I swear he smiled at Miss Padgett before turning his attention back to Ernie and me.

"Am I allowed to open the door yet?" asked Ernie.

"Yes, thank you," I said. "I didn't mean to hit you so hard."

"That's all right," said Ernie in a longsuffering voice. "I'm used to it."

"Nuts," I said.

So Ernie drew the cage door open, then took my arm and assisted me into the hallway. Boris's tail wagged faster. If we didn't have such a good custodian in Mr. Buck, that tail would have created a massive fug of dust.

"May I pet him?" I asked cautiously.

"Yes. Please do," said Miss Padgett. "He loves people."

There she went again. Tentatively, I reached out to pet Boris behind an ear. "Oh, he's so soft!" I said.

"He is," said Miss Padgett proudly. "He's only nine months old, but he's already taken best of breed at two shows."

"My goodness." Boris evidently liked having his ear scritched, because he kind of leaned into me. He was so heavy, I had to take a step sideways so as not to fall over. Ernie braced my shoulder, which helped. "What kind of dog is Boris? He seems like a sweetheart."

Pride radiated from Miss Padgett's voice when she said, "He's a Russian wolfhound. Isn't he darling?"

"He seems to be sweet," I said. "So you have an Irish wolfhound and a Russian wolfhound. Do they speak the same language?"

Miss Padgett looked at me as if I'd gone 'round the bend.

"Sorry," I said. "Bad joke."

"Oh," she said, getting it. She tittered once, which was more than my silly sally was worth.

"Well, come on inside the office," said Ernie. I could tell he was less than ecstatic to have a client greet him at his own door before he'd read the *Times* or drunk even one cup of coffee. "I presume there's a reason you're here at this hour?" He didn't sound as snide as his comment reads. He valued his customers.

"Yes. I…" Miss Padgett gulped audibly. "I got another death threat, only this time it threatens *my* life. Which, if I'd ever done anything to which Mrs. Swale could take offense, makes more sense than her threatening my dogs, but I haven't. Unless I did it by accident, but what could it have been?"

We'd reached his office. "Don't know," said Ernie, shoving the door open. I stepped aside to allow Miss Padgett and Boris to enter before Ernie and me.

Boy, having a dog as big as Boris or Bevan—or the two mastiffs, Caesar and Augustus—in the office made the room seem really small. I stepped around Miss Padgett and Boris, got behind my desk and felt a sense of great relief. Even though Boris loved people. Ernie and Miss Padgett danced together for a couple of seconds before Ernie finally cleared the hurdle of woman and dog. He took off his hat and overcoat and laid them over the chair beside my desk.

"Please take a seat, Miss Padgett," he said, gesturing to one of the chairs in front of my desk. She did so, sitting in the chair closer to Ernie's office door and allowing Boris to drape himself over the second chair. "Did you bring the note with you?"

"Yes, I did," said Miss Padgett, who looked as if she'd been crying again, poor dear. Feeling threatened is no darned fun, as I knew well. Holding tight to Boris's leash, Miss Padgett put her handbag on her lap, unfastened it, and fiddled around inside it for a second. She removed an envelope.

"This is a departure," said Ernie, holding his hand out to receive the envelope. He turned it over, squinting. "It was mailed to you. None of the other notes have been mailed, have they?"

"No. They were all stuck in my belongings at different dog shows."

"Hmm. There's no return address on the envelope."

"No, but it *must* be from that awful Swale woman!" Miss Padgett squeaked. "Nobody else has ever threatened my dogs or me before she started doing it."

Picking up his hat and overcoat, Ernie said, "Just let me get rid of these. I agree, it's probably Mrs. Swale who's doing the threatening. I have an idea I might know why."

Giving a visible start, Miss Padgett gasped loudly.

Boris, taking this as an indication that Ernie was somehow endangering his mistress, stood and rumbled low in his throat. He had sparkly white teeth. I saw them when he drew his lips back in a snarl.

I sat back in my chair, dropping the hat I'd been about to put in my desk drawer along with my handbag. "Good Lord, don't let him bite Mr. Templeton!"

"Boris!" said Miss Padgett sternly to her dog, who was as on-guard as any dog had any right to be. "Sit. Mr. Templeton is not a danger to me."

"Cripes," said Ernie, looking at Boris with distaste. "I'll be right back."

"Down, Boris," Miss Padgett said again.

Boris, after one last threatening glance at Ernie's retreating back, decided to obey his mistress's command and sat again.

Thank God!

TWENTY

W hen Ernie returned to my room, he straddled the chair from which he'd removed his hat and coat, folded his arms over its back and looked askance at Boris. I think he sat that way so he could pick up the chair and try to fend Boris off with it, as I've seen animal trainers in circuses do, should such an action become necessary. "Is he calm now? I don't want to be chewed to death by a Bolshie dog."

"Boris is *not* a Bolshevik, Mr. Templeton!" Miss Padgett said, offended by Ernie's mention of the current bloodthirsty regime subjugating Russia.

"Just keep him calm, okay?"

"Of course, I shall. Boris is extremely well-trained for so young a dog."

Deciding intervention would not be amiss here, after retrieving my hat, putting it in my desk drawer and removing a couple of dollars from my handbag, I carefully and slowly rose from my chair behind the desk. Boris peered at me, interested, but he didn't growl. Therefore, I decided it would be safe to speak. "I was just going to get Mr. Templeton and me some morning coffee, Miss Padgett. Would you care for a cup of coffee or tea?"

"Don't go out," Ernie commanded, scowling at me.

"I won't," I told him. And I did it sweetly, too, by gad. "I'm sure Mr. Buck will be able to send someone across the street for coffee or tea and…what else? Donuts? Pastries?" I was full to the brim with Mrs. Buck's good breakfast, but poor Ernie probably hadn't had the opportunity to eat anything yet.

After hesitating for a second or two, Ernie nodded. "Yeah. Thanks, Miss Allcutt. I'd like a couple of sinkers to go with my Joe." He glanced at Miss Padgett. "Would you like anything, Miss Padgett?" He sounded almost sweet, too.

I'd have rolled my eyes had we been alone in the office. Since we weren't, I merely smiled. Sweetly.

"Thank you," said Miss Padgett. "Um…are you sure it's no bother? I don't drink coffee, but I'd love a cup of tea."

"I'm not sure if the diner across the street makes a good cup of tea, but I'll be happy to get you one," I told her. "Would you like a donut or anything?"

"No, thank you, Miss Allcutt. This is awfully kind of you."

Nuts to that. I wanted Ernie to get some food and coffee in his stomach to help improve his disposition. I knew my boss. He didn't like surprises first thing in the morning. In fact, I think he stopped at a diner for breakfast most mornings.

"I'll be right back," I said, then scurried past Ernie, Miss Padgett and Boris to the door, exited same, and walked quickly down the hall. Since Ernie wasn't with me, I clattered down the staircase to the lobby.

When I burst through the door leading to the lobby, Lulu and Mr. Buck turned to see who was interrupting their chat.

"Miss Mercy!" said Mr. Buck, looking concerned. "What's the matter?"

"Nothing, but I have to get some coffee and donuts for Ernie. Miss Padgett is upstairs in his office with her Russian wolfhound, and Ernie's not in a good mood about it.

"That's the lady with the big dog?" asked Mr. Buck. "Wondered what she wanted so early in the morning."

"She wanted Ernie," I said. "Say, Mr. Buck, Ernie doesn't want any of us to go out by ourselves, but you know most of the folks in the building and the neighborhood. Know anyone who can get coffee, tea and maybe donuts for us?"

"Try Junior," suggested Lulu.

"Who's Junior?" I asked.

"Kid works as a runner for the lawyer on the second floor," said Lulu.

Thus enlightened, I said, "Great. If you can get Junior to go out on a coffee and food search, Ernie would really appreciate it. So would I."

"You want more food?" Lulu looked at me as if she thought I'd lost my mind.

"No. *Ernie* needs food. I'll take a cup of coffee. Miss Padgett wants tea." I held out the two bucks I'd taken from my handbag. "If Junior can find anything more substantial than a couple of donuts for Ernie, that would be even better. A sausage in a bun or something like that would be great. Tell Junior to keep the change."

Taking the money, Mr. Buck said, "I'll go get the lad right now." He strode to the door to the staircase.

"He's so nice," I said.

"Yeah, he's nice," agreed Lulu. "He also knows you and Ernie saved his kid from the electric chair. He owes you both."

"Nonsense. Both Ernie and I—and you, too—were happy to help the Bucks."

"That's true," said Lulu, leaning over to open a drawer in her desk. As I'd expected, she withdrew a bottle of nail varnish and an emery board.

"Guess I'd better go back to work now," I told Lulu. "That dog of Miss Padgett's has already growled at Ernie once, and I don't know how well Ernie will be able to protect himself with a chair if Boris decides to attack."

Lulu gasped. "Cripes! A dog that big shouldn't be allowed in the building! Especially if it's mean."

"Miss Padgett says Boris is a sweetheart and loves people, but Boris growled at Ernie."

"Well, take this with you. If the dog gets out of hand, bash it with this." Darned if Lulu didn't hand me a bowling pin!

"Why in the name of heaven do you keep a bowling pin at your desk?"

"To conk mashers on the head if they come in here and try anything. I'm usually alone here in the lobby, you know." Lulu assumed a ferocious expression.

"I never even thought of that. Maybe you could...I don't know."

"Neither do I. That's why I keep the bowling pin, but you can use it for a while. Just bring it back when that dog leaves, okay?"

"You probably need it more than I do," I said, worried about Lulu now that she had pointed out her state of isolation. What if Checked Suit or Cheap Sack Suit should enter the lobby and kidnap her or something equally vile?

"Don't worry about me," said Lulu. "I have the telephone, and I know how to use it. Besides, Mr. Buck checks up on me all the time."

"How nice of him. All right. Thanks, Lulu. I'll bring this back as soon as Ernie's office is free of dogs."

Shaking her head, Lulu said, "Why are all the dog people suddenly hiring Ernie?"

I'd opened my mouth to tell Lulu about the dog people when the word "confidential" slithered through my brain. Shoot. What kind of confidential P.I.'s assistant would blab as I'd been about to blab? A lousy one, was what kind. "I'll tell you all about it after the cases are closed," I promised instead.

"Okay. Have fun." Lulu waved her emery board at me, and I crossed the lobby and tromped up the stairs once more.

When I returned to the office, Boris hadn't bloodied any part of Ernie's person. Miss Padgett had a hand on his long, long head and drew a silky ear through her hand as she and Ernie talked. Ernie still straddled the chair, but he looked up hopefully when I opened the door from the hall.

"Any luck?" he asked.

"Mr. Buck is getting the runner from the second-floor attorney's office to go to the diner across the street for coffee, tea and either donuts or something more substantial," I told him.

"Thanks, Mercy—Miss Allcutt." Ernie sounded as if I'd told him he'd just inherited a huge fortune. Poor guy.

"Thank you, Miss Allcutt," said Miss Padgett.

"You're both welcome," I said, steering as wide a path as I could around Miss Padgett and Boris, past Ernie and to the comfort of my desk chair. I felt oddly safe there, although I'm sure Boris could have put his front feet on my desk, leaned his huge body across same and ripped my throat out if he suddenly took it in his head to do so.

"Is that a bowling pin?" asked Ernie, peering at the item in question.

"I'll tell you about it later," I said.

Ernie shrugged. "All right. So, here's what I've been telling Miss Padgett."

"Would you like me to take notes?"

"No reason to," said my sometimes annoying employer. "You already know this stuff."

In that case, I decided not to be irked. I nodded graciously.

"I was just telling Miss Padgett that, from the sound of the notes she's been getting, I believe Mrs. Swale is mistaking her for someone else."

I blinked. "Oh?"

"Yes. Remember when that other gentleman came to the office? He was worried because he was being blackmailed?"

"Oh! Mr.— Yes, I remember him."

"I think perhaps Mrs. Swale has come to the mistaken conclusion that her husband and Miss Padgett are having an affair."

"Good heavens," I said, flabbergasted that anyone would want to have an affair with either Mr. Swale or Miss Padgett. Or Mrs. Swale, for that matter.

Whoops. Unkind, Mercy Allcutt, however true.

Ernie went on. "Or perhaps Mrs. Swale thinks Miss Padgett is the one who saw her..." Ernie's words trailed off. Guess he didn't want to say the words "bribe the dog-show judge" aloud. "You know, about that other problem."

"Ah, yes," I said, thinking that made more sense than Mr. Swale having an affair with Miss Padgett. On the other hand, he married Mrs. Swale, so one probably shouldn't judge such things without adequate information. But wait a minute. "I thought you knew who…uh…did that other thing." Mr. Gallagher was behind that blackmail, wasn't he? Although what he had with dog shows hadn't yet been made clear to me.

"We're not sure about that," said Ernie.

If he said so.

"It seems so ridiculous," said Miss Padgett. "I've never even met Mrs. Swale's husband, and I'd certainly never have an affair with a married man." She sniffed. "Although, after meeting Mrs. Swale, I wouldn't blame Mr. Swale for seeking comfort elsewhere."

"Nor would I," I said before I could stop myself.

"Ladies, ladies," said Ernie, grinning. "Let's be kind, shall we?"

"She's been threatening the lives of my dogs and me," said Miss Padgett indignantly. "I'll save my kindness for a more worthy object, thank you very much."

"All right," said Ernie, giving up on the let's-be-kind idea, which was ridiculous to begin with. "I do think I've figured out a way to solve the threat problem, however."

"Oh?" I said.

"Oh?" said Miss Padgett.

"Yes. I aim to invite Miss Padgett and Mrs. Swale to my office, and have the whole thing out. Right here, where there will be two disinterested parties to observe."

I wasn't disinterested, but I didn't say so.

Her brow furrowing, which made her look kind of like one of those Chinese pug dogs, Miss Padgett said, "Do you really think she'll believe me when I tell her I'm not running around with her husband?"

"Yes, I do," said Ernie with what I considered unwarranted optimism. Mrs. Swale, who looked as much like one of her mastiffs as made no matter, didn't appear upon first—or even second or third—acquaintance to be particularly malleable and open to sensible truths.

On the other hand Ernie had been a private investigator for much longer than I'd been a P.I.'s assistant, so maybe he really did know what he was talking about.

"Well..." Miss Padgett, still running Boris's silky ears through her fingers, thought some more. I wish she'd stop, because her resemblance to a pug was making my innards tickle, and I didn't want to giggle. She might sic Boris on me.

"For what it's worth," I said, "I think Mr. Templeton's idea is a brilliant one."

Ernie muttered, "Aw, shucks," but I didn't frown at him.

"You do?" asked a clearly skeptical Miss Padgett.

"Yes, I do. In truth, you and Mrs. Swale have much more in common than most people do. I think, once this misunderstanding is cleared up, you might even become friends."

Miss Padgett and Ernie looked at me as if they both thought I'd lost the few wits remaining to me. I forged on in spite of the two of them. "After all, very few people are involved in the dog-show world. I should think, as your dogs aren't in direct competition with each other, it might be pleasant to have a friend to talk to about various shows and dog breeds and so forth."

Miss Padgett tilted her head to one side and murmured, "Hmm."

Ernie actually said, "That's not a half-bad idea, Miss Allcutt."

"Thank you," I said with just a trace of irony.

The three of us discussed the matter for several more minutes. Because she wasn't a stupid woman, in spite of appearances, Miss Padgett voiced a couple of problems with the rosy scenario I'd painted.

After one of them, I nodded and said, "Yes, she doesn't seem the most pleasant person upon first acquaintance. In fact, she resembles her mastiffs a little too much for my taste."

Giggling—which was an improvement over sobs and tears—Miss Padgett said, "Yes, she does, doesn't she? She's nearly as massive as her dogs." Then she sighed. "I wish I resembled Bevan and Boris more than I do. I wouldn't mind being tall and svelte and leggy."

"Miss Allcutt bears a remarkable likeness to her miniature poodle," said Ernie, all innocence.

With a scowl for him, I said, "I do not. I don't have curly blond hair."

Miss Padgett giggled some more.

A knock sounded at the door, and it opened, revealing Mr. Buck and a lad I'd seen in and around the Figueroa Building several times. Mr. Buck carried a tray, upon which sat a few large bumpy things covered with a towel. The kid carried what looked like napkins rolled around flatware.

"Where would you like us to put these things?" asked Mr. Buck.

Ernie quickly stood up from the chair he'd been straddling, and I moved everything on my desk aside, settling my pagoda clock in the same drawer as my handbag, hat and gloves, and sticking my pencil cup on the floor beside my chair along with my calendar.

"Why don't you lay everything out here," I suggested. Then I remembered Boris. "Boris won't eat our food, will he, Miss Padgett?"

"Good heavens, no," said she, clearly shocked by the mere suggestion that Boris might take a bite out of a donut or whatever Junior had found to fill Ernie's empty innards.

As if reacting to the thought of food, I heard Ernie's stomach growl. He placed a hand over same and said, "Sorry. No breakfast, and I'm starving."

"Good. We'll get you all fixed up in a minute, Mr. Ernie," said Mr. Buck with a wide smile.

And boy, was he correct! Moving the chair next to Miss Padgett aside, he slid the tray onto my desk and whipped off the towel to reveal three heavy white mugs containing dark liquids, a small sugar bowl and cream pitcher, and a plate upon which sat a sandwich on toasted bread.

"Oh, boy, looks like you'll actually get something more substantial than a donut, Ern— Uh, Mr. Templeton." I smiled at my boss, who looked happy.

"Yes, indeed. Thank you, Mr. Buck and Junior," said Ernie,

clearly happy as a pig in slop. Which is a disgusting saying. Not sure why I used it.

"Fried egg sandwich," Junior piped up. "And I had 'em put bacon on it."

"You're a true gentleman, Junior. So are you, Mr. Buck."

"That's okay," said Junior, grinning.

I don't know how old the lad was—he seemed too young to be working for a living, but what did I know? At least we didn't use little children to go down into coal mines any longer. Unless we did. Oh, dear. I wish I hadn't thought about that.

"Let me see what we have here," I said, standing and eyeing the white mugs. I correctly deduced the lighter liquid to be Miss Padgett's tea, so I slid it over to her. Junior handed me the napkins and flatware, so I also gave her a napkin and a spoon.

Ernie sorted out his own food.

"We'll leave you to your breakfast," said Mr. Buck, putting a hand on Junior's shoulder.

Junior looked mighty pleased with himself. I deduced from this that he'd managed to do his duty by us and keep enough money to make his efforts worthwhile.

"Thank you both," said Ernie heartily.

"Yes, thank you very much," said Miss Padgett, giving the two laborers a sweet smile.

"Yes. Thank you both. Shall I ring the reception desk when we need to have the table cleared?"

"That would be perfect, Miss Mercy," said Mr. Buck.

"You betcha," said Junior. "And any time you need me to fetch anything else, just let me know."

"How?" I asked.

Junior looked as if my question had stumped him, but Mr. Buck saved the day. "Just call Miss Lulu, she'll call me, and I'll get Junior."

"Thank you both," said I.

Junior saluted. Chuckling, Mr. Buck led the lad out of the office.

TWENTY-ONE

As Ernie dug into his breakfast, Miss Padgett and I talked about Russian wolfhounds, Irish wolfhounds, mastiffs and poodles. Now that her terror for her dogs and her own person had been subdued a bit, Miss Padgett turned out to be a nice-ish person.

As I sipped my coffee and she sipped her tea, she said, "I've never had anything to do with poodles, although I understand they're quite intelligent dogs."

"Buttercup is brilliant," I told her with what I believe was pardonable pride. "She actually saved a couple of friends and me from an armed intruder a few months ago."

"Good heavens!" Miss Padgett looked appalled.

"Well, she distracted the person with the gun until someone else could knock him out and tie him up."

"My goodness, Miss Allcutt! Where did this happen? How dreadful!"

"This was in my home, which is on Bunker Hill not far from here."

"I had no idea Bunker Hill had such problems!"

"Well, it doesn't ordinarily," I said.

"Miss Allcutt attracts problems," Ernie managed to say in between bites of his sandwich.

"I do not!"

"Huh," said Ernie, lifting his coffee mug and taking a swig to wash his sandwich down.

"Hmm," I said. "Perhaps I should have used another example of Buttercup's superior intelligence. I suppose most people don't have to fend off armed intruders."

"I should hope not," said Miss Padgett with more fervor than I'd believed she possessed until then.

"That particular problem was a big mess, mostly my fault, but everything ended well."

Busy with breakfast, Ernie only grunted, but I knew he wanted to add a few reproachful comments to my bald narrative.

Therefore, I rushed to say, "Buttercup is also quick to learn tricks," I assured Miss Padgett, who looked as if she'd like to escape from the room.

"That sounds better than fending off armed intruders," Miss Padgett said, relaxing slightly. For what it's worth, Boris looked bored. "She can heel when we walk, shake hands, sit and stay, and all sorts of other things."

"Obedience training is so necessary," said Miss Padgett.

"I suppose it's especially necessary with dogs as huge as yours and Mrs. Swale's," I opined. Then, because she frowned, I added, "I mean, you wouldn't want one of your wolfhounds or one of Mrs. Swale's mastiffs to run around the neighborhood. Even if the dogs are friendly, they'd probably frighten little children and so forth."

"Anyone with a dog with a pedigree like Boris or Bevan's would never allow it to roam loose in any neighborhood." Miss Padgett spoke with unexpected firmness and still eyed me as if she thought I was at least a little loony.

"I should never have told you about the armed intruders," I muttered, wishing myself elsewhere. "I didn't mean to frighten you."

To my surprise, Miss Padgett reached across my desk and put the hand not stroking Boris's ear on my arm. "It's all right, Miss

Allcutt. I'm sorry I reacted so strongly. I just…Well, I've been so nervous since I began receiving those awful notes."

"I can understand that," I said, gratified by her evident change in attitude.

Suddenly Ernie wadded up his napkin, tossed it onto his empty plate and said, "All right, ladies. Let's get down to business here." He eyed me benevolently, which was a pleasant change. "Thanks for thinking of sending Junior for food. Mind calling the front desk and asking for someone to pick up the leftovers?"

"Happy to," I said, noticing there were no leftovers. "Need more coffee? I'm sure Junior can get you more if you feel the need."

"No, thank you. I think I'll last until lunchtime now."

"Thank you for thinking of tea, too, Miss Allcutt," said Miss Padgett with a soft, small smile.

I swear to heaven, Boris snored. He gave a little start when I moved the candlestick telephone closer to me and lifted the receiver. Then he yawned in my face. Honestly, he might be a purebred Russian wolfhound, but his breath stank something awful.

However, that's not the point. I called Lulu's desk and asked her to send someone up to haul off the dirty dishes and table linens.

"Will do. Did Junior do right by old Ern?"

"He sure did. Fried egg sandwich with bacon. And tea and coffee. Mr. Templeton isn't ravenous and snarling from hunger any longer."

"Hey," said Ernie, but he didn't mean it. Rather, he rose from his chair and spoke to Miss Padgett. "Why don't you come into my room, Miss Padgett, and we'll see if we can work out a solution to your problem. With luck, we'll solve Mrs. Swale's woes at the same time." He might have noticed my expression of panic about being left behind, because he added, "Will you join us to take notes when the office is tidied up, Miss Allcutt."

"Certainly," I said, tossing him a grateful smile.

The man rolled his eyes at me.

Boris didn't look as if he much wanted to move, but he obeyed his mistress and lounged into Ernie's room in the wake of Miss

Padgett. I finished chatting with Lulu and set all the plates, mugs and napkins together tidily at the front of my desk.

It wasn't long before both Junior and Mr. Buck showed up. They took the breakfast things away, and Mr. Buck even wiped down my desk for me. I thanked them both and said, "Somebody should open a diner in this building, Mr. Buck. It would sure be handy."

"That it would, Miss Mercy."

"Say, that's a great idea!" said Junior.

I still couldn't tell how old he was. He was lanky and had a mop of light brown hair, hazel eyes and freckles forming a rainbow across his nose and onto his cheeks, making him appear a hearty specimen of boyhood. He wasn't precisely good looking, but he had an amiable quality that was endearing. Upon first acquaintance. Perhaps if I knew him better, I wouldn't like him at all.

He chattered like a magpie when he and Mr. Buck carted off the leftovers from breakfast. I didn't listen too hard, but it sounded to me as if he had an aunt or a sister or some other relation or friend who would love to open up a diner in the Figueroa Building. It only then occurred to me how much trouble it would be to rip out offices and set up kitchens and counters and so forth. Oh, well, I guess Junior's sister or aunt could figure it out. I set my desk to rights once more, picked up my secretarial notepad, grabbed a couple of pencils and went to Ernie's office.

"Want me to shut the door?" I asked.

"No need," said Ernie. "We're not expecting anyone for a while, are we?"

For once I'd remembered to check our calendar before entering my boss's office. "Not this morning. You have an appointment at one-fifteen and another at two-thirty."

Wrinkling his nose, Ernie said, "Who's coming in for those two?"

"A Mr. Hamilton and a Miss Quatermaine. Hamilton's the one-fifteen, and Quatermaine's the two-thirty."

"Quatermaine," murmured Miss Padgett in a dreamy sort of voice. "I loved *King Solomon's Mines* and *Maiwa's Revenge*."

Aha. Underneath Miss Padgett's dull exterior lay a romantic, sentimental soul. "I enjoyed those books, too," I told her. It was nominally the truth, I generally preferred a rip-roaring detective novel to romantic novels.

"Quatermaine's an unusual name," mused Ernie. "Any idea what she wants?"

"She gave me few specifics," I told him, thinking he shouldn't be talking about clients in the presence of another client. "Although I doubt she wants you to lead her to a lost goldmine in Africa."

Miss Padgett tittered. Ernie squinted at me.

"You can tell me later," he decided.

"Good idea," I said.

"All right, so let me see if we can figure this out so you, Miss Padgett, no longer feel threatened and perhaps Mrs. Swale will be satisfied at the same time."

"If you really think you can do that, I would greatly appreciate it," said Miss Padgett. "I've been a nervous wreck for weeks now."

"Understandable," said Ernie. "All right. Why don't you give me some dates and times when you'd be available for a meeting of...what do you think, Miss Allcutt? Will an hour do it, do you think?"

How the heck should I know? I didn't say so. What I said was, "I think an hour would be enough time to get everything sorted out."

"Excellent," said Ernie.

"You really think a meeting will stop her from threatening my precious dogs?" Miss Padgett sounded and looked doubtful.

"I think it's a strong possibility," said Ernie.

"Very well. Let me look at my calendar." Opening the handbag on her lap, Miss Padgett rummaged in it for a second or two and withdrew a beautiful little book with what looked like an embossed Egyptian design on it. Ever since those archeologist fellows found King Tut's tomb, you could find Egyptian influences everywhere. Even on little date books. "Let me see here," muttered Miss Padgett, thumbing.

Ernie and I exchanged a glance over her bowed head, and Ernie twisted his mouth into a comical moue. Because I didn't believe it would be appropriate, I didn't laugh.

"Okay," said Miss Padgett. "How many dates and times do you need?"

"I won't know that until you give me a few and Miss Allcutt gets in touch with Mrs. Swale and finds out if she's available at those same times."

"Ah," said Miss Padgett. "Yes, I see. All right, then." She flipped pages and ultimately said, "Very well, here are four dates and times during which I'll be available. They're for tomorrow and the day after. I hope that's all right, because I'd *really* like to stop receiving threats."

Made sense to me.

"That will be just fine," said Ernie, fibbing. He hadn't seen our calendar filled with upcoming appointments. But that was all right. I could call and put off clients if necessary.

Therefore, Miss Padgett rattled off four dates and times, and I dutifully wrote them down in my own dull green secretarial pad, which held no adornment of any kind. When she finished, she glanced up, first at Ernie, then at me.

"Thank you. Miss Allcutt?" Ernie smiled at me.

"I shall telephone Mrs. Swale and be back as soon as possible," I said, rising from my chair and aiming myself at the door to Ernie's room.

Boris, whom I'd forgotten about because he'd been snoring gently at Miss Padgett's side, rose up on all fours and took a huge step my way. I stopped mid-stride, suddenly terrified of the gigantic hound who appeared menacing just then.

"Down, Boris," said Miss Padgett gently.

Darned if Boris didn't yawn in my face again and fold up into a curly white blob—an enormous curly white blob—at Miss Padgett's side again. My goodness, but that Russian wolfhound was huge!

My heart had stopped pounding like a drum by the time I got to my own safe desk chair. I decided to buy some doggie treats for Buttercup. *She* wasn't huge and terrifying. *She* wouldn't go anywhere near a wolf. Or a poacher, for that matter. Although she was brave and stout-hearted, *she* didn't scare the daylights out of people just because they forgot she was in the room and decided to stand up.

Where in the world did a person get doggie treats? Well, probably Lulu would know. Or Miss Padgett, actually.

I telephoned the Swale residence. A maid answered the wire on their end, which came as no surprise to me. I already knew the Swales lived in the lap of luxury in a relatively new development in Los Angeles called Hancock Park. According to Ernie, they lived on Mrs. Swale's money. And Mr. Swale was playing around on her. Mind you, I didn't care for Mrs. Swale, but any man who'd live on a woman's wealth and not be faithful to her was lower than dirt in my estimation. Darned shame nobody cared about my estimation. Oh, well.

I asked to speak with Mrs. Swale and, when questioned by the well-trained maid, gave her my name and told her for whom I worked.

"Thank you," she said. "I'll see if Mrs. Swale is home."

She didn't already know? Well, maybe the house was huge or something. Or maybe this was a ploy, and if Mrs. Swale didn't want to speak to an underling, she'd tell the maid to lie and say she wasn't home. Not much would surprise me about Mrs. Swale. Well, if she suddenly turned nice and polite, I'd be surprised, but that's about it.

"Yes. What do you want, Miss Allcutt?" came Mrs. Swale's voice as I was pondering the nature of fibs.

No fibs today. And no politeness either. "Mr. Templeton asked me to telephone, Mrs. Swale. He'd appreciate it if you could visit his office."

"What for?"

"He will be able to discuss the matter with you if you can come in. I have several dates and times during which he will be available to see you."

"Why should I bother going to see *him*?"

I should have asked Ernie what kind of excuse to give this nasty woman in order to get her to visit the office. But I hadn't, so I had to play it by ear. I think that's a musical term.

"Mr. Templeton needs to discuss the matter of threatening notes another person has been receiving. The person has hired Mr. Templeton to look into the matter of who is sending the notes."

After a long silence, Mrs. Swale snapped, "And he thinks *I'm* sending the notes?"

"Mr. Templeton will have to discuss the matter with you, Mrs. Swale." After all, *I* was a mere underling.

"*You* can't tell me?"

"I fear I can't. Mr. Templeton's business is confidential." I could fib as well as she could, by golly.

More silence. Then a grudging, "What are the dates and times. I'll look at my calendar."

So I recited the dates and times Miss Padgett had said she'd be available. Mrs. Swale snapped, "I'll telephone you," and she hung up. Rude, rude, rude!

Back to Ernie's room I walked. Softly, so as not to upset Boris. Both Ernie and Miss Padgett looked at me hopefully. Boris continued to snooze.

"I gave her your dates and times, Miss Padgett. She said she'll call back to let us know if one of them is convenient for her."

"She would," said a sarcastic Miss Padgett. Boris uttered a muffled growl, but didn't bother rising, which was fine by me. Besides, I'm sure the growl was meant for Mrs. Swale.

TWENTY-TWO

Miss Padgett departed about twenty minutes later, Mrs. Swale not having deigned to telephone us back by then. Ernie saw her and Boris to the door.

"Cripes," said Ernie, flopping into one of the chairs set before my desk. "I hope to God clients don't start showing up before the day begins on a regular basis. And what's with all the damned gigantic dogs women have."

"I don't have a big dog," I reminded him.

"True." He sat in the chair, his long legs stretched out in front of him, his hands in his trouser pockets and, I presume, mused about the dog situation in Los Angeles because when he spoke again, it was to say, "Why would any woman want a dog bigger and heavier than she is?"

"For protection?" I offered.

Ernie's gaze had been, I presume, aimed at his scuffed shoes because when he lifted his head, his startling blue eyes held a skeptical cast.

"Who in their right mind would want to attack either of those women?"

"I don't know why anyone would want to attack anyone," I said.

206

"I should think Mrs. Swale could stave off an attacker with one of her glares. I guess if a glare didn't work, she could have one of her mastiffs eat any lingering perpetrators of crime in her vicinity."

"You ever been to Hancock Park?" asked Ernie with seeming irrelevance.

"No. Why?"

"There's a fence around most of the development. You can't get in except by going through a guarded gate. In other words, if you want to see either of the Swales, you have to make an appointment, kind of like with my office. Only nobody with a Russian wolfhound could surprise either of the Swales at their front door."

"Goodness, I had no idea Hancock Park was so...ritzy."

Squinting at me, his eyes two almost-turquoise slits, Ernie said, "You could install a gatekeeper at your place. It's big enough, and you've got the fence for it."

"It's just a short stone wall," I reminded him. "It's not, like, a six-foot black wrought iron fence or anything. Besides, I don't want a gatekeeper. I don't need one."

"I suppose not. Anyhow, you've got that ferocious watch dog."

"Buttercup is a very good watch dog, and she helped catch a couple of criminals, don't forget."

"How could I ever forget? You keep trying to get yourself killed. Maybe you should get Buttercup a roommate. One of Mrs. Swale's mastiffs or something along those lines."

"Never."

"Figured as much. Wonder who'd come out the winner if you sicced a mastiff on an Irish or a Russian wolfhound."

"I have no idea, and don't want to find out," I said, revolted by the notion of dog fighting. Yes, I know people still conduct dog fights. And cock fights. I think both of those practices are inhumane and barbaric.

"Yeah. It would probably get pretty bloody. I don't even like watching boxing matches."

"Really?" For some reason, his attitude about boxing gratified me. Silly, I know.

Ernie yawned. Honestly. "When's the next person coming in?"

"Not until one-fifteen. That's a Mr. Hamilton. Your two-thirty is Miss Quatermaine."

"Hmm. What's Hamilton want?"

"He thinks his fiancée is cheating on him."

"Ah, cripes. What about Quatermaine?"

"She believes one of her household staff is stealing from her."

"Good God. People have too much money for their own good sometimes."

"I agree."

"Yeah?" With a grin that told me he thought I was being disingenuous, Ernie stood and stretched. "Well, hell, I think I'll take a walk around the neighborhood. Maybe go to those boarding houses in back of this building and see if I can sniff out the murderers' lair."

"Really?" I asked, surprised but happy. "You really *do* care about poor murdered Mr. Davis and his poor beaten-up son? Even though no one is paying you to help solve the case?"

"Figured I'd better care. If I don't, my secretary will probably get herself and her entire household killed."

"I will not!"

"Looks like it from here."

"Darn you, Ernie Templeton."

"Yeah, I know. I'm a bad guy." He sauntered into his office and came out again wearing his hat and coat. "Don't take any wooden nickels," he told me, then tipped me a wink and left the office.

Well, honestly!

I didn't have much time to fume, because Mrs. Swale telephoned a few minutes after Ernie's departure. "Mr. Templeton's office. Miss Allcutt speaking," I said in my professional secretary's voice. Heck, *one* of the members of this team should behave like a professional.

"Miss Allcutt, I should like to speak with Mr. Templeton." No please. No good day. No nothin', as Lulu sometimes said.

"Mr. Templeton is not in the office right now. May I take a message, Mrs. Swale?"

"How did you know who I am?" she demanded suspiciously.

"I spoke to you not long ago," I said in honeyed tones. "I recognized your voice."

"Hmph. Well, tell Mr. Templeton I can be at his office at ten-thirty tomorrow morning."

"Very well."

"You wrote that down?" Another demand.

"Yes, I wrote it down."

"Good." She hung up on me. Twice in the same morning. What a horrid woman!

Fortunately for my mood, Chloe called not long after Mrs. Swale and told me she and Mr. Francis Easthope were going to pick me up and take me out to lunch at Musso and Frank's Grill.

"D'you think Ernie and Lulu would like to go with us?" asked my lovely and kind-hearted sister.

"I'm not sure about Ernie, but I'll bet Lulu will. Ernie's not in the office at the moment."

"Well, if Ernie comes back before twelve-thirty, he can come along. What's Lulu wearing today?"

With a laugh, I told the truth. "She's subdued today. She doesn't want to be noticed, so she's wearing black. With red trim."

"Why doesn't she want to be noticed?" asked Chloe with a hint of suspicion in her tone.

"I'll tell you all about it when you get here," I promised.

"You'd better. Bet you've managed to get mixed up in another murder, haven't you?"

"That's not fair, Chloe," I told her, slightly miffed. "You sound like Ernie."

"Just tell me about it when we pick you up. Twelve-thirty all right with you and Lulu?"

"Fine, thanks. We only get an hour for lunch, don't forget."

"How could I ever forget? Never fear. Francis and I will get you back to your place of work in an hour. He knows all the waiters at Musso and Frank's."

"Good for him!"

We hung up, and I called the reception desk to see if Lulu would like to be taken out to lunch by one of the most handsome men in the known universe. Along with my sister and me, of course.

"Sure! Thanks, Mercy. Thanks. Well, thanks to your sis and Mr. Easthope. Too bad he's a fairy. I could really go for him."

"If he wasn't one of those, he probably wouldn't be so nice," I reminded her.

"That's true," she said cheerfully. "He's great to Rupert, and he's never laid a hand on him, either."

Her comment surprised me. "Why would he lay a hand on Rupert?"

"Don't be naïve, Mercy. He's a fairy, and Rupert's a pretty good-looking young man."

"But Rupert isn't…one of those."

"Doesn't matter," said Lulu in a world-weary voice.

Irrationally nettled, I said, "I don't suppose men of Mr. Easthope's stamp are any more eager for rejection than any other stamp of man—or woman—on the planet, so unless he knows a fellow is likewise inclined, I doubt he'd make any overtures."

"Hmm. Never thought about it that way. You're probably right," said Lulu. "He wouldn't want to get beat up, either."

"Rupert wouldn't beat anybody up!"

"I didn't mean Rupert. I mean another guy. Anyhow, yeah, it makes sense that Mr. Easthope wouldn't go around making passes at other guys unless he's pretty sure they won't haul off and slug him."

"Right," I said acerbically.

"Don't get huffy, Mercy. Didn't mean to make you mad."

I sighed. "You didn't make me mad, Lulu. I guess I'm touchy lately, what with all the bad stuff going on."

"Yeah. That makes sense. Plus you've had all those monster dogs coming and going all week long."

"Yes. We're liable to have four of them in the office tomorrow at ten-thirty."

"Gar, really?"

"Don't know if the ladies will bring their dogs, but I suspect, given the circumstances, they will. They'll probably try to outdo each other."

"I don't know what you're talking about, but you can tell me later," said Lulu.

Upon that note, we hung up. I felt better about the day after Lulu and I talked. I'd get to see my sister and one of the nicest and most handsome men on the face of the earth, and Lulu and I would get to dine at a restaurant popular with the Hollywood crowd.

I was a little disappointed that Ernie didn't make it back to the office before twelve-thirty, but Lulu and I had a wonderful time at lunch. *Plus*, Lulu got to see three (count 'em) giant stars in the Hollywood firmament: Gary Cooper, Charlie Chaplin and Douglas Fairbanks. We ultimately persuaded Lulu not to stare at the trio, who seemed to be deep in some discussion or other, probably about an upcoming flicker.

"Gary Cooper is *so* glorious," said Lulu, nearly swooning in the aisle.

I kind of had to agree with her.

Oh, and I'd returned her bowling pin when I joined her in the lobby to meet Chloe and Mr. Easthope.

Darned if Mr. Easthope didn't take Lulu by the arm and walk over and introduce her to the trio of famous actors. If she'd been clad in one of her violent yellow or purple garments, he might have hesitated. He was such a nice fellow, however, he probably would have introduced her even if she'd been in full flower.

The three men were gracious to Lulu, and each gave her an autograph.

Lulu, who fairly floated back to our table, was silent for the rest of the meal. Her silence gave me the opportunity to tell Chloe what had been going on in the office—and out of the office.

"Good heavens, Mercy! How come it's always *you* who sees people getting murdered?" Chloe gasped at one point.

"I don't *always* see people being murdered," I protested.

"You stumble over bodies all the time, which is bad enough," she countered.

"I work for a detective," I pointed out. "Perhaps I see more... what would you call them? Sordid deeds? Well, whatever they are, I probably see more of them than other people because I work for a detective."

"Nuts," said Chloe. "Ernie'd *much* rather you stop finding dead people. Or seeing people being murdered."

Couldn't argue with her there, because it was true. "I know, but he's out detecting right this minute. He left the office this morning in order to check out the boarding houses across the alley from the Figueroa Building. We figure the crooks must live in one of them."

"Good," said Chloe. "I hope he finds them while we're out to lunch and they can't bother you any longer."

"I do, too," said Mr. Easthope.

"So do I," I told my wonderful sister and Mr. Easthope. "I'm tired of not being able to walk outside by myself."

"You can't walk outside by yourself?" Chloe sounded—and looked—aghast. "Why not? Mercy, have you been snooping around and getting into trouble again?"

"What do you mean, *again?*"

"You know very well what I mean."

"Well, Lulu and I saw the two murderers in the diner across the street from our building a day or two ago. Ernie is just being careful in case they saw us."

I expected an interruption from Lulu telling the luncheon party *she* hadn't seen any murderers, but she was evidently still in the clutches of her dream about movie stardom.

"How is he being careful?" asked a too-suspicious Chloe.

"He's taking us to work and driving us home again, is all, and he won't let us out of the building by ourselves. Mr. Buck is having to be careful, too, because..." Oh, bother. It was too complicated to explain. "Anyway, he's being careful, too, in case one of the crooks saw him. He gets a police escort to and from work."

"My goodness!" said Mr. Easthope. "Our police department in action. That's mighty nice of them."

Was it? I suspect my fury and Ernie's persuasion had more to do with the police department's cooperation than their overall niceness. On the other hand, Phil was nice. For the most part.

And then Mr. Francis Easthope almost caused me to have a heart seizure.

"Oh, will you look there," he said happily.

I turned to peer in the direction he'd looked. And there, big as life, stood Mr. Gallagher, owner of the haberdashery down the street from the Figueroa Building. I tried to slide down in my chair, but it did no good. As soon as Mr. Gallagher saw Mr. Easthope, he smiled and walked over to our table. I thought about throwing a napkin over my face, but the notion of embarrassing my sister to death stopped me. I glanced in a different direction from Mr. Gallagher, however.

"Francis!" said Mr. Gallagher cordially as the two men shook hands. "Good to see you! I see you're taking lunch with three lovely ladies, too, you sly dog."

Mr. Easthope and Chloe laughed. Lulu was still lost in a dreamy fog. I wanted to suddenly discover the ability to become invisible. Didn't. Darn.

"Speaking of dogs, how are yours doing these days?" asked Mr. Easthope, after he'd introduced us to Mr. Gallagher, who showed no sign of recognition when he smiled at me. Good. I hoped he wasn't just acting.

But wait a minute. What about dogs? I paid attention to my luncheon plate, but I listened hard.

"They're fine, thanks. We're getting ready to attend a show in Santa Barbara. I have high hopes for Lady Jane."

"Good luck to you," said Mr. Easthope.

"Thanks." Mr. Easthope and Mr. Gallagher shook hands once more, and Mr. Gallagher turned to follow the waiter to his table. The waiter had paused as the two men spoke.

When he was out of sight, I cleared my throat and said, "Um, how do you know Mr. Gallagher? Just curious. He has a hat shop in the neighborhood of my workplace."

Smiling, Mr. Easthope said, "Indeed, he does. He makes great hats. He did all the hats for *The Fire at Midnight* a couple of years ago."

"Oh. And you say he has dogs?"

"He does, indeed. He's deeply involved in the dog-show world."

"He is, is he?" Merciful heavens, whatever did this mean?

"Oh, yes. He can scarcely talk about anything besides his Italian greyhounds. He just adores those dogs."

"I-Italian greyhounds?" I asked feebly.

"Yes."

"Are they anything like Russian wolfhounds or Irish wolfhounds?"

"Lord, no! Italian greyhounds are tiny dogs. Very delicate. They look like miniature greyhounds. I keep telling him he ought to teach them ballet. His dogs would look great in pink tutus." Mr. Easthope laughed. So did Chloe. I succeeded in choking out a chuckle. Lulu was still wrapped up in her dream of becoming Mrs. Gary Cooper, or at least starring with him in a flicker. "You'd never know it to look at him, would you? I mean, he's such a big fellow. You'd expect him to own huge dogs, but not he. Italian greyhounds are his life."

"Fascinating," I managed to murmur.

Why did so many countries claim separate hound breeds as their own? And why was an Italian greyhound tiny but an Irish wolfhound huge? Were there any middle-of-the-road-sized hounds extant? I knew Mrs. Majesty, the lady at whose house Ernie and I had taken Thanksgiving dinner, owned a hound, but it was a dachshund. It was short and long-bodied and looked as if it needed another set of legs in the middle to support its back.

According to Mrs. Majesty, dachshunds had originated in Germany, but she said her hound was born in Altadena, California, insisted he was a liberty hound, and had nothing to do with Germany or Germans. Her husband had been shot and gassed by Germans during the war, so I understood her point of view. It still seemed odd to me that so many different countries had so many different kinds of hounds to call their own. Did we here in the United States have a hound breed of our own?

Darned if I knew.

But this astounding revelation might put a whole new light on everything! If Mr. Gallagher participated in dog shows, perhaps he was only peeved when he saw Mrs. Swale bribe a dog-show judge.

Perhaps he wasn't a vicious criminal mastermind. Maybe he only had a dirty murderer working for him in his back room. It was possible.

Fudge. I no longer knew what to think.

Anyhow, except for having nearly died of fright, lunch was lovely. Not only had Lulu managed to get three autographs from three *major* stars of the silver screen, but Ernie had come back to the office by the time Mr. Easthope drove up to the Figueroa Building, and Mr. Buck opened the door to his Daimler for us to exit.

"Say hi to Ernie for me!" said Chloe, who had taken a shine to Ernie from the moment they'd met.

"I shall," I told her.

Nobody shot at us as Mr. Buck escorted Lulu and me to the building and held the door open for us. I considered this a positive sign.

TWENTY-THREE

When I hurried into the office, I was irked to see Ernie's office door closed. I wanted to tell him about Mr. Gallagher, curse it!

Although I tried not to interrupt my boss when he was busy, I also didn't trust him not to be napping in his room or shooting elastic bands at his waste-paper basket. Therefore, I quietly tapped on the door.

"Yeah?"

Yeah? Was that any way to answer a knock at the door? I guess for Ernie it was.

"Are you busy?"

"Yeah. Phil's here and we're talking about the Davis case. Cases."

"Oh, good!" I shoved open the door and marched into Ernie's office. Phil needed to hear what I had to say, too.

Both men frowned at me. They would. I decided to begin politely even if Ernie had been rude. "Did you discover anything when you visited the different boarding houses?"

"Yes, but I'm not going to tell you what I found out, because I don't want you nosing around and getting yourself killed."

216

"Darn you, Ernie Templeton. I won't go *nosing around* and getting myself killed! What kind of idiot do you take me for?"

The glance the two men exchanged didn't gratify me one itsy bit. "Anyhow," I said, forging on in spite of their low opinion of my detectival and survival skills, "I discovered Mr. Gallagher, the man who runs the haberdashery down the street, is a big dog-show fancier. He shows Italian greyhounds!"

"What the devil is an Italian greyhound?" asked Ernie.

"A tiny, delicate dog, according to Mr. Easthope."

"You been hanging out with that fairy again?" Ernie. Rudely.

"For your information, Chloe and Mr. Easthope took Lulu and me to lunch at Musso and Frank's Grill today, which I think is extremely nice of them both."

"Oh," said Ernie, interested for the first time. "Is your sister going to be in town for a while?"

"No. She was just here for lunch. She said to tell you hi."

Ernie lifted a hand in a gesture of…I don't know. Acknowledgment? Whatever. I went on. "At any rate, Mr. Gallagher entered the restaurant while we were there, and Mr. Easthope introduced us and told us he shows Italian greyhounds."

"How do Gallagher and Easthope know each other?" asked Ernie, totally changing the subject.

"He makes hats for the pictures sometimes. He made all the hats for *The Fire at Midnight*. That's how they became acquainted. Mr. Easthope is a costumer, you know."

"Yeah. I know," said Ernie, wrinkling his nose in distaste.

"Honestly, Ernie Templeton, you're the most annoying man I've ever—"

"Yeah, I know," said Ernie, interrupting me. "So what about Gallagher and his little dogs?"

After huffing out an aggrieved breath, I said, "According to Mr. Easthope, Mr. Gallagher's whole life is centered around his dogs."

"Good God," muttered Phil.

"Yeah?" said Ernie, sounding totally uninterested. "So that makes…what? Two middle-sized women with gigantic dogs and one gigantic man with itty-bitty dogs?"

"Exactly." I nodded.

"Seems odd." Ernie's mouth twisted into a grimace meant, I think, to indicate distaste.

"Maybe it isn't," I said. "Maybe it explains why the man who met you at the Melrose told you he came for Mr. Gallagher. Maybe Mr. Gallagher was only angry at Mrs. Swale for bribing a judge and has nothing to do with the petty crime racket thriving in the neighborhood."

Ha! I'd finally managed to capture the two men's attention. This time when they exchanged a glance, it was one of interested inquiry.

"Huh," said Phil. "That actually makes sense. We couldn't figure out how Gallagher fitted into the numbers racket the Baker woman's involved in."

The name made me stiffen up and take notice. "Mrs. *Baker?* Isn't that the woman with the boarding house? *She's* the mastermind behind the racket?"

"Now you've done it, Phil," said Ernie, sounding disgusted. "You shouldn't have told her the woman's name."

"Whoops," said Phil. He looked chagrined.

Furious, I asked, "What do you expect me to *do?* Race over to her house and demand to meet her sons? Honestly, you two men drive me *crazy!*"

"Just don't want you taking any chances, is all," said Phil. "We've got the Baker woman in custody, but we don't have the men you saw killing Huey Davis."

"Also," said Ernie. "She's not the mastermind. There's someone else involved who's directing traffic, so to speak."

"Who is it?"

"We don't know," said Ernie. "Which is another reason I'm not going to let you out on your own. Not until we have the person behind the throne locked up."

I huffed again.

"Interesting about Gallagher," said Phil to Ernie.

"One of the murderers works in his back room," I reminded the two annoying men. "I saw him there, operating some kind of machine."

Ernie narrowed his eyes and squinted at me. "Which one was that? The one in the checked suit or the other one?"

"Not Checked Suit. The one I saw was Cheap Sack Suit."

"Ah," said Phil.

"You didn't pick up either Checked Suit or Cheap Sack Suit?" I asked, feeling wildly disappointed. It seemed to me we were *so close* to solving the crimes, yet those two horrid men remained elusive. And, curse it, they were both too *big* to hide anywhere!

Phil stood up. "Well, thanks for the tip, Mercy."

That was nice. I ignored Ernie and said, "You're welcome," to Phil.

"I might as well take a couple of guys and go to the haberdasher's place. If one of the murderers works there, we might be able to pick him up."

"If his mommy hasn't figured out how to warn the bastard," said Ernie.

"Mrs. Baker is that man's *mother?*"

"Yeah," said Ernie. "She's the other one's mother, too."

"Yes," said Phil.

"Gee, she seemed nice when Lulu and I went to her place," I said. Then I wished myself to the moon when both Ernie and Phil turned on me as if I'd just admitted to killing Huey Davis myself.

"*Damnation!*" thundered Ernie. "I *knew* you'd been snooping around! Don't you have any sense at all? That woman's two sons are murderers! You *saw* them kill Huey Davis!"

"Yes, I—"

"And you also saw what they did to Louie Davis," said Ernie relentlessly.

"I know, but—"

Phil, still standing, glowered at me. "No buts, Mercy. We're dealing with a band of dangerous criminals here, and we still don't know who the head of the ring is. The Baker woman and her sons are puppets in this drama, but there's some evil person behind them, pulling their strings."

Golly, how poetic. I sensed it would be unwise to say so. Anyway, I didn't have time, because Ernie resumed ragging on me. "For

God's sake, Mercy Allcutt, how many times have you been in trouble because you've sneaked around or done something stupid in the presence of a killer?"

"Not that many times!" I said. I got no further with my defense of myself—which, when I thought about it later, was relatively lame—because the outer office door opened.

Because I didn't think it would be appropriate for Ernie, Phil and me to be caught by a client having a vicious argument, I turned on my heel and walked into my room. I even smiled at the well-dressed gentleman holding his gloves in his left hand and fondling them with his right.

"Mr. Hamilton?" I asked perkily.

"Um...yes. I'm Mr. Hamilton," he said. "Is this the private investigator's office?"

Hadn't he read the information painted on the office window? Thanks to Mr. Buck, it was there, big as life: Ernest Templeton, P.I. I didn't ask.

"Yes, it is. If you'll take a seat, I'll get Mr. Templeton for you. He has someone in his office right now."

Not that this man and anyone with good ears in the vicinity of the office didn't already know there was someone in Ernie's office. I'm sure Mr. Hamilton had heard Ernie and Phil scolding me ever since he'd left the elevator. But I was a consummate professional, and I knew my duty. Therefore, I turned, intending to step back into Ernie's office, but Phil stood there, slapping his hat on his head, so I didn't.

"I'm just leaving," Phil said unnecessarily.

Ernie, standing right behind Phil, said, "Come right on in, Mr. Hamilton." He didn't ask me to take notes.

Which was fine by me. I didn't feel like taking any stupid notes about stupid Mr. Hamilton's stupid fiancée. If I were she, I'd run around on him, too. I disliked the man on sight. He looked like the kind of prig my mother would force me to marry if she could, which she couldn't, thank God, because I'd had the good sense to move to Los Angeles and wouldn't have married a man I didn't like even if I still lived in Boston. Also, he had one of those ugly skinny mustaches and slicked his hair back with too much oil.

Ahem. Where was I? Oh, yes. In my office. I shut the door behind Mr. Hamilton and turned to face Phil, who wasn't facing me, so it didn't matter.

He turned at the door, however, gave me a frown and said, "Just don't go anywhere by yourself, Mercy. You and Lulu and Mr. Buck need to stay as out of sight as possible until we get the whole gang rounded up."

"Yes, I understand. Will the police department be escorting Mr. Buck to and from work, as you did yesterday evening and this morning? If you don't, there's no way he can keep out of sight, you know. Unless, of course, the L.A.P.D. doesn't care about any but the white residents of the city."

"That's not fair, Mercy." Phil tried to shut me up with a stern look.

He ought to have known better. If my mother, known by Chloe and me as the Wrath of God, hadn't yet been able to shut me up— and she hadn't—there was no way Phil could. He was a rank amateur compared to my mother.

"Horse feathers! It is, too, fair. You know it's the truth, Phil Bigelow!"

After rolling his eyes at me—he and Ernie were *so* much alike sometimes—Phil said, "We'll give Mr. Buck a ride to and from work. Will that make you happy?"

"No, it won't make me happy! It will make me think you're making a stab at treating all of L.A.'s citizens the same! You should *always* do that."

"We do our best."

"Huh. And what about Mr. Davis's newspaper kiosk? Do you still have an officer there, or are you going to let Mr. Louie Davis work his father's stand until he gets murdered, too?"

"Mercy! You're not being fair. We've got a plainclothes man at the news stand."

"Huh. Good thing."

"See you later, Mercy," Phil said, sounding defeated.

He didn't deserve Pauline. I decided not to tell him so. "Yes," said I. "Later."

Unless I saw him first.

But that was silly, and I knew it. Still, the inequities abounding in this life made me angry.

I know. I know. So what, Mercy Allcutt? So what?

So nothing, was what.

I'd pretty much stopped fuming when Ernie's door opened and Ernie escorted Mr. Hamilton out of his office.

"Miss Allcutt will make out a receipt for you, Mr. Hamilton," said Ernie, sounding pleasant. For this awful man. Me, he yelled at. Hmph.

"I'll be happy to write up a receipt, Mr. Templeton," I said in a tone so sweet, I hoped he'd gag on it. Naturally, he didn't.

He only said, "One hundred fifty dollars, Miss Allcutt. A retainer."

All righty, then. I took out the receipt book residing in my middle drawer, which saw very little service. In fact, the same receipt book had been in my middle drawer since I first came to work for Ernie. Pitiful.

"Very well. What is your first name, Mr. Hamilton?"

"Albert."

I wrote out a receipt to Mr. Albert Hamilton for one hundred fifty dollars as a retainer for the work Ernie aimed to do for him. Prying into Mr. Hamilton's fiancée's activities. Sordid job.

What was I thinking? One couldn't be a private investigator without doing those jobs. Not every case could be interesting.

Therefore, when I said, "Here you go, Mr. Hamilton. Have a lovely day," and handed him the receipt, he looked at me as if I were an idiot.

As soon as the office door closed behind him, I told Ernie, "I hate that man."

With a grin, Ernie said, "Why? What's the matter with him?"

"He reminds me too much of Boston."

Tilting his head to one side, Ernie seemed to ponder this statement. Then he said, "Yeah. He does look like a damned prig, doesn't he? He acts like one, too."

"If I were his fiancée, I'd kick him to the curb," I told my boss.

Ernie roared with laughter. It was better than when he roared in anger, I guess.

When he'd quieted enough for me to make myself heard, I told him, "And Mrs. Swale will come to your office at ten-thirty tomorrow morning. I'll telephone Miss Padgett and give her the news."

"Oh, boy. Well, with any luck, we'll be able to get those two off our backs."

"And each other's," I said.

"Yeah." Shaking his head, Ernie said, "What's up with everyone wanting to enter their dogs in shows? Whoever decided holding bathing-beauty pageants for dogs was a good idea?"

"I don't have a single clue. I do doubt they wear bathing costumes, however."

"Wouldn't you like to see one of those mastiffs in a bathing suit?"

After thinking the matter over for approximately two seconds, I said, "No."

Ernie laughed again.

TWENTY-FOUR

Miss Quatermaine, Ernie's next client, turned out to be a young, lovely woman and, while I didn't hate her on sight as I had Mr. Hamilton, I didn't appreciate it when Ernie took her into his office with a big, smirky grin and didn't ask me to take notes. At least she wasn't a slinky man-eater like a couple of Ernie's former clients had been.

I hoped.

If she was a slinky man-eater, she didn't stay awfully long in order to perpetrate her seduction, unless she was an extremely fast worker. About five minutes after the door had closed on her and Ernie, it opened again. Miss Quatermaine was holding an embroidered hankie to her eyes and appeared distressed. She turned in the door and said, "Are you *sure* you can't help me?"

"I'm awfully sorry, Miss Quatermaine, but that's one kind of job best left to the police. The police can be discreet."

"I don't trust them," said she. "You know how those gossip magazines latch onto stories like mine and trumpet them to the world."

"I'm very sorry, ma'am, but I'm not the one for you."

"Are you *sure?*"

"I'm afraid I am."

"Oooooooh!" Miss Quatermaine wailed. Then she tucked her hankie into her handbag and marched to the front door, where she turned and said, "Well, you have my telephone number. Please call if you change your mind."

"I won't change my mind, but thank you for your interest in my services."

With a sigh of utter despair, Miss Quatermaine opened the door and left the office. I turned in my chair and stared at Ernie.

He held a finger to his lips, so I didn't burst out with my inquiry. What the heck had the woman wanted that Ernie couldn't do? I mean, I had faith in my irksome employer. He was a good detective.

Leaning over and whispering, Ernie finally said, "She's not telling the truth. Not sure what her game is, but it's not what she said it is."

"Game?" I whispered back, confused.

"Wait here." With those words, Ernie ambled to the front door to my room, opened it, stepped out in the hallway and stretched elaborately. Then he stood there, peering this way and that, and seemed to be waiting for something, although I had no idea what. After I don't know how long of stretching and peering, he came back into my room and shut the door behind himself.

"Well?" I demanded. "What was that about?"

After moseying over to my desk, planting himself in one of the chairs there and stretching out his long legs, he said, "She lied to me, and I don't know why."

"You already said as much, but you didn't say what she lied about."

"She said she wanted me to find the man who promised to marry her and then backed out and left the city. She wants to file a breach-of-promise suit, but she says she can't find the fellow."

After pondering this for a moment or two, I said, "Why can't you find the two-faced rat of a man?"

"That's not what she wants."

"How do you know that?"

"I recognized her voice."

"What?"

"She's the woman Mr. Swale called Mrs. Guernsey and whom he said was blackmailing him."

"*What?*"

"You heard me."

"But…but what's the point?"

"I don't know, but it sounds to me as if either she or Mr. Swale, or both of them, are trying to send me off on a wild-goose chase—she claims she thinks her fake fiancé bunked off to Bakersfield—and get me out of Los Angeles for a while."

"But why?"

With an elaborate shrug and a yawn, Ernie said, "Beats the hell out of me."

"Sometimes *I'd* like to beat the hell out of you, Ernest Templeton! Why would Mr. Swale and his honeybunch want you to leave Los Angeles?"

Holding his arms out wide, Ernie said, "I'm as puzzled as you are, believe me. But there's got to be a reason. If I just stay put, maybe one or the other of them will make a move and show us why they want me out of the way."

I stared at my boss for a few seconds. "I don't like how you phrased that. 'Want you out of the way'? That might mean permanently, you know."

"Yeah, I know, but I don't think it does. Swale doesn't strike me as a robust character, unless he feigned his dizzy spell in the office here, and I don't think he did. I'm pretty sure those were real nitroglycerine tablets he stuck under his tongue. I doubt he'd try to tackle me literally. And Miss Quatermain-Guernsey is about as big as a minute. She couldn't do me any harm if she tried."

"Either one of them could do you a good deal of harm if they used a gun. Or—" A notion suddenly struck me. Then I decided it was too ridiculous to say aloud.

"Or what?"

"Or…I don't know. A bow and arrow? I know! A crossbow."

"Or maybe if they hired a couple of big thugs?"

"You mean you thought of those fellows, too?" I gaped at Ernie.

"I thought about those two big brutes, but then decided the idea of Mr. Swale being mixed up with them was silly."

"I don't think it's any sillier than killing someone with a crossbow. Or somebody blackmailing a woman for bribing a dog-show judge."

"Well, I guess that's so." After thinking for another second or three, I added, "Or anybody suing anybody for taking Mr. Swale away from her. I'd run away from him as fast as I could. Mrs. Swale, too. I can't even picture the two of them together as a couple."

"If I'm right about the so-called Guernsey woman and the so-called Quatermain woman being the same person, the Swales probably won't be a couple for too much longer."

"Guess not. How are you going to find out if she's both women, and if she and Swale are trying to pull a trick on you?"

"I'm not. I already solved Mr. Swale's purported problem. It's up to him to deal with the women in his life."

"I suppose so."

Ernie looked at the little pagoda clock on my desk. "It's about five o'clock. Want to see if Lulu and your other pal is downstairs ready to go home?"

"Sure. Why not? Phil said there's still a policeman at the news kiosk. Do you know how Mr. Davis is doing? He was sure beaten badly."

"Yeah, I went to see him earlier today with Phil." He gave me a twisted grin. "When we were out detecting."

"Huh."

Oh, Lord, now I was sounding like Ernie!

Nevertheless, while Ernie went to his office to get his coat and hat, I retrieved my handbag and hat from my desk drawer and rose to take my coat off the rack by the door. As soon as I lifted it from the hook, Ernie said, "Here, let me hold that for you."

I hadn't heard him come up behind me, and I jumped about three feet and whirled around. "Don't *do* that!"

Stepping back and looking shocked, he said, "Don't do what? Hold your coat for you? I thought holding ladies' coats was the gentlemanly thing to do. I'm sure gents in Boston hold ladies' coats for them."

"You crept up on me and nearly scared me to death."

"Did not!"

"Did, too!"

"Aw, fer God's sake, stick your arms into your coat and let's see if Lulu and what's her name are ready to go home."

Although my heart still thudded painfully, I did as commanded, turned and stuck my arms into the sleeves of my coat Ernie still held for me. "I didn't hear you. Make a noise before you sneak up on me next time, all right?"

I turned in time to see Ernie's gaze pay a trip to the ceiling. "I'm too big to sneak," said he.

"You're tall, but you're not big," I retorted.

"Tall's big."

"Fiddlesticks."

We didn't continue our fuss, but took the elevator down to the lobby in silence. When we stepped out of the elevator cage, I was surprised not to see Lulu filing her nails. In actual fact, she had a pencil in her right hand and seemed to be studying a newspaper lying on the reception desk before her. If she were anyone but Lulu, I'd say she was in a brown study, but that day Lulu wore black and red, so her study could only be called...I'm sorry about this...scarlet. "A Study in Scarlet"! Get it?

Never mind.

"Whatcha doing, Lulu?" asked Ernie as we both approached her desk.

Her head jerked up and she uttered a frightened squeak. "Stop creeping up on people, Ernie! You scared the daylights out of me!"

"Ha. Told you so," I said.

"Crumb," said Ernie, frowning. "You women are all alike. Like I told Mercy, I'm too big to sneak and creep. What are you so enthralled with that you didn't even hear the elevator land?"

"Shoot," said Lulu. "You took the elevator? I must have been concentrating real hard."

The elevator made a lot of noise, in case you wondered.

"Anyhow," Lulu continued, "I'm trying to solve the crossword puzzle in the *Times*. I can't do these things. They're too hard."

"I love doing crossword puzzles," I said and then wished I hadn't.

"Well, of course, *you* like doing them. You're educated and good with words." It looked as if Lulu aimed to crumple the newspaper up and toss it, but she stopped herself, folded it and handed it to me. "Here. Have at it. I'll stick to movie magazines."

"Movie magazines are fun, too," I said in a feeble voice. "I'm not really all that educated. I only took shorthand and typing. My parents wouldn't pay for Chloe or me to go to college or anything."

"Huh," said Lulu. Fortunately—because I'd begun to feel like a pampered Boston socialite—she brightened and said, "Say, you two are early. Caroline's not here yet."

Lifting his arm and shaking his coat sleeve down to expose his wristwatch, Ernie said, "Well, it's just about time. Guess we can hang out here and wait for her."

So saying, he planted himself on Lulu's reception desk, dangling one leg and bracing his other foot on the floor. I gazed at him with some disfavor, although I tried to hide it.

"Did you want to go to college, Mercy?" he asked. He would.

"Did I?" I thought for approximately six seconds, then told the truth. "Not really. I mainly wanted to get out of Boston. Thanks to the Boston YWCA and Chloe and Harvey, I could." I smiled brightly at my two best friends in Los Angeles.

Ernie chuckled. "Thought maybe you wanted to be the first female to graduate from Harvard or something."

Staring at my boss in surprise, I said, "Why'd you think that?"

"Yeah, Ernie," said Lulu. "And what's Harvard?"

"Rich man's college," said Ernie.

"Oh," said Lulu. Then she turned to me. "Did you really want to go to Harvard, Mercy?"

"No! Ernie's being silly. I didn't want to go to any college. I honestly and truly just wanted to get away from Boston and my parents. And my brother." I gave what I hoped was an eloquent shudder.

"Understandable," said Ernie.

"You betcha," said Lulu. And she'd only met my mother. Ernie had not only met, but had dealt with, both of my parents, poor guy.

"Amen. And neither one of you has met my awful brother George. He'd put anyone off Boston in a flat second."

"Your mother did that to me," said Lulu.

"You should meet her father," said Ernie.

"No, you shouldn't. Neither one of you should ever have to deal with any members of my family except Chloe and me."

Five o'clock must have struck, because people who worked in other offices in the Figueroa Building began filing into the reception area. Not everyone left work at five, of course, but most of the tenants in our building did. A clatter on the staircase revealed Junior from the second floor when the door to the stairway opened. He gave the three of us a big, friendly wave.

"Thanks again, Junior!" I said to him.

He tipped his cloth cap and said, "Any time, Miss Allcutt."

"He's a good kid," opined Lulu.

"Seems like one," I agreed.

Suddenly, Ernie slid from the reception desk and said, "Hey, Junior! C'mere for a sec, okay?"

"Sure, Mr. Ernie." Junior swaggered up to the reception desk, sweeping his cap from his head as he did so. Polite young man, if remarkably jaunty.

Puzzled by Ernie's sudden interest in Junior, both Lulu and I stared at him. Ernie, for the record, still had his newly redeemed hat firmly on his head.

"Say, Junior, you know the Davises who run the news stand down the street from here, don't you?"

"Yeah." Junior's young face lost his cheery aspect. "It was awful when Mr. Davis got killed."

"It sure was," agreed Ernie. "But it just occurred to me that you might have helped him in the little numbers game he had going on."

Taking a step back and pointing dramatically to his chest, Junior said, "Me? Why'd'ya think that, Mr. Ernie?"

"Don't put on an act with me, Junior. I don't care what sort of arrangement you and Huey Davis worked out. What I want to know is if *you* know if he was worried about anyone or anything in particular. I know you know what I'm talking about."

"Unh…I…um…"

"Spit it out, Junior. You took money from people in this building and ran it to Huey Davis, didn't you? 'Fess up. I won't tell another soul. But I do want to find out who killed him and beat up his son, Louie. And it'd probably be better for you to spill the beans, too. They might come after you next, you know."

Gaping at Ernie, I said, "Oh, Ernie, no! Not even those monsters would hurt a child." I scanned Junior's face and then Ernie's. Then I peered at Lulu, who had tilted her head to one side and looked as if she wondered why *she* hadn't asked Junior such a pertinent question before now. "Would they?" I asked in a tiny voice.

"Yeah," said Ernie, "they would."

"Yeah," said Lulu, "they might."

"Cripes," muttered Junior.

In a cajoling tone, Ernie said, "Spill it, Junior. I sure won't tell anyone what you tell me, except the coppers who want to arrest the murderers. And I *really* don't want those guys—have you seen them? They're *huge*—to stomp you to death and throw your mangled corpse into a Venice canal."

Ew. I decided it wouldn't be prudent to scold Ernie for his crudity, since it seemed to be having the desired effect on Junior.

"I wouldn't like that, either," said Lulu.

"Nor would I," I said, then wished I hadn't when they all turned to stare at me. "What?" I asked.

"Nothin'," said Junior. "Just not sure what you said."

"She's a college girl," said Lulu. "She doesn't talk like regular people."

Knowing it would be unproductive to protest, I didn't, although I aimed to take up the subject with Lulu later.

"C'mon, Junior," said Ernie.

"Aw, jeez," said Junior. He moved a step or two closer to Ernie. "Promise you won't tell nobody but the coppers?"

"Promise," said Ernie. "I want to keep you alive to grow up."

"Aw'right," said Junior. "The guy who works for Mr. Gallagher at the haberdashery and his brother are the enforcers for the bimbo who runs the racket."

"Yeah, we already know that. What we don't know is who the bimbo who runs the racket is."

"Well, I can point him out to you, but I don't know his name. He lives a ritzy life's all I know for sure. He don't show up here very often because he has those two goons to do his dirty work for him."

"Is Gallagher involved in the rackets?" asked Ernie

"Gallagher? Heck, no! He's a pansy who has pretty little dogs. He don't know what the guy who works for him does. And he sure as heck doesn't know the guy who's behind the racket."

"And you don't know his name?" Ernie.

"Naw. Don't think I ever heard it." Junior.

"You sure?" Lulu.

"Yeah. I'm sure," said Junior. "I never heard him called anything but 'the boss'."

"Shoot," said Ernie. "Well, thanks for that, Junior. If you hear his name or find out what it is, let me know, okay?"

"Sure, Mr. Ernie!" Junior fairly ran to the door of the Figueroa Building, looking as if he'd just escaped execution or something.

"Damn," said Ernie.

Caroline stared after Junior as she same into the Figueroa building. "That child looks as if he just saw a ghost."

"I think Ernie scared the daylights out of him," said Lulu.

Ernie said, "Hey!"

TWENTY-FIVE

E rnie stayed for dinner again that night, which was smart of
him. Mrs. Buck served a delicious ham along with her
wonderful biscuits; sliced potatoes with cheese in them; a magnifi-
cent salad made with apples, walnuts, celery and I don't know what
else; and a dessert she called raspberry Charlotte. Not sure what was
in it, but it sure tasted good. All I know for sure was the crust was
made from those soft cookies called lady fingers.

"Mrs. Buck, would you be willing to teach me to cook?" I asked
her at one point. "I'll pay for lessons."

"Pshaw, Miss Mercy."

"I mean it! I don't have any useful household skills, and I want
to learn to cook!"

"I'd take lessons from you, too, Mrs. Buck," said Lulu. "About all
we ever ate in Oklahoma were beans. Maybe we had a ham every
now and then. We raised chickens, so we always had eggs. And we'd
eat chickens. My mother would fry the feet, but I didn't like them
much."

An entire dining room full of people stared at Lulu.

"You mother fried chicken feet?" I asked in a weak voice.

233

"Yeah, but they were tough. I'd love to learn how to fix all this fancy stuff."

Dropping the fried-chicken-feet issue, I said, "I know you're busy," suddenly feeling guilty for adding to her duties. "But maybe we can work something out."

"I can teach you how to make a few things," said Caroline. She was an accomplished girl, was Caroline Terry.

"I know how to fix split-pea soup with ham," said Sue Krekeler. "I can teach you that."

"Thank you all," I said, wishing I hadn't brought up the subject in front of everybody. "It was just a thought."

"Good one, too," said Ernie. "The only places I ever get good home cooking are here and at Phil and Pauline's house."

"I'll just keep on cooking for you ladies," said Mrs. Buck, bringing in dessert. "And I'll be happy to teach you to cook, Miss Mercy. And you, too, Miss Lulu."

"Thank you, Mrs. Buck."

"Yeah. Thanks!" said Lulu.

"If they have time," said Ernie. "These gals have to work for a living."

Giving Ernie a squint-eyed stare, Mrs. Buck said, "As do I, Mr. Ernie."

"Whoops. Yes, you do, Mrs. Buck. I beg your pardon."

"No need to beg, Mr. Ernie," said Mrs. Buck as she swept all the empty plates off to the kitchen.

"Guess she told you," I said, chuckling.

"She sure did." Ernie didn't seem bothered by Mrs. Buck's acerbic comment. He just dug into the dessert she'd placed in front of him.

Ernie left shortly after dinner, and I paid my usual after-dinner visit with Mrs. Buck. We always had a meeting after dinner, ostensibly so I could help her plan meals for the next day. We both knew this was something in the nature of a joke. Mrs. Buck didn't need my help with anything at all relating to food, but she insisted she needed my approval of what she expected to feed us. I was always happy to give my approval, believe me.

Mrs. Buck never let anything go to waste, bless her. The morning after our ham dinner, she served us ham biscuits for breakfast. I'd never heard of a ham biscuit before I ate one, when I realized my sheltered Boston life had deprived me of even more than I'd already discovered it had.

"I think people from the southern states eat ham biscuits," said Lulu, chomping on one of her own.

"Really?" said Sue. "They're sure good."

"My father's parents live in Virginia," said Caroline. "Once when we visited them we had ham biscuits."

"Why don't they just call them ham sandwiches?" I wondered.

"Because they're made with biscuits?" suggested Lulu.

"As good an explanation as any," said Sue, happily taking a bite out of her second sandwich. I mean ham biscuit.

Not that breakfast has much to do with anything relating to the day, except it got us all off to a good start, and Lulu and I, at least, needed it. Mrs. Buck handed me a brown paper sack before we left.

"For Mr. Ernie," she said. "I don't expect he's eating much before he picks you ladies up these days."

"Thank you, Mrs. Buck! You're absolutely correct about Ernie. Poor guy didn't get breakfast yesterday until Mr. Buck and a kid named Junior brought him some."

She nodded. "Yes, Mr. Buck told me about it. Well, you just give Mr. Ernie that sack, and give him this, too." And darned if she didn't hand me a thermos bottle. "Got coffee in it," she said.

"You're wonderful, Mrs. Buck! Thank you!"

"Thank *you*, child. And Mr. Ernie, too."

So I kissed her on the cheek, thereby startling her into a gasp and a hand slapped to her heart. Sometimes I didn't know what was going on in the world, if a white girl couldn't kiss a black woman on the cheek without darned near giving her a heart attack.

At any rate, Ernie was delighted with the sack of ham biscuits and the thermos flask of coffee. In fact, the frown on his face when he pulled into the driveway in order to drive all of us ladies—or maybe women, depending on your definition—tipped upside down as soon as I handed him his breakfast.

"From Mrs. Buck," I told him. "Breakfast. Ham biscuits and coffee."

"I'll be damned," said he. "What a fine woman Mrs. Buck is. What's a ham biscuit?"

"First of all," I said in a prim Boston voice, "I have no doubt whatsoever about your first sentence. And a ham biscuit is...well, ham in a biscuit."

"With a little mustard," added Lulu.

"What a kind thing to do for a poor old suffering bachelor," said Ernie.

Four varieties of chortle greeted this declaration. Nevertheless, Ernie smiled as drove a contented crew to their workplaces now that he knew his tummy would be taken care of before the big meeting—or small meeting; didn't know yet—between the two dog ladies at ten-thirty. Ernie became even cheerier when Mr. Buck greeted us at the front door of the Figueroa Building holding out a *Los Angeles Times* for Ernie to peruse as he dined.

Those Bucks sure knew how to make people happy.

Leaving Lulu, as usual, at the reception desk, Ernie and I took the elevator to the third floor. When we got to the office, I unlocked the outer door because Ernie's hands were full. From the front door, Ernie sauntered to his room to devour his breakfast and read the *Times*, and I performed my usual morning chores.

Along around nine o'clock, Phil strolled in. I greeted him, and he greeted me, and then he went into Ernie's office and closed the door. I swear. You'd think I didn't have any stake at all in the ongoing investigation, curse Ernie and Phil both.

However, I'd wasted a curse. About thirty seconds after the door closed, it opened again, and Phil said, "Ernie wants you to come in and hear what I have to say, Mercy."

"Thank you. Shall I bring my pad and pencil?"

"Beats me," said Phil unhelpfully.

"Yes!" came Ernie's voice from the nether reaches of his office. His *yes* sounded as if it had managed to make itself heard around a lump of ham biscuit.

I grabbed my secretarial pad and a few pencils and joined the men in Ernie's office, where Ernie was stuffing the last of Mrs. Buck's breakfast offering into his mouth.

"Morning again, Mercy," said Phil.

"Morning again, Phil," said I.

"Ernie said Mrs. Buck fixed breakfast for old Ern today."

"She did. She's a fine woman and an excellent cook."

After swallowing his last big bite and chasing it down with a cupful of coffee from the thermos flask's screw-on metal cap, Ernie said, "She's both of those things. And Mr. Buck's a prince among men."

"Oh?" Phil lifted an eyebrow or two.

Because Ernie was still trying to swallow, I said, "He had a *Times* waiting for Ernie when he drove up to the building."

"Aha. Yes, the Bucks are good people."

I squinted at him to see if he was being sarcastic, but he looked as if he'd meant his comment.

"Aaaaah," said Ernie at last. "That's better. All right, Phil, please tell Mercy what you found out."

"You found out something?"

"You don't have to sound so surprised," Phil told me, frowning.

I only shrugged.

"We arrested one of the Baker boys."

"Wonderful!" I said. "Which one?"

"Cletus Leroy Baker," said Phil. "Age twenty-four. Height six feet, two inches. Weighs two hundred fifty pounds."

"Which one is he?" I asked. "Checked Suit or Cheap Sack Suit?"

Peering at me narrowly, Phil said, "I can't rightly answer that question, Mercy. He was wearing pajamas and a bathrobe when we picked him up at his mother's boarding house. His brother was nowhere to be found, and Cletus isn't talking."

"Oh." I felt a little let down. "So you don't have any idea where the other one is?"

"Not at the moment, but I think we'll be able to wear Cletus down."

"I know a way you might be able to find out," I told him.

"When the haberdasher's shop opens, see if the brute who works in the back room is there. If he's not, he might be not-Cletus." After pondering for half a second, I added, "Although, if he's not not-Cletus, he might not show up for work anyway because he knows you're after him. Curses. I'd hoped it would be easy to figure out which was which."

"Well, it was a good idea," said Phil, not sounding condescending, which I appreciated. "We can at least check at the haberdasher's."

"Yeah, it is a good idea," said Ernie, being supportive for once.

"It's good to know you got at least one of them," I said. "Will you have any trouble pinning the murder on him, do you think? I mean, he hasn't confessed or anything, has he?"

"No, but we have his fingerprints on file—he's been in trouble with the law for most of his life—and they were all over the news kiosk, so he can't deny he was there. Plus, we found Louie Davis's wallet in his room at the boarding house."

"My goodness! That sounds like excellent evidence." I smiled at Phil, who had been a little exasperating of late. But he'd redeemed himself. I'm sure he'd be thrilled to know I thought so.

Yes, that was meant sarcastically.

"Glad you approve," said Phil, who seemed to have deduced my thoughts.

"Do you know when the hat shop opens, Mercy?" Ernie sat back in his chair, looking happy and replete, which was a whole lot better than how he'd looked yesterday morning.

"Nine o'clock, I think. Mr. Buck probably knows. He gets out more than I do, and he knows more people in the neighborhood."

Standing, Phil plopped the hat that had been residing on his lap onto his head. "I'll see if I can find him."

"All this sounds promising," I said to my boss when we heard the outer office door close.

"Yeah," said Ernie. "It does. Now if I can get those two blithering women off my back, it will have been a good week."

"Unless something else awful happens," I said.

"Always a blooming ray of sunshine, aren't you?"

"I do my best."

"Well, do your best at typing up a couple of invoices, one for the Swale woman and one for Miss Padgett."

"Happy to. How much are you going to charge them?"

"Hmm." Ernie tilted his swivel chair back, plunked his feet on his desk and shut his eyes, I presumed to think and not take a nap. I was right. After a few seconds, he opened his eyes and said, "Two-fifty each. They can afford it, and we deserve it for putting up with them and their confounded dogs."

"You mean two hundred fifty dollars and not two and a half dollars, right?" I asked, wanting to be sure of my ground.

"Yes."

"Don't you dare look at me as if you think I'm an idiot, Ernie Templeton. For all I know you've gone soft on Miss Padgett or something."

The look of horror in Ernie's face made up for his doubt about my mental acuity. I left his office, feeling fine, went to my desk, and stuck a piece of paper in my typewriter. I was merrily typing away when Phil returned, appearing pleased with himself.

"Did you check the hat shop?" I asked, deducing the reason for his smirk of satisfaction.

"You betcha. And you were right. The other killer was there, as if he hadn't even heard we were looking for him, which is impossible. Mr. Gallagher was shocked. Guess he had no idea he'd employed a murderer."

"Is he really stupid? Not Mr. Gallagher. I mean the other Baker brother."

"He's a few convolutions shy of a working brain, yeah. That's actually one of the reasons Mr. Gallagher hired him."

"Why's that?" I asked.

"Says he felt sorry for the guy. Nobody else would hire him, because he had trouble following directions. But Gallagher had him doing simple tasks in the back room of the haberdashery, and he managed."

Ernie had come to his door to hear Phil's story. He laughed. "So Gallagher's a genuinely good guy and not a villainous mastermind."

With a sigh, Phil said, "Yes, he's a good guy, and no, we still don't have the mastermind."

"What's this brother's name?" I wanted to know.

"Theodore Grover Baker," said Phil. "Says everybody calls him Teddy."

"So you have Cletus and Teddy. Now all you have to do is discover who's behind the racket," I muttered.

"Exactly," said Phil.

"Crap," said Ernie.

A clatter of feet preceded Junior's eruption into the outer office. Ernie, Phil and I all turned to look at him, probably agape. I know I was, anyway.

"I remembered!" cried Junior, excited as all get-out. "I remember the name of the swanky guy in charge of the racket!"

"Wonderful, Junior!" I said, thinking what a bright lad he was.

"So what's his name?" asked Ernie and Phil together.

"It's Swale! I remembered last night, because I kept thinking about a whale!"

"Bright kid, aren't you?" said a venomous voice behind Junior.

And wouldn't you know it? There stood not merely Mr. Swale, but also Miss Quatermaine. Worse, both of them held big shiny guns.

TWENTY-SIX

"Get in there, you," said Mr. Swale, poking Junior in the back with his gun.

Junior leaped like a gazelle into my office. Ernie, Phil and I stared in horror at the two people holding us all at gunpoint. I stood slowly, thinking to gather poor Junior to my bosom and offer him comfort, but sat again instantly when Miss Quatermaine turned her gun on me and growled, "Sit down!"

And then the telephone rang, startling me into a tiny scream and the closest thing to a heart attack I hope ever to get. Reflexively, I reached out my hand, but then paused and glanced at our captors. They exchanged a glance, then Swale said, "Answer that. Don't say anything about us, or your pals here die."

"We ain't pals," griped Junior. See if I ever long to give *him* aid and comfort again.

"Shut up, you," said Swale.

So I answered the telephone, trying in the maybe five seconds I had with which to think how to do so as to tip off the caller that we were in trouble without letting the trouble know I was telling on them. I failed miserably.

"Mr. Templeton's office. Miss Allcutt speaking."

"Mercy!" came Lulu's voice in a grating whisper.

"Good morning, Miss Mullins," I said.

"Huh?" Lulu.

"May I help you, Miss Mullins?"

"Oh, gar, you know, don't you? Junior was just here telling Mr. Buck and me about that man and woman who went up the elevator, and I wanted to call you then, but the darned 'phone rang, so I had to get *that*."

"It's perfectly all right," I said, glad she at least had figured out why I'd called her Miss Mullins instead of Lulu. She'd probably forgive me for it. Eventually.

"I called the coppers, and Mr. Buck is going to see if he can snag the one at the newspaper stand. Is Junior there with you?"

"Indeed, yes. Thank you."

"Oh, dear. They're there, too, aren't they?"

"Yes, I'll be happy to make an appointment for you, Miss Mullins. When would you like to come in?"

Both Swale and Quatermaine were getting antsy. I could tell by their deepening frowns, and Miss Quatermaine's gun swerving from being aimed at Junior's head to my chest. Therefore, I said, "Two o'clock will be fine, thank you, Miss Mullins."

"Oh, hertz!" cried Lulu. "Those two dog ladies are here now! Should I tell them to go away?"

"Do they have their children with them?"

"If you mean those monster dogs, yes."

Miss Quatermaine hissed, "Get off that telephone."

"Send them right along, thank you."

"Huh? You mean tell them what's going on and send 'em up there?"

"Thank you. That will be perfect." I hung the receiver in the cradle, praying like mad that Lulu, who was whip-smart if not well-educated, would figure out what I hoped she would do. Then I prayed even harder that the two women, who weren't friends at the best of times, would bury their troubles and figure out a way to help us.

From his office door, Ernie squinted at me and said, "Miss Mullins?"

"Yes. She'll be here at two p.m."

"Is that so? Well, she won't find you two when she gets here," said Swale.

"I'm an officer of the law," said Phil, sounding stern. "You won't get away with this."

"The hell we won't," said Swale. He didn't deserve to be called *Mister* Swale.

"Dicky?" said Miss Quatermaine. "We can't shoot them here. It'd make too much noise."

Dicky? She called him *Dicky*? She didn't deserve to be called anything at all.

"Don't worry. Thanks to my darling wife, I have all the dog leads we'll need to tie them up. And gags. I brought lots of clean handkerchiefs."

"Um...there's only two of us, and there's four of them," the person with Swale pointed out.

"We'll take them one at a time, starting with the kid."

"The hell you will!" hollered Junior, unexpectedly lunging at Swale's legs.

The woman with Swale, surprised by this unusual behavior on Junior's part swung her gun away from my chest and shot a bullet into the floor. I ducked under my desk and wondered what to do. I heard a lot of scuffling, so I dared creep out and peer over the desk.

Then my eyes almost bugged out when I heard a voice from down the hall shout, "Caesar, sic! Augustus, sic!"

Another voice shrieked, "Bevan, attack! Boris, attack!"

And darned if four massive dogs didn't pound into the office. One of the mastiffs went for Swale. Junior had knocked him down with his shocking lunge. I couldn't tell if the hero dog was Caesar or Augustus, but Swale didn't stand a chance.

Neither did the female entity who'd entered the office with him. When the two hounds barreled into the office, they plowed into her, her gun hand hit my desk, and the gun went sailing, nearly clobbering me as it flew past my head.

Ernie and Phil instantly went into action. So did I, lest you think diving under my desk was cowardly on my part. Well, I guess it was, but I was trying to think of a way to help. Found it. As the two mastiffs mauled Swale and the two hounds stood on top of his accomplice's prone body, I lifted the telephone receiver and dialed O, as fast as I could.

When Mrs. Swale's large body finally appeared in the office door, I was already asking the operator to connect me with the Los Angeles Police Department. Miss Padgett, who was a tiny bit taller—and much skinnier—than Mrs. Swale, peered over Mrs. Swale's shoulder to watch the carnage unfold.

Fortunately, there wasn't much of it. Carnage, I mean. After I reported to the police and hung up the receiver, I raced around my desk, steering clear of the melee. Junior, I noticed, had run to the door as soon as he'd played his trick on Swale. He couldn't get through the door because of the canines charging in. So he stood with his back against the wall and stared at the ruckus. He enjoyed it, too, if I were any judge.

I have to admit it was kind of satisfying to see two people who had lately threatened the lives of two of my friends and me—and Junior—at the mercy of some dogs who clearly took their ancestry as mighty hunters to heart.

"Richard Swale, get up this instant!" barked Mrs. Swale. She noticed one of her mastiffs about to grab him by the throat and said calmly, "Down, Caesar. Good boy. Come along, Augustus. Good boy."

I don't think Mr. Swale could talk. As soon as the slobbering dog backed reluctantly away from him, one of his hands went to his throat, and the other one lifted and he tried to get it into his jacket. Believing this to be an inauspicious movement on his part—for all I knew he had another gun in his jacket somewhere—I bounded over to him and stamped on the arm attached to the grasping hand.

He hollered in pain.

"Oh, no, you don't," I snarled, feeling fierce. I also had no pity for this perfectly awful man.

Swale gasped, "My...pills. Need...pills."

"Pills? What pills?" I demanded.

"Nitro. In my inner pocket."

I glanced at Ernie, who was in the process of persuading Boris and Bevan to get off the female's body. He said, "You get them for him. Phil, make sure he doesn't try anything."

"Will do," said Phil. "Okay, Mercy. Go for the pills."

Thinking a more deserving heart patient probably existed in the Figueroa Building, but not knowing where he or she might be, I said, "Oh, all right." And I reached into Swale's jacket. Sure enough, in an inner pocket of his expensive jacket—paid for either by his longsuffering wife or his ill-gotten criminal profits—I found the envelope containing tiny pills he'd had to use on his first visit to our office. "How many?" I asked harshly.

"Two," whispered Swale.

"He doesn't deserve them," said Mrs. Swale.

"I agree, but Ernie said to give them to him, so I will."

"Huh," said Mrs. Swale.

And then suddenly Lulu and Mr. Buck appeared at the office door! Boy, if I'd been asked before this happened if I believed four massive dogs, a massive woman, two skinny women, a thirteen-year-old boy, two tall men, Lulu, Mr. Buck and I would all fit in my smallish office, I'd have said, "No." But I'd have been wrong.

I got even wronger a second or two later when two uniformed policemen barged into Lulu's back. She reeled around and clobbered one of them on his shoulder. He said, "Hey!" but didn't retaliate. He took one look at the scene before him and stopped short, as if he didn't know what to do. Which he probably didn't.

"Get the man and the woman cuffed, Oakley," snapped Phil, who'd been dragging Swale's hands together after Swale had stuck the pills under his tongue.

"Which woman?" asked the officer I presumed to be Oakley.

"The one on the floor," said a clearly exasperated Phil.

Ernie, standing and dusting off his hands, said, "Yeah. I got the dogs off her for you. So *you* put the cuffs on her."

"Here, Boris," whispered Miss Padgett, sounding frightened. "Here, Bevan."

The two hounds obeyed her instantly, so she praised and petted them. I noticed Caesar and Augustus sitting one on each side of Mrs. Swale, too. Well-behaved dogs, all of them. I was impressed. And relieved.

"Holy shit," breathed Junior from where he stood with his back to the wall. "That was the *berries!*"

I deplored his language, but I totally agreed with the sentiment.

And thus ended another case. A couple of cases. Well, a whole lot of cases actually got tied up that day. Both of Ernie's dog-lady clients were satisfied; two vicious murderers and their mother got locked up; the mastermind behind them and their evil deeds didn't last long in jail, but nobody much cared. The female who'd abetted him in his wicked deeds was set to stand trial as an accessory. To what, I wasn't sure. She might not have known about the murders, but she sure knew Swale was a criminal, and she had aimed to help him kill three people. Four, if you counted Junior.

Mrs. Swale began divorce proceedings against her husband, but Mr. Richard Swale died from his heart condition before she could have the papers served on him in jail. Good riddance, is what I say.

Oddly enough—or maybe it isn't—Mrs. Swale and Miss Padgett became fast friends. I guess the dog world drew them together. Well, and a misunderstanding, but it got cleared up in a flash even before they reached Ernie's office that fateful day.

No one could bring Mr. Huey Davis back from the dead, but his son Louie recovered from the vicious beating the Baker brothers had delivered unto him, and he was soon manning his father's old news kiosk. I have no idea what happened to the news stand he used to run on Temple and Hill near the courthouse. I suspect the friend he'd mentioned in Ernie's office still operated that one.

I didn't know if Louie Davis was operating a numbers-running racket. What's more, I didn't want to know.

So life went on. I decided Buttercup was the absolute most perfect dog on the face of the earth.

And then, on the Friday after the clearing up of all the cases associated with Mr. Huey Davis's murder, Ernie drove Lulu and me home from work, and I asked him to stay for dinner.

"Happy to, if it's all right with Mrs. Buck."

I walked to the kitchen, asked Mrs. Buck if there was enough food for everyone if Ernie stayed for dinner and she said, "Laws, Miss Mercy, there's *always* enough food for that man here."

I grinned at her. "Thanks, Mrs. Buck."

"He can dine here every day, as long as you don't mind footing the bill for him, Miss Mercy."

Laughing, I said, "I don't mind at all."

The telephone rang as I left the kitchen and headed to the living room. Fearing I might not make my way to the telephone, which sat on the desk I used as an office downstairs, before I could get to it in time, Lulu answered it.

"Mercy's Manor," she said in a cheerful voice. Then her eyes opened wide, her happy smile turned into a grimace of dismay, and she said, "One moment, please." She held the telephone receiver out to me.

Worried by the sudden change in her demeanor, I got even worried-er when she mouthed, "I'm sorry," as I took the receiver.

Deciding that sounding formal was probably my best bet under uncertain circumstances, I spoke firmly into the receiver, "Miss Allcutt speaking."

"Mercedes Louise Allcutt, what *are* you playing at? Mercy's Manor? Can you think of a more demeaning thing to call that house of yours?"

"M-mother?" I said faintly.

"Yes, it is I. Your mother. And I expect you to come to Pasadena for Christmas week and stay with your father and me."

Standing in my office holding the receiver away from my ear, with Lulu, Ernie, Sue, Caroline, and Mr. Buck looking on in consternation because I must have appeared so dumbfounded, I ultimately shook myself back together.

Then I said, and firmly, "No, Mother, I will not be spending Christmas week with you and Father in Pasadena."

I hung up the telephone with my mother's outraged, "Mercedes Louise Allcutt, how *dare*—" thundering throughout the office.

Gazing at my friends in distress, I said, "Oh, my God, whatever will I do *now?*

Good old Ernie walked over to me, slung an arm over my shoulder, and led me to the living room. "Don't worry about it, kiddo. Your mother doesn't stand a chance against you."

Everyone in the room agreed with him. Except me.

CHRISTMAS ANGELS

A MERCY ALLCUTT MYSTERY, BOOK 7

The chilly air nipped our noses, but the rest of our bodies were all snuggled up in scarves, coats and hats as Lulu and I made our way to Angels Flight, the tiny, almost vertical funicular railroad a couple of blocks away from my home. In a minute flat, it would take the two of us—and everyone else riding the car we occupied—from Bunker Hill to Hill Street. From paradise to…well, downtown L.A. That morning we gave the engineer our nickels and made the quick trip on the car called Olivet. The other car was called Sinai. I'm sure there's a reason for the names, probably having to do with the railroad existing in the City of Angels, but I hadn't bothered to look it up yet.

"What's on your list?" I asked Lulu as we took seats on the wooden benches.

"I already sent Mom and Dad their presents. I wanted to make sure they got to Oklahoma in time for Christmas. What about you? I guess you don't have presents to send now that your folks are here in California."

Mom and Dad? Lulu called her parents *Mom and Dad*. My eyes got all misty for a second as I contemplated a family occupied by children who felt safe and happy enough to call their parents Mom and Dad. How lovely.

"Mercy? Mercy! What's wrong?"

"What?" I jerked out of my reverie and realized I hadn't answered Lulu's question. Or questions. I'd lost track of what she'd said after the "Mom and Dad" references.

"What's the matter with you? All of a sudden you drifted off somewhere. Daydreaming about a certain fellow, perhaps?"

"What? No!" It irked me that both Lulu and my sister thought I was fonder of my boss than I actually was. "I was . . ." My voice kind of trailed off. Lulu would think I was being silly. On the other hand, she'd met my mother. "I was thinking about how nice it would be to belong to a family where the kids called their parents Mom and Dad. That sounds stupid, doesn't it?"

Cocking her head to one side, Lulu contemplated my words for a second or two. Then she said, "Naw. If I had parents like yours, I'd run away, too. I wouldn't call your mother 'Mom' on a bet."

With a sigh, I said, "Nor would I. Anyway, I think I know what I'm going to get for Chloe. I want to see if they have some of those embroidered silk Chinese pajama sets for kids. You know. Wouldn't it be darling to see a wee baby dressed in a pair of red silk pajamas embroidered all over with dragons? Or maybe butterflies."

"That would be cute. When's the baby due?"

"Chloe and Harvey think it will be born in February."

"Two months from now," Lulu mused. "I guess you could get tiny pajamas in green or yellow since you don't know if it'll be a boy or a girl."

"I think red is considered a lucky color for the Chinese." I wrinkled my nose, trying to remember where I'd learned this tidbit of information. Maybe I'd made it up, but I didn't think so.

"Yeah," said Lulu thoughtfully. "I think I've read that somewhere. Maybe you should get some of those paper Chinese lanterns in red and hang them in your house."

"Where would I hang paper Chinese lanterns?"

With a shrug, Lulu said, "I dunno. In the entryway? They'd be pretty with those black and white tiles. You have the prettiest house, Mercy. You know that, don't you?"

"Yes." I smiled. "I'm so lucky! Very well, red lanterns and red silk embroidered pajamas. If they have baby sizes."

"Get some for yourself. Heck, I'll get some, too! We can all wear red and usher in the new year in a lucky fashion."

"Sounds good to me."

Olivet landed at the small station on Hill Street, and Lulu and I clambered out. Chinatown was a short walk from the station, and it was our primary goal for shopping that day. Plus, we could have lunch in Chinatown. Lulu and I both loved Chinese food.

Most of the shops on both sides of Hill Street in Chinatown sold similar merchandise, but some carried goods of a generally higher quality than most. I headed to a shop where I'd found a lovely dress once. I knew this shop sold clothes, so I hoped they'd have some baby things.

By the way, Chinatown in Los Angeles wasn't really much of a place. I only knew about it because Ernie liked to dine at a little dive called Charley's. In fact, he'd taken me there on the very day I'd gone to his office to ask for an interview. Still, it was where a lot of Chinese people had gathered, and they had food markets, butchers' shops—which always had dead, naked ducks hanging on hooks— clothing shops, trinket shops, and even a Chinese opera. I'd visited the Chinese opera with Ernie once. Let me just say the Chinese opera isn't like anything I'd seen—or heard—before. Nevertheless, Lulu and I liked to mosey through its various shops when we had a day to ourselves.

Ha! It was my lucky day! No sooner had we walked into the shop than I saw a rack of Chinese silk garments. I hurried over to it, reached for a red silk robe embroidered with butterflies, and looked around to see if there was a clerk anywhere handy.

Then I was nearly upended when a girl ran past me to the open door of the shop, shoving Lulu out of her way in her mad dash, too. Trying to remain upright, I grabbed onto a pole at one end of the garment rack.

Lulu hollered, "Hey!"

And a man surged out of a back room in the shop—I guess it was the same room from whence the girl had charged—and raced past me. He also blundered into Lulu as he ran.

"What the heck?" Lulu said, shoving her hat back into place. It had been knocked askew when she'd been bumped by two running people.

"I don't know," I said, answering Lulu's unasked question. "That man is chasing that girl."

"Yeah, I saw that," said Lulu. "Let's go see what's up."

So we did. Leaving the rack of Chinese silks, I joined Lulu, and together we raced out of the shop. There we were just in time to see the man grab the fleeing girl in what one might call a bear hug, if one was feeling charitable. It looked as if his hug wasn't one of friendly concern, but rather as if he were capturing bank robber or an escaped slave.

Oh, dear, why did I think of slaves? I'd read about Chinese traffickers in young girls and women. This girl wasn't one of those girls, was she? I glanced frantically around, hoping to see a uniformed copper. Of course, there's never a policeman around when you need one.

Other people were gathering in the street to watch the scuffle. The girl, struggling violently, shrieked something in Cantonese. The man holding her, trying valiantly to keep her long fingernails from scratching his face, hollered something back at her in Cantonese.

Mumbles and mutters from gathering throng came at us, all in Chinese and all sounding disapproving.

"Let me *go!*" the girl screamed in English.

I have no idea what the man bellowed back at her, because it was in Cantonese. But he somehow managed to subdue the wriggling girl—now that I could see more of her, I'd estimate her to be fifteen or sixteen years old—and, still holding her tightly, march her back to shop they'd emerged from. I got a good look at both of them as they neared Lulu and me.

As a chorus of two, Lulu and I, shocked, said loudly, "*Charley!*"

Charley Wu, owner of Ernie's favorite Chinese dive, paused on his way to the shop from whence he'd come, frowned at Lulu and me, and continued his encumbered journey back to the shop.

Having heard Lulu's and my duet, the maiden in Charley's arms looked frantically at us and hollered, "Help me! *Please!*"

Oh, dear. Whatever did this mean?

I didn't get to find out, because as soon as Charley Wu and his captive entered the shop where hung the Chinese silk garments I'd been fingering moments before, he slammed the door, and I heard the lock click.

Available in Paperback and eBook from Your Favorite Bookstore or Online Retailer

ABOUT THE AUTHOR

Award-winning author Alice Duncan lives with a herd of wild dachshunds (enriched from time to time with fosterees from New Mexico Dachshund Rescue) in Roswell, New Mexico. She's not a UFO enthusiast; she's in Roswell because her mother's family settled there fifty years before the aliens crashed (and living in Roswell, NM, is cheaper than living in Pasadena, CA, unfortunately). Alice would love to hear from you at alice@aliceduncan.net

www.aliceduncan.net